Flipped

Rock and Roll Gymnast Book Three

By Margena Adams Holmes

This is a work of fiction. Names, places, characters and events within this novel are from the author's imagination. Any resemblance to actual people, living or dead, or to any event is purely coincidental, or has been fictionalized.

Prologue

"Has Greg been found yet?" a newspaper reporter shouted.

"Oh, God, did you have to go there?" Kelly asked. "No, he hasn't been found yet. Last I heard he was still in Mexico. He can stay there for all I care unless he's extradited back for trial and put away for a long time."

Kelly's ex-boyfriend Greg had been giving the band, but mostly Kelly, trouble after calling the Indonesian police to detain the band while they looked through their luggage for drugs on their world tour. The police didn't find any, but Greg had been harassing Kelly since then, sending her text after text, saying to watch her back. He'd been spotted in Mexico while they were there for a show, but he didn't make an appearance there, at least not to Kelly's knowledge. Not knowing where he was set her on edge, and she thought she saw him everywhere.

Kelly Brennen, lead singer for the band Fate Struck, glanced around at the crowd. She'd never seen so many people in one place—for the band—with the exception of their shows. So many cameras and reporters. Kelly took it all in, and grabbed her phone from her purse to take a quick photo of the crowd there. She wanted to remember this feeling, of people wanting to see her and the band. It overwhelmed yet excited her. A few of their fans waved to them and tried to get close enough to snap a photo, but security pushed them back. Kelly and Ian, the band's bass player, stopped in front of them and asked security to let them take a few photos. The fans cheered and about fifteen people took their photos, then Kelly and Ian moved on. Kelly caught something out of the corner of her eye and thought it was Greg. She turned to look again, but didn't see anything.

Chapter One

One Week Earlier

Kelly and Jayna pulled up to Kelly's brother David's house. Kelly and her bandmates—drummer Isaac Landry, guitarists Jake DeHerrera and Paul Slaney, and bassist Ian Ketchner—had had their concert in England recorded to be released to streaming and DVD. David, Kelly's older brother, had offered to give the band a preview of the completed video before the premiere, so there were no surprises.

Marty had just arrived and they walked up to the house together.

"How'd the fitting go?" he asked, then kissed Jayna, Kelly's best friend and personal assistant, and Fate Struck's merchandise manager.

The ladies had just spent three hours at a dress store with a stylist friend of Dean's trying on dresses. The guy's girlfriends were there, too, and it was a very relaxed atmosphere with glasses of wine, finger sandwiches, and lots of laughter and girl talk. They'd all picked out gorgeous dresses for the premiere being held at the end of next week.

"Good!" Jayna said. "You're going to love the dress I picked out."

"She looked gorgeous in it," Kelly said.

"She looks gorgeous in everything." Marty smiled.

Kelly rang the doorbell and David opened the door a moment later.

"Come on in!" David said, stepping aside to let them in. Dean, Isaac, and Ian sat in the living room with their beers.

"Hey, guys," Kelly said.

When everyone had arrived, David popped the DVD into the player.

"This is what Jim has approved to be released," David said, hitting *Pause* while he spoke. "We had probably a good five hours of material to use, which is edited down to about two hours, with the other edited stuff in the bonus section. So pretty much everything we shot is there, it just won't be shown at the premiere, but will come out on the DVD and there are two versions for streaming. It will have an M rating because of the swearing and drinking, but I think that's okay. Kids will catch it on Hulu or wherever it ends up. You all did an amazing job."

David hit *Play*, and the video began with one of their songs as the title came up, *Fate Struck in England*. The music faded down as the video showed them coming into the venue.

The movie ended just over two hours later, and Kelly saw her name along with her bandmates' and Jayna's names in the credits, and she squealed as the others cheered and applauded. Kelly then saw David's name scroll past.

"Woo hoo, Davy!" she shouted.

"Well done, David!" Dean said.

David hit Stop on the remote and turned the TV off.

"What do you think?" David asked.

"That was fan-fucking-tastic!" Isaac said.

"That was awesome!" Kelly said.

"Bloody brilliant," Ian said.

"Well done, David," Dean said, shaking his hand. "I believe it shows the band how they really are—down to earth and approachable, as well as great musicians."

"That's what I tried to do," David said. "I've known most of you almost as long as I've known Kel so I wanted to show that you're regular people also."

"The concert footage was great," Jake said.

"I love how the fans started to cheer once they saw Kelly take her shoes off," Ian said.

"They knew what was coming," Paul said.

Kelly didn't realize she'd had two bottles of Mike's while she watched the video. David must have brought out another one with the beers for everyone else.

"So, I guess we'll see each other again at the premiere next weekend," David said. He ejected the DVD from the player and put it back in its case.

When Kelly arrived back home, her parents had just sat down for dinner.

"The video is awesome!" she said in a sing-song voice as she sat at the table.

"That's wonderful!" Mom said. "I can't wait to see it."

"You both are going to the premiere, right?" Kelly asked.

"Of course, pumpkin," Dad said. "We wouldn't miss it."

Kelly ate dinner, then went to her room. She sat on her bed and scrolled through the band's social media pages. She and Isaac kept them updated, but fans also posted very frequently with photos they'd taken and some of them got really great shots of the band. It always surprised the fans when she or any of the band members posted on there.

One post mentioned how much better Kelly had gotten onstage from the first time he'd seen them at The Taste of Long Beach four years ago. Kelly had to laugh. She remembered being onstage for those, and not moving around as much as she did now. She used the stage, but didn't really connect with the audience. Now she'd pick out faces in the crowd and look at them while she sang. It helped her connect to the fans.

***

Isaac Landry picked up his girlfriend Hayley and took her to dinner.

"How was the dress…thing you went to?" Isaac asked.

"It was fun," Hayley said. "Remind me to thank Dean when I see him next."

"That was really nice of him to arrange that for you ladies," Isaac said.

"I felt very pampered, with the wine and the personal attention. No one else was there but us and the two ladies working there."

"I can't wait to see you in that dress."

After dinner, they went to Huntington Beach to walk along the water's edge, carrying their shoes. They walked the beach for an hour, kissing, hugging, and playing in the water before they stopped to watch the waves roll in. They watched until the sun seemed to sink into the ocean, leaving an orange, pink, and dark blue sky. They had the beach almost to themselves, the crowds from earlier in the day having left as the sun started its descent, with only a few people walking on the beach, or getting their fire rings ready for the evening.

The evening was beautiful and perfect for what Isaac had in mind. He reached into his pocket without Hayley noticing, and then knelt down in front of her.

"Oh my God, what are you doing?" Hayley asked quickly.

He took hold of her hand as the breeze blew through her hair.

"Hayley, I love you so much," Isaac said. "Will you do me the honor of marrying me?" Isaac held the ring out in front of him.

"Oh my God," she whispered as she brought up her shaking hands to her mouth. Then a little louder, "Oh my God! Yes! I'll marry you!"

He slipped the ring onto her third finger on her left hand, then stood, picked her up and kissed her.

"You have made me the happiest man in the world!" Isaac said.

"Oh my God," she said again, wiping happy tears from her cheeks as he set her down again. "I love you so much."

They put their arms around each other and watched the waves as the sky grew darker. Isaac couldn't believe his luck. He had the most beautiful woman in the world by his side, and she'd said yes! All seemed right in the world at that moment.

They walked back up the beach to his car. He drove her home and they both went inside to tell her parents.

"That's wonderful!" her mom said, looking at the diamond in the ring. "That's a beautiful ring!"

"I guess I should've asked this earlier," Isaac said, "but you know what you're getting into, right?"

"I survived one tour," Hayley said. "I think I can survive the others."

Hayley's dad brought out a bottle of champagne and four glasses. When they all had a glass, he raised his.

"Congratulations," her father said, "and welcome to the family, although you've pretty much been family for six years."

Hayley's seventeen-year-old sister Jenna came out from her room.

"What's all the cheering for?" she asked.

"Isaac asked me to marry him," Hayley said, "and I said yes!"

"My friends are going to be so jealous," she said as she grabbed her phone from her back pocket and started to text.

"How about congratulating your sister?" their mom asked.

"Oh, yeah, congrats," Jenna said, her thumbs moving quickly over her phone.

"I guess we'd better let Dean and Jayna know sooner rather than later," Isaac said with a laugh. "You know how teens are."

They finished their champagne, and after kissing Hayley, he drove home.

"I did it!" Isaac said to Jake as he came in the door. Jake sat in the living room watching the Dodgers play the Cardinals. "And she said yes!"

"That's fantastic!" Jake said as he stood to shake Isaac's hand, then hugged him.

Isaac sat down on the couch to watch the game with Jake.

"I'm sure you haven't set a date yet," Jake said.

"No, we'll need to talk about that soon. We've got a bit of a break now, so I'm hoping within the next few months. I don't want to be like Jayna and Marty—get married and then leave on tour right away."

"At least he got to come on tour with us for a little while," Jake said. "Kind of like a second honeymoon."

"Except with a lot more people," Isaac said with a laugh.

Isaac texted Dean to let him know the deed was done.

"Congrats! About time!" Dean texted back.

***

The day before the premiere all the girls went back to the stylist to pick up their dresses, giggling excitedly about walking the red carpet for the first time.

"I just hope I don't trip and fall," Paul's girlfriend Alexa said.

"Right?" Jayna said. "It'd be my luck to do that right in front of the cameras."

"You're very graceful, Jayna," Kelly said. "Your dance elements in gymnastics were always beautiful."

"Until I get nervous. At least I'll have Marty there to catch me if I do stumble."

"Who are you walking with, Kelly?" Missy, Jake's girlfriend, asked.

"Probably Ian, since neither of us are attached," Kelly said. "We're good friends so hopefully no one reads anything into it."

"You know they will, Kel," Jayna said.

"Yeah, I know. Can't get away from what the reporters report."

"Jessica will really read something into it," Hayley said. "She doesn't shut up about you."

"I'm so glad she still thinks of me," Kelly joked. "I've stopped trying to figure her out."

"I've also had some jewelry sent over for you to choose from," Maddie said. "Necklaces and earrings."

The ladies looked over all the jewelry, *oohing* and *aahing* over each piece. They finally all decided on which pieces they liked with their dresses.

"Remember, ladies," Maddie said. "You need to bring the dresses and accessories back the day after tomorrow."

"We will!" Kelly said. "Again, thank you so much for helping us with this."

"You're very welcome! You ladies were easy to work with."

Premiere day arrived, and Jayna went to Kelly's house to get ready. Marty stayed home where the limo would pick him up, then Ian, then come by to pick up Kelly and Jayna.

Kelly sat in her bathrobe while she put on her make-up. She toned down the make-up a bit from her stage make-up, but still made her eyes stand out with purple eye liner and shadow. Next, she attempted to put on her dress, but had some difficulty pulling it into place. She'd had help at the dress shop, and Jayna tried her best to help, but in the end they had to use cornstarch to pull the latex bodice into place. Kelly pulled the short Spandex skirt into place, then smoothed out the floor-length lace overskirt. She had gone with a black dress, as the stylist thought it was edgy and perfect for a lead singer of a rock band. Kelly had to agree.

She left her pink- and purple-streaked brown hair down around her shoulders, just clipping back the sides with the barrette she'd bought at A Taste of Lakewood the first time they played there. Kelly had chosen a black diamond pendant necklace on a silver chain, and matching earrings. She wore her black platform Mary Janes with her dress.

Jayna looked beautiful in her red dress with a thigh-high slit over her left leg. She applied her make-up then put her dark brown hair in an up-do, leaving tendrils to frame her face. Her diamond and ruby necklace and matching earrings completed the look.

"Whoa, girl," Kelly said. "You're not supposed to upstage me," she joked.

"No one can upstage you," Jayna said, smiling.

"I don't know, you look fabulous."

They stood together and admired themselves in the mirror. They both looked gorgeous.

"We're all gonna knock 'em dead tonight," Kelly said.

The other band members and their girlfriends would take another limo and they'd meet them there. Dean would ride with Ian, Kelly, Marty and Jayna.

An hour and a half later, the girls went to the living room to show Kelly's mom.

"Wow!" Mom said. "You both absolutely look the part."

"It's not too much, is it?" Kelly asked. She hated to draw attention to herself when she wasn't onstage, though with something like this, it was inevitable.

"You look great," Mom said. "I was expecting something like prom dresses, but of course you want to look like the celebrities you are. Can I take some pictures?"

"Of course," they said in unison.

"Just like always," Mom said with a smile.

Kelly and Jayna put their arm around each other's waist and Mom took the pictures. When Marty and Ian arrived, they got out to meet the girls.

"Wow," Ian said. "You are breathtaking."

"Thank you," Kelly said shyly. "You look great, too."

Ian wore a black Tom Ford suit, with a gray button-down shirt with the top four buttons unbuttoned and a gold chain around his neck. Kelly had a hard time not looking at his smooth, well-defined chest. He had left his dark blond hair loose, and it just brushed his shoulders. He totally looked the rock star part.

"And you!" Marty said. "Kelly wasn't wrong when she said how great you look."

They went outside for a couple of quick photos before the girls grabbed their handbags and jackets and headed to the limo.

"We'll be about half an hour behind you," Mom said.

"You have the parking instructions I sent you?"

"I do, sweetheart," Mom said. "Dad will get us there, don't worry."

"Love you, Mom," Kelly said, and she stepped inside the limo, pulling the Spandex skirt down to stay comfortable and keep everything covered. She greeted Dean and his girlfriend Rosa with a wave as she sat down.

"It's like prom all over again," Jayna said.

"Yeah," Kelly said. "My mom's so cute."

Dean poured champagne for them and gave a toast as the driver pulled away.

"To Fate Struck," he said. "I hope that fate keeps striking in the same good way."

"I'll drink to that," Ian said, and they clinked their glasses and drank.

None of them drank more than one glass. They wanted to be fully sober for the walk on the carpet.

"You know," Ian said, "that dress really shows off your legs."

"That's what Maddie, the stylist, said, too," Kelly said. "To both Jayna and me."

"She's not wrong," Marty said, kissing Jayna's neck.

"You could always 'strike a pose' and let everyone see how great they are," Ian said with a naughty grin.

"Or just show them off gracefully," Dean said.

"I'll think about it," Kelly said, looking at Jayna, who smiled.

Chapter Two

The driver got in line forty-five minutes later with the rest of the limos and other vehicles waiting to drop off their occupants at TCL Chinese Theatre. It took about fifteen minutes to get to the drop-off place. There, a doorman opened the car door. Dean and Rosa stepped out first, then Kelly, who discreetly adjusted her dress again, followed by Ian, and both waved as the fans cheered, then Jayna and Marty, the photographers snapping photos in rapid succession. Dean and Rosa stepped back to let Kelly, Ian, Jayna and Marty walk ahead of them.

Ian held his arm out to Kelly, who put her hand through and they walked with Jayna and Marty up the red carpet. She'd never seen so many photographers and reporters in one spot, and they were there for Fate Struck! Kelly hadn't realized just how popular the band had become until that moment. The butterflies started up in her stomach as they walked on the red carpet toward the media, taking tiny steps to keep the skirt from riding up. *I should have practiced walking in this,* she thought.

"I am so nervous," Kelly said as they slowly walked up the carpeted walkway, cameras flashing around them, Jayna and Marty sticking next to them.

"You? After being onstage all this time?" Ian asked.

"This is very different," Kelly said. Luckily no one could hear them. The butterflies worked overtime in her stomach, it fluttered so much.

"Kelly! Ian! This way," someone shouted. Kelly and Ian turned and smiled toward the voice.

"Kelly! One of you and Ian together, please?"

"Kelly, one of you by yourself?"

Kelly's heart stopped for a moment. She wasn't used to doing stuff like this on her own, but Ian stepped aside and Kelly put her hands on her hips, bent her leg gracefully, only the toe of her shoe touching. She looked over her shoulder, then confidently turned her head toward the other photographers, smiling the entire time.

"Can we get the four of you together?"

"How about you two friends together?"

"Let's get the band together in one."

The guys stepped up to Ian and Kelly, their ladies standing back a bit while the photographers took photos of the band. Jake, Paul, and Isaac all looked great in their suits. Jake had his dark brown hair pulled back into a ponytail, and he had even shaved off his perpetual stubble, and had on a dark red suit with a blue shirt and no tie. Isaac had his short blond hair, usually in a faux hawk, parted on the side and combed smooth, wearing a dark gray suit and dark purple shirt with a lavender tie, while Paul's shaggy short brown hair still had the wind-blown look, and him in a pinstriped gray suit with a charcoal gray shirt and blue tie. The photographers then got a photo of their ladies together.

"Kelly! Are you gonna do any flips tonight?"

"Not in this dress!" Kelly said, laughing.

Kelly and Ian stopped every few feet to turn toward whomever called out to them, then Kelly and Jayna stopped for a photo together, putting their arms around each other's waist, bending one leg just a bit, and their free hand on their hip. They finally got up to the interview area.

"Are you and Ian dating?" one reporter asked.

"No," Kelly said. "Neither of us had a date so we came together."

"But isn't that a date?"

"No, we're more like Rey and Finn in Star Wars," Kelly said. *God, I'm such a nerd.* "We're just friends."

"With benefits," Ian whispered in her ear. Kelly giggled.

"Where is Lena Hendricks?"

"She couldn't make it tonight," Ian said.

"Did you get your brother the job making videos?"

"He did our first video, and Tyrian Records liked his work so they asked him to do our concert video. He's doing other music videos now. I think we've kind of helped each other."

"Ian, your ex-girlfriend's gymnastics videos have gone viral. Have you watched any of them?"

"Not really," Ian said. "Only a couple. She's a great gymnast so she deserves the attention, but I just don't have time to watch them."

Jayna and Marty had gone into the theater, and Kelly and Ian, after answering a few more questions, followed them.

"That was crazy," Kelly said.

"You look really relaxed and confident despite the reporter's questions about Greg," Ian said.

"I'm shaking on the inside. I thought I saw him out of the corner of my eye, though," Kelly said.

"Are you kidding?" Ian asked, grabbing her arm.

"I looked again and didn't see him, so it must have just been my eyes playing tricks on me. I'm paranoid about him turning up so now I'm seeing him everywhere."

Kelly saw David come inside the theater and went over to him.

"Hey, big brother," Kelly said. David had also dressed in a designer suit in blue, wearing a gray shirt and a bright red tie.

"Wow, you look a-MAZ-ing!" David said. "Total rock star in the dress."

"Isn't she gorgeous?" Ian asked.

"Absolutely. I see you survived the animals out there," David said.

"That was great fun," Kelly said sarcastically. "I guess I'll get used to it the more I do it."

They stood and talked in the lobby, which continued to fill up with people and celebrities Dean and the record execs had invited. Kelly saw Maggie and her band there, and Erik with his wife. Kelly went over to greet them.

"I'm so glad you could come," Kelly said, as she and Catalina kissed each other on the cheeks, then Erik. "Are the rest of the band here?"

"Stevie's here," Erik said. "But the others couldn't come."

"Are you staying for the after party?"

"We're planning on it," Catalina said.

"Great! Well, I hope you enjoy the movie." Kelly gave them both a brief hug, then moved on to say hello to Maggie.

"This is fantastic," Maggie said.

"This is—really weird to me," Kelly said, nodding her head "Surreal."

"I can imagine. This is my partner, Melanie."

"Oh, nice to meet you," Kelly said, shaking Melanie's hand. "I've seen you in pictures but never knew who you were."

"Yeah, we try to keep things private," Melanie said.

"Of course. After being in this business for this short amount of time, I get it."

Kelly saw her parents standing off to the side with Ian's parents. Kelly, Ian, Maggie and Melanie went over to talk to them.

"Hey, Mom and Dad," Kelly said. "I want you to meet my friend, Maggie, and her partner, Melanie."

Maggie held out her hand, and Kelly's mom, after getting over her shock over meeting a real celebrity, held out a shaking hand.

"Nice to meet you both," Maggie said, smiling.

"It's uh, wow, nice to meet you, too," Mom said when she found her voice. "Kelly has told us a lot about you. Thank you for helping her with everything."

Maggie shook Dad's hand.

“I know what it’s like to be a newbie in this business,” Maggie said. “Kelly’s a good girl and very talented. I kind of see a bit of me in her.”

“What? No way,” Kelly said.

“I was shy when I started. I still am, offstage. I’m happy to help however I can.”

They stood and talked until the manager of the theater came out and asked everyone to come and take their seats. They followed him into the auditorium and saw that all the seats had been reserved with their names. The band, David and his crew, and Dean would be in the first row, with all the families seated behind them. Everyone else found their seats using the seating chart they’d been given. Once everyone had settled, Dean stood up to say a few words and introduce David, who also said a few words, before giving the signal to start the movie. The lights went down and the opening credits and title came up and everyone cheered, then quickly quieted down.

Kelly hadn’t realized the first time they watched how much they all swear. The boys did it a lot, and both Kelly and Jayna let the occasional F-bomb fly. She cringed with each one once she noticed. Her parents wouldn’t approve, but she was an adult after all.

During the concert footage, Kelly heard a few people clapping along to some of the songs. She thought that was a good sign. When Kelly did the flips at the end of the concert, the entire auditorium cheered. Kelly waved her hand to acknowledge them.

One thing Kelly did notice was the footage of the guys popping their pills had been cut out. Probably a good decision by the record execs, to keep their image intact. Yeah, they drank quite a bit, but that was legal. Technically the pills were legal, too, but they’d always projected a semi-clean image. Greg’s little stunt in Indonesia almost killed that, and Jim at Tyrian Records had had to do a lot of damage control after that.

The final thirty minutes of the movie was the after show, with the band winding down and talking to the fans, then heading to the hotel. It ended with them all heading to bed one by one, and the credits started to roll. The audience applauded and when the movie ended, the lights came up.

David stood up to address the audience.

"I want to thank all of you for coming tonight," David began. "It means a lot to me and I know it means the world to Fate Struck and Dean. I've been lucky to be able to watch the band grow from the beginning, and they have gotten so much more confident onstage." David then addressed the band directly. "Jake, your leads have gotten faster and more melodic, Isaac's showmanship is off the chain. Ian and Paul, you two have really found your groove with each other. And I know I'm biased when it comes to Kelly, but you've started to own that stage! I'm very proud to be your brother."

"Aaaww," Jake and Isaac said in unison.

"Oh, and Jayna," David said. "I don't want to leave you out! You are very personable at the table. I love how you talk with everyone and don't try to upsell everything."

"I just try to avoid what I hate having done," Jayna said. "The fans are going to buy what they want, so I don't need to pressure them to do it."

"It was a real pleasure to do this for Fate Struck, Dean Landry, and Tyrian Records," David said, nodding at Jim, the A&R rep.

The General Manager of the theater stood up to speak again.

"On behalf of Tyrian Records, Fate Struck, and David Brennen, I want to thank you all for coming tonight," he said. "If you'd like to stay for the celebration, there are refreshments in the lobby and an open bar."

The din of voices started as people made their way out of the auditorium. Kelly and the band and their dates stood and gathered up their belongings. Kelly, going into usher mode for a moment, reminded everyone to take their trash out to the trash cans as they filed out to the lobby. She ran over to her brother and gave him another hug. Dean had invited a number of members of the press, and they stopped to take a picture of Kelly and David while they talked.

"That was even better the second time," Kelly said. "Though I still think I look like a dork."

"No one else thinks that," David said. "I had a couple of my crew want to marry you."

Kelly's grew hot as she blushed and she put her hand up to her face.

"Oh my God," she said. "How embarrassing."

"Anyway, you all looked great onstage, so you don't need to worry," David assured her.

Kelly went over to the bar and got a bottle of hard lemonade, then talked to more people. Maggie came over to her and gave her another hug.

"That was brilliant!" Maggie said. "I wish someone had done that for us when we were new."

"You've had concerts recorded before, haven't you?" Kelly asked.

"Yeah, but it was just the concert and nothing else. You are just adorable offstage."

"I think 'nerdy' is the word," Kelly said.

Maggie laughed.

"Well, whatever it is, well done," she said. She clinked her glass to Kelly's bottle and they drank.

Kelly saw most of the band and Dean over by the parents. Isaac's parents once again looked like they'd rather be elsewhere, and kept trying to slip away, but someone stopped them each time to talk. Kelly excused herself from Maggie and went over to talk to them all.

"Wasn't that great?" Kelly asked. "Davy did such a fantastic job!"

"Yes, he did," Mom said. "You all put in a lot of hours to your shows."

"Yeah, it's a lot of work," Jake said. "But it's fun."

Isaac's parents stopped trying to sneak away and stayed to talk while the band was there, though Kelly noticed Isaac steered clear of them.

"It was really interesting to see what goes on behind the scenes," Ian's mom said. "A lot of down time when you're not onstage."

"Sometimes we can go do things in the area after sound check, but we stay in if the weather's bad or we're tired," Ian said.

"I just never realized how much time is spent on the show," Dad said. "The roadies do a hell of a job getting everything ready for you."

"And I never knew what a sound check was," Paul's mom said.

"It's great that you all play around sometimes," Mom said. "It's not so serious when you're working."

"We try to keep it light but professional," Kelly said. "We don't want to waste anyone's time."

They talked for a few more minutes, then Jake's dad looked at his watch.

"I think we parents are going to go," Mr. DeHerrera said.

"Aw, already?" Kelly asked, looking at her parents.

"This really isn't our scene, as you kids say," Mom said. "We'll let you all have your fun. I've got some things to say about the film when you get home, though."

Kelly sighed.

"I'm sure you do," she said. She wasn't being disrespectful, she just knew what her parents would say.

"Thanks for coming!" Dean said, shaking the parents' hands. "Thank you for your continued support."

"It's our pleasure," Mrs. Slaney, Paul's mom, said.

They all said goodbye to their parents, and Kelly's parents stopped to talk with David for a moment before leaving through the back exit.

Kelly went around and talked to the people she knew, and some of the guests came up to her to introduce themselves to her and they spoke for a few minutes. She looked around for Jayna and finally saw her and Marty talking to David and one of his crew and walked over to them when she was free.

"Hey," Kelly said. "Are you guys doing okay?"

"Yeah, we're good," Jayna said. "Marty's a bit overwhelmed, though."

"Not used to rubbing elbows with famous people," Marty said.

"I still get star-struck sometimes. Like, I never thought I'd be at the same party as Christy Moreland," Kelly said.

Christy Moreland was a pop star who'd done the Disney circuit for a while, then branched out to do her own thing. A hot commodity, she was always on this or that show, and was currently on a big dance tour.

"She's great, isn't she?" Jayna said.

"Who's great?"

Kelly turned and saw Christy standing behind her.

"Um, you!" Kelly said. "Hi, I'm Kelly."

"Nice to meet you, Kelly," Christy said, shaking hands. "I just wanted to stop and say Hi. We'll probably never be on the same bill, but I do like your music. I like to work out to it."

"That's amazing! Thank you so much!" Kelly said. Kelly introduced everyone there.

"I actually want to talk to you, David, if you don't mind," Christy said.

"Not at all," David said, and he and Christy excused themselves to go talk privately.

"More work for him, probably," Kelly said.

"He's in demand, it sounds like," Marty said. "He was telling me he's got a job doing the music video for Safe Horizon."

"Oh, wow! They opened for us on our mini-tour," Kelly said. "That's fantastic!"

***

Ian felt like he needed to be more attentive to his parents there. This was their first big celebrity production they'd been to and he knew they were out of their element there, so he wanted to make sure they weren't neglected. Ian saw all the parents sticking together off to the side of the lobby, and went over to talk with them for a few minutes before they decided to leave.

Once they left, he went to talk with Stevie from The Disciples of Man, who was talking to Maggie's guitar player.

"Hey, we've got our bass player here," Stevie's said. "We just need a singer now," he joked.

Ian shook hands with them both since he hadn't had a chance to talk with them earlier.

"Tyrian Records must really like you guys," Nick said. "They shelled out a lot of money for this."

"I don't know what makes us so special," Ian said. "But I'm glad they like us."

"Just be careful they don't try to lure Kelly away for a solo career," Stevie said.

"They wouldn't do that," Ian said. "Would they?"

"I've seen it done before," Nick shrugged.

"No way Kelly would do that to us," Ian said. "We're all in it together."

"She doesn't really seem like the type who would do that, either," Nick said. "Just be warned."

With that, Nick shook hands again and wandered off.

"Come with me to the restroom," Stevie said.

"I thought only girls did that," Ian said with a laugh.

"Nope, not just girls."

They went into the men's room and Stevie did his business, then washed his hands and pulled a small plastic bag out of his pocket.

"Is that what I think it is?" Ian asked.

"If you think it's baby powder, no," Stevie said. "But if you think it's coke, then yes, it is. Want to join me?"

"Um," Ian started.

Stevie took hold of Ian's arm.

"What? You've been on tour and not tried this?"

"Nope," Ian said. "I mean, we had quote-unquote energy drinks in Peru that were made from coca leaves, but no, haven't tried coke."

"What did you guys take, then?"

"Ritalin."

"Oh, man, this is so much better," Stevie told him.

He watched as Stevie took his credit card and chopped out a couple of lines, then snorted it through a small metal tube he had hanging around his neck. He looked at Ian expectantly.

Ian had never even smoked pot before. It's not that he was anti-drug, he just had no interest in pot. Alcohol, on the other hand, he'd been drinking since before he graduated high school. It was such a rock star thing to do, snorting cocaine, and he *was* one. He also wanted to fit in with the rest of their friends.

"I guess, sure?" Ian said hesitantly.

Stevie made one short line for Ian and showed him how to roll up a dollar bill into a tube to snort it through. Ian snorted it and his nose and throat became numb immediately. He rubbed his nose a few times, trying to get the feeling to go away.

"It'll go away quickly," Stevie said.

"And you do this willingly?" Ian asked.

"You'll see why very soon."

What did I get myself into?

He followed Stevie back out to the lobby and stuck with him until he knew how he'd react to the drug.

Fifteen minutes later, he knew.

"Oh, my God," Ian said. "This is fantastic! I feel like I could go onstage and play for three hours, or-or-or write a great song."

"That's what I'm sayin'," Stevie said.

Ian hung around with Stevie for a while, talking a mile a minute, then he finally chilled out after drinking another Jack and Coke. He wondered if Kelly would want to have a quickie somewhere in the theater. *Eh, probably not.*

At one in the morning, Ian got a text from Dean, asking all of them if they were ready to leave.

Yeah, I'm ready to leave whenever, he replied.

The others replied similarly. Dean texted back, asking them to start their goodbyes.

Ian went over to tell Stevie and Erik goodbye.

"Let us know when your next show in SoCal is and I'll be there," Ian said.

"Sure!" Erik said.

"Here," Stevie said, handing him his small bag of coke. "See if your friends want to try it."

Ian shoved the bag into his front pocket.

"Sure," Ian said. "Thanks. Great to see you guys."

"Likewise," Erik said.

The band made their way around to the guests, thanking them for coming. Most of the guests had left, but a couple of photographers had hung around, and they took photos as the band left. Ian walked out with Kelly and they, along with Jayna and Marty, and Dean and Rosa, walked out to the waiting limo. The crowds had gone, but a few people waited to see them leave and perhaps get another photo of them. The band stopped one last time so the photographers and the fans could get a few photos before they got into the cars and drove away.

Ian had a hard time keeping his mind and his hands off Kelly. She looked really good in that dress. The Spandex skirt barely covered her as she sat there, even though she'd tried pulling it into place. He lay his hand on her thigh, caressing it through the lacy fabric of the overskirt. Kelly covered his hand with hers and squeezed it. He looked up at her face and she smiled at him. He leaned over and kissed her gently, then a little more eagerly, putting his hand up in her hair, then running it down her neck to her breast. With the latex over it, it felt strange but sexy.

"Do we need to get you two a room?" Dean asked, laughing.

"I thought they weren't dating," Rosa said.

"They aren't."

Ian stopped kissing Kelly and let his hand fall to her lap.

"I can't help it! Look at her," Ian said.

Dean didn't say anything, but chuckled and brought Rosa's hand to his lips and kissed it.

The driver stopped to let Jayna and Marty off first at Jayna's house, then drove around the corner to Kelly's house.

"I'll walk her up and make sure she gets in okay," Ian offered.

The driver opened the door and Kelly stepped out followed by Ian. They walked up to the front porch and Kelly dug out her key from her purse. She put the key in the door, then turned to Ian.

"Thanks for walking me up," she said.

"You're welcome," Ian said. "See ya!"

Ian kissed her on her cheek, and she opened the door and went inside. He got back into the limo and they drove on to drop him off at his house.

"Who gave you the coke?" Dean asked.

"What?" Ian asked with mock surprise.

"I didn't come down with yesterday's rain, Ian," Dean said, looking pointedly at him.

I guess I didn't hide it as well as I thought.

"Stevie," Ian said.

"Stevie," Dean repeated. He ran his hand through his short gray-streaked brown hair. "It figures. Well, I'm not going to ask you how you like it because I know from experience what it's like. As your manager, I'm supposed to tell you to not use drugs, et cetera, but I also know that none of you will listen to me. So, just—be careful."

"Yes, sir!" Ian said with a mock salute as they pulled up to his house. "See ya later."

Chapter Three

Kelly went into the kitchen for a late breakfast. She'd slept in after getting home at 2AM and it was more like lunch by the time she got up. Mom had already done the laundry and swept the floor.

"Good morning, sleepy-head," Mom said.

"Good morning," Kelly said. "What a night last night."

"Yes, it was very exciting," Mom said. "David said that he may have another music video to do with someone he met last night."

"Christy Moreland," Kelly said. "She came up and talked to us, then she and David went to talk shop."

"He's getting a lot of work these days."

"Yeah! I'm so happy for him."

"Speaking of films, your movie was great, but something bothered me."

Here it comes.

"There was a lot of unnecessary profanity in the movie," Mom continued.

"The guys have always talked like that," Kelly said, "and it's started to rub off on me."

"Yes, it has. You've always been so good with your words, Kelly. Just be mindful."

"Okay," was all Kelly said. She didn't want to talk about it. Yeah, it made her cringe last night, but only because her parents were there. No one else cared how she spoke, but maybe she'd make an effort to not swear as much.

Later in the week, the guys and Kelly met at Dean's house to work on writing some new songs. Kelly brought some partial lyrics and Jake and Ian had a few things worked out on guitar.

They went out to Dean's garage, which he had converted into a studio once they started rehearsing there all the time. Dean had it sound-proofed, and there was a couch and several chairs grouped together in a corner, and a computer with a digital recording program so they could play and save what they'd worked on. A fridge stood along the wall with bottles of water, beer, and hard lemonade as well as soft drinks.

The guys got their beers and Kelly her hard lemonade and they sat in the corner to work on their music.

"Hey, before we start," Ian said. "I have something you might want to try." He pulled the small bag of cocaine from his pocket and tossed it onto the table.

"Very rock and roll," Kelly said, glancing at it then looking back at her notes on her tablet.

"How very laidback of you," Ian said.

She shrugged.

"Nothing fazes me anymore, though I am a little surprised."

"This from the guy who won't even smoke pot? I'm surprised, but I'm in," Isaac said enthusiastically.

"Sure, why not?" Jake said.

Paul took a minute before he answered.

"I might as well," he finally said.

"Kelly?" Ian asked.

She looked up again.

"Really? You know that's a nope from me."

"Not even a little?" Isaac asked.

"I'll let you know if and when I ever need it, but you guys go ahead."

"Does Uncle Dean know about this?" Isaac asked.

"He does," Ian said as he carefully cut out short lines for each of them on the table with his credit card. "He called me out on it. Stevie let me try it at the premiere the other night, then gave me this for you guys to try."

"How thoughtful of him," Isaac said, and he snorted a line.

"No wonder you were so touchy-feely on the way home," Kelly said with a smirk.

The others followed suit then Ian put the bag back in his pocket and they sat for a few minutes to see how the drug affected them. They initially reacted like Ian did at first, rubbing their nose at the numbing sensation. The guys talked a lot more than usual, but they all worked on the songs, and by the end of the night, they had gotten the basic parts for two songs worked out and recorded. They had also played a couple of songs just to keep in practice with them.

Ian sat down next to Kelly on the couch while she made some notes on her tablet.

"Want to stay for some extracurricular activities?" he whispered in her ear.

"Here?" she asked quietly.

"Yeah, why not?" he said, pulling her hair back to kiss the back of her neck. "Just continuing where we left off the other night."

"And with that, I'm outta here," Isaac said, tossing his empty beer bottle in the trash. "You two have fun."

Jake and Paul also said goodbye, and Isaac pulled the side door shut.

Ian continued to kiss her neck.

"I haven't said 'yes,' you know," Kelly said, but she didn't push him away.

Ian smiled.

"You haven't said 'no,' either."

She put her tablet down on the table, then turned and kissed him, giving him an answer to his question. They didn't bother taking all their clothes off, just unbuttoned, unzipped, or unhooked and moved them out of the way.

Half an hour later, Ian and Kelly pulled their clothes back into place, Ian helping Kelly hook her bra.

"Coke makes me really horny," Ian said. "I wanted you at the video premiere, but figured you probably wouldn't want to then."

"You're just horny, period," Kelly said, tying her shoes. "You figured correctly, though that didn't stop you in the limo. Don't expect this every time."

"I know, I know," Ian said, holding his hand up. "I'll wait until you want to do it next time."

"Okay," Kelly said.

They locked the side door and pulled it shut and walked into Dean's house.

"See ya later, Dean," Ian called out. Dean came out of his work room.

"Have a good night," Dean said. "But then, you already did."

Kelly blushed. She should be used to all the sexual innuendoes by now, but she still got embarrassed by them sometimes.

"Good night," she said, and she and Ian left.

When Kelly got home a few minutes later, she told her parents good night, and went to her room. She grabbed her book and turned to the marked page, but before she could start reading, her phone dinged. She opened the message from Jayna and read it. With each word her face burned hotter. She quickly punched in Jayna's number.

"Are you fucking kidding me?" Kelly asked, forgetting about her vow to not swear as much.

"Nope," Jayna said. "Jessica saw the photos from the premiere and of course jumped to the wrong conclusion. Ian has told her that there is nothing between you two, but you know how she is—she's like a dog with a bone. She's posted on Facebook how you two are secretly seeing each other, blah, blah, blah."

"Well that's nothing new from her," Kelly said.

"No," Jayna said. "But she saw you and Ian leave rehearsal after everyone else and posted about it."

"We just left fifteen minutes ago! Is she spying on him?"

"Apparently."

"Holy shit," Kelly said, rubbing her forehead. "Well, we just stick with what we've been saying—we're just friends. It's no one else's business what we do."

"That's what Dean said, too. I called him first—Jess must have posted from her car, or wherever she's watching you from because it was so fast."

"I'll have to talk to my parents, because they'll hear about it somehow. They always do."

"Parents know these things," Jayna said. "Well, I just wanted to give you the heads-up about this."

"Yeah, thanks, Jayna. You are fantastic at your job."

"You're my friend and I don't want her to mess with you."

"Love you, sweetie," Kelly said.

"I love you, too. Talk to you later."

They disconnected, and Kelly went to talk with her parents.

"Jessica is at it again," Kelly said when she went into the living room where her parents sat watching TV.

"What now?" Mom asked.

"She posted on Facebook that Ian and I are secretly seeing each other, because we left after everyone else after rehearsal."

"I've kind of stopped caring about what she says," Mom said. "She causes so much trouble for all of you."

"She's still jealous and thinks she can get back with Ian. She's not helping her case with all this."

"Why *were* you and Ian last to leave?" Dad asked.

"We were working out some harmonies to a couple of songs." It surprised her how fast that lie came out.

"I figured as much," Mom said. "Well, I hope those who know you and the guys know that she's just stirring the pot."

"Yeah," Kelly said. She stood up to go back to her room. "Just wanted to let you two know."

"Thanks, sweetheart," Mom said.

Back in her room, Kelly sat on her bed and opened her Facebook app. She went to Fate Struck's page and saw what Jessica had posted. A lot of people defended Kelly, with only a few people agreeing with Jess. It warmed her heart to know that she had friends and fans out there who thought enough of her to do that. She saw that Ian and Isaac had already posted, denying Kelly and Ian were dating. Which was true; they weren't dating. *Semantics*.

Kelly wrote out her reply, also denying what Jessica said. At least that wasn't a lie. A few minutes later, replies to her comment popped up.

"*See? Straight from the source*," one fan commented.

"*Kelly would say something if they were dating*."

"*Three people who would know are saying they're not dating. Can you drop it now?*"

Jessica is really off the deep end with this, she thought.

Kelly texted Ian.

"*Jess needs to grow the hell up.*"

Ian replied a few moments later.

"I don't know what else to do about her."

"Maybe Dean will have an idea," she tapped out.

"Perhaps."

Kelly tried to read her book but couldn't focus on it now, her mind running a mile a minute. She took out the bag of gummy bears Isaac had given her during their tour and ate one. She'd need it to fall asleep.

"What is it with these exes you guys have?" Dean asked when the band met at the next meeting and writing session two days later.

"I thought Jess had moved on," Ian said. "She had some guy with her at the gymnastics exhibition and I thought she'd finally gotten over me. I actually thought I'd gotten through to her last year before we went on tour."

"Still no word on Greg?" Kelly asked.

"No," Dean said. "I'm sorry. It's like he's fallen off the face of the earth."

"Damn it," she said. She hadn't been able to shake the feeling that he'd been at the premiere, waiting outside.

"So, Jayna, you and Marty good?" Isaac asked.

"Yes! No psycho-asshole there," she said.

"And Hayley knows what she's getting into by marrying you, Isaac?" Dean asked.

"I've asked her several times," Isaac said. "She's good."

"Okay, then," Dean said. "I'll try to figure out something to do about Jessica, and if I get any updates on Greg, I'll let you know."

"Thanks," Kelly said.

"In the meantime, David's almost got the gymnastics exhibition finished," Dean told them.

"Awesome!" Kelly said.

"After it gets the okay from Jim at the offices, and the okay from Miss Susie, it'll be released to streaming and DVD."

"Fantastic," Jayna said.

"So, you guys gonna work on writing today?" Dean asked.

"Yeah, that was the plan," Isaac said. "Hopefully finish the songs we started last week."

"You don't mind if we 'indulge,' do you?" Ian asked as he pulled out his bag of cocaine.

"As Isaac's uncle, yes, I do care," Dean said, glancing at Isaac. "As your manager, I know it comes with the territory."

"I'll go get things set up in the studio," Kelly said as she stood up.

"You don't indulge?" Dean asked.

"Kelly's brain works just fine without it," Isaac said. He took the studio keys out of his pocket and tossed them to Kelly.

"Thanks," she said. She went out and unlocked the studio, Jayna going with her.

"When did they start doing that?" Jayna asked.

Kelly unlocked the door and they stepped inside.

"Ian tried it at the premiere and he shared with the others at the last rehearsal," Kelly said. "I have no desire to try it." Kelly turned on the lights and got a bottle of hard lemonade from the fridge. "This works just fine for me."

When the guys came out to work on songs, Jayna left. They worked on a song inspired by their detainment in Indonesia, and got music for two of the songs they had worked on previously.

"Well, we're a quarter of the way to another album," Jake said.

"Only nine more to go," Isaac said.

"No biggie," Paul said.

They decided to come back the next day for another writing session. Dean also had some things to tell them.

"A couple of magazines want to do a photo shoot with you," Dean said. "There is one, however, Kelly, that I doubt you're going to want to do."

"What's that?" Kelly asked.

"*Playboy*."

"Nope! Nope, nope, nope, no way in *hell* that's going to ever happen," Kelly said emphatically, leaning forward. "I draw the line at that. Hell no."

Dean laughed at her reaction.

"I knew that would be your answer," he said. "Okay, how about *Rockin' the Sport* magazine? They've seen you doing your flips onstage and want to do a story on you."

"If it includes the band, then yes," Kelly said. "I'm not going to do an interview or photo shoot alone."

"See? This is why we like you," Ian said, kissing her cheek.

"What do you mean?" Kelly asked.

"At the premiere party, Stevie and Nick said that you'd get lured away from the band for a solo career, and I told them you'd never do that. This proves it."

"The band isn't Kelly and the Fate Struck," Kelly said. "I don't want a solo career. We're a band and we're going to stay a band."

"Okay, I'll let them know," Dean said. "Also, *Music After Dark* wants to have you on the show. I told them you'd do it."

Music After Dark was a late night music show that usually had harder rock acts as guests.

"Sure!" Isaac said. "That's a popular show for our demographic."

"I'll firm up with everyone and get back to you with the dates and times," Dean told them as he entered notes into his phone.

"Cool!" Jake said.

Ian brought out his little bag of white powder; that was Kelly's cue to head out to the studio to get things turned on for their writing session.

They spent the next four hours working on songs, ending the night with three more completed songs. They finished the detainment song, and got words and music for another two.

"Are you going to be okay with the lyrics to The Hunted?" Isaac asked.

"Yeah," Kelly said. "But my parents may not be."

"You're such a nice girl to think of your parents," Jake said.

"And I don't care what my parents think," Isaac said.

"It's amazing how you and Dean came from the same family, but you're both so different from your dad," Paul said.

"Rebellion, I guess." Isaac laughed.

They saved their work on the computer and then shut everything down to leave.

When Kelly got home she told her parents about the upcoming events.

"And I told Dean to tell *Playboy* absolutely no way in hell I'd ever do that," Kelly said. "That's just…ew!" She shuddered.

"Good for you!" Mom said. "That's just pushing it too far."

"I agree," Dad said. "I can't even imagine you doing that."

"It's pretty gross," Kelly said. "But the other photo shoot will be better."

Two weeks later, the band, Jayna, and Dean met in the gym at Cerritos College in Norwalk. Jonathon, the writer of the article for *Rockin' the Sport*, had gotten permission to use the gym to take photos of Kelly doing some gymnastic skills, and Kelly and Jayna had signed the waivers.

"We're going to focus on you and your gymnastic skills," Jonathon said, "but we'll get some fun action shots of all of you at the beach tomorrow, because I understand you wouldn't do the shoot unless the band was involved."

"Yes," Kelly said. "I'm sorry to be a pain, but I'm not comfortable with it just being about me, when we're a band, not a singer and a back-up band."

"No, it's fine, and you're right, though I have to say that you've got to be the first singer who doesn't want the spotlight."

"That's our Kelly," Isaac said.

"Do whatever you need to do to warm up, then we'll take some photos," Jonathon said.

"Cool beans," Kelly said.

Kelly and Jayna sat down on the mats and stretched. Jayna wasn't going to be in the photos, but wanted to work out while she was there. After stretching for fifteen minutes, Kelly and Jayna ran around the gym a couple times, then Kelly got on her favorite apparatus, the uneven bars. Since the exhibition had only been a month ago, Kelly remembered her routine, and the photographer Jonathon brought with him took lots of photos. The guys applauded her routine, but Dean turned away a few times, not wanting to watch in case she fell.

Next, Kelly went over to the balance beam.

"I can't do a whole lot on here," Kelly said, "since I haven't really trained on this in a long time, but I can do a couple of turns and such."

"Whatever you can do, we'll photograph it," Jonathon said.

Kelly hopped up onto the beam and did a couple of different leaps. She lifted her right leg up into a split and held it while she did a Y-turn, then got into position for a Wolf turn. She spun around twice and the guys and Jayna applauded again.

"Beautiful, Kel!" Jayna said.

"How about a vault?" Jonathon asked.

"I'm afraid the vault is off limits to me," Kelly said as she jumped down. "Dean would have a heart attack."

"No vault," Dean said.

"Okay, we'll move to the floor," Jonathon said. "That's okay, right?"

"After seeing her routine, yes, she can do that," Dean agreed.

"Kelly's really good on floor," Ian said.

Kelly got the CD with her music out of her gym bag and handed it to Jayna, who went over to the sound system and put in the music for Kelly's floor routine.

"You should've been at the exhibition a few weeks ago," Jake said. "You'd have gotten some good stuff from there."

"That's actually what inspired us to do this article," Jonathon said. "It got back to us about the exhibition and they wanted someone to get on that right away."

"Are we ready?" Jayna called out from the booth.

Kelly chalked up her hands and feet and got into position, telling Jayna to play the music.

The photographer took a lot of shots of Kelly, then after she'd done the routine once, asked if she could do it a second time as he changed position.

"Yeah, I think I've got one more in me," Kelly panted.

"Don't overdo it," Dean said.

"I'm okay," Kelly assured him. She got into position again and Jayna started the music once more. During her last tumbling pass, however, she opted to do an easier skill, taking out the layout and leap.

"Nicely done!" Jonathon said.

"You changed that last thing you did," Isaac said.

"I was too tired to do the layout," Kelly said.

"Smart move," Dean said.

"I think we've got what we need," Jonathon said. "We'll see all of you tomorrow at Huntington Beach at 11 o'clock."

"We'll be there," Dean said.

When they got to the beach the next day, they found that Jonathon had roped off an area of beach to use with permission. The sun beat down on the sand and a slight sea breeze blowing onshore—a perfect day for the shoot. Kelly put on sunblock to protect her skin from getting sunburned, and told the guys they should do the same.

"If you don't I guarantee you'll be red by noon," Kelly said.

They put on the sunblock as they waited for the photographer to get ready.

Kelly wore her pink one-piece swimsuit with shorts and a tank top over it, and her flip-flops. The guys had on their swim trunks and a t-shirt, and Jayna had on a one-piece black and teal swimsuit under her shorts and top. Kelly had braided her long hair into two braids, and Jayna had hers pulled back into a ponytail. Jake and Ian had their hair pulled back into a ponytail as well.

"Thanks for agreeing to do this," Jonathon said. "We'll take some stills and then some action photos of all of you. I reserved the volleyball court here. Do you guys play volleyball?"

"I have in the past," Jake said.

"Back in high school," Isaac said.

"Well, it's not a hard game, so I figured we'd do that, and we can split you up evenly with Jayna here," Jonathon said.

"Fantastic!" Kelly said.

"And then maybe all of you in the water playing around."

"Sounds great," Isaac said, looking at the others.

"I thought for the cover photo is we'd have you, Kelly, doing a split and the guys holding you up, and Jayna on the ground in a split," Jonathon said.

"We're gonna need to stretch first," Kelly said.

"Do what you need to do while we get things set up," Jonathon said.

Kelly and Jayna spread out a towel on the sand and began to stretch while the guys tossed the volleyball around. Ten minutes later, the girls were ready.

"No funny business, you guys," she said to the guys.

"Wouldn't dream of it," Isaac said.

Jonathon told them where to stand, and then Kelly got into position, lifting her left leg up for Jake and Ian to hold, then she pushed off and did her split, Isaac and Paul grabbing her right leg.

"You're so light," Jake said. "No wonder you make your flips look easy."

Jayna got into position in front and they both put their arms in the air, toes perfectly pointed, and the photographer took several photos, having the girls in different positions with their arms.

"Okay, you can set her down," Jonathon said.

The guys carefully let each leg down as Kelly put her arm around Ian's shoulders to keep from falling, and Jayna stood up and brushed the sand off.

Jonathon next had them split into teams to play volleyball—Kelly, Ian, and Paul on one team, and Jayna, Isaac, and Jake on the other. The guys took off their shirts to play and Kelly donned a pair of sunglasses, as did Jayna and Jake. Isaac served the ball and was so surprised that he'd hit it that far that he wasn't prepared for the return and missed it, landing on his stomach on the sand. Ian and Paul laughed, and Isaac flipped them the bird.

Jayna served next, and they got a good rally going finally. As the game progressed, several people came by when they noticed the photographer and the roped-off area.

"Who are they?" one of the bystanders asked Dean.

"The band Fate Struck," Dean told her.

"Oh, how cool!" she said. "I went to a couple of their shows, but I didn't recognize them without their make-up and stage clothes. Do you think we can get their autographs?"

"Sure, when we're all done with the photo shoot."

Kelly had a lot of fun playing volleyball, even though she wasn't very good at it. She did manage to get the ball over the net a few times. She and Jayna both laughed when Jake spiked the ball into the net three times.

"You two are terrible," Jake said, but he laughed with them.

They played for just over half an hour, with Jonathon asking them questions as they played, keeping it very informal. Next, Jonathon wanted to get photos of them in the water. They all grabbed their bags and walked down to the water, the group of people following a short distance behind. They set their bags down on the sand and Kelly and Jayna took off their shorts and shirt, much to the delight of every guy there, even the band.

"God, those abs," Ian said, as both Kelly and Jayna tossed their shirts aside. They both still had flat stomachs with some muscle definition from their years as competing gymnasts, and their workouts at the community college. The people standing around clapped and whistled.

"Don't encourage them," Kelly said jokingly to the crowd. She took off her sunglasses and put them in her bag, then they all walked to the water's edge and tested the water. It wasn't warm, but it wasn't very cold, either—just right after playing volleyball. Jonathon brought out a couple of boogie boards for them. Isaac and Jake grabbed them and headed out into the water with them, then rode the wave back in. Kelly and Jayna stayed at the edge of the water, cheering the guys on as they took turns on the boards.

"Aren't you two going to get on them?" Jonathon asked.

"I've never actually been on one before," Kelly said.

"You grew up in Southern California and never tried boogie boarding?"

"Nope."

Jonathon whistled to the guys.

"Kelly and Jayna are trying them now," he said.

Ian and Paul brought them up and handed them to the girls.

"This is going to end badly," Jayna said.

"Agreed," Kelly said as they walked into the water.

They got out just past where the waves were breaking, about waist deep.

A wave came and they mounted the board. They caught the wave and rode it in, to a round of applause from everyone watching. They stood up and Kelly took a bow, Jayna just waving quickly.

"Well, that didn't suck," Kelly said to the guys.

"Going again?" Jake asked.

"Yeah! That was fun."

Kelly and Jayna rode the waves two more times before turning the boards back over to the guys.

After the guys had finished, Jonathon asked Kelly if she and Jayna would do a couple of flips in the sand.

"Yeah, I probably could here," she said, indicating the hard wet sand. "I wouldn't try it on the beach, though. Too hard to walk on let alone run and do flips. What do you think, Jayna?"

"Should be okay," Jayna said.

The guys came out of the water to watch when Kelly checked out the sand by running on it.

"Yeah, we can do it here, no problem," Kelly said.

Kelly and Jayna put their shorts and shirts back on before doing the flips.

"If you start at that end, I'll start at this end, and with any luck, we'll do our flips at the same time right in front of the photographer," Kelly said.

They discussed what they would do, then took their positions as the crowd applauded. When the photographer was ready, Kelly and Jayna started their run and did their flips perfectly in front of the photographer. The crowd cheered as the girls walked back.

"Nicely done," Jonathon said. "I think we have everything we need now. Thanks, everyone."

"You're welcome," Dean said, shaking his hand. "You'll let us know when it will be out?"

"Yes, I'll shoot you an email," Jonathon said.

"Thanks, Jonathon," Isaac said. The rest of them chimed in their thanks.

Jonathon and the photographer left, and the band signed a few autographs for the people standing there, or took photos with them. By the time they finished, it was 2 PM and they wanted to eat.

"There's a Jack In The Box up the street," Ian said.

"Okay, we'll drive through," Dean said. "What do you guys want?"

"Tacos!"

They got into the van and Dean drove through to get their food, and they ate on the drive back home.

"How was the photo shoot, honey?" Mom asked when Kelly walked in.

"It was really fun!" Kelly said. "We played volleyball and then played in the water, Jayna and I did a few flips on the hard sand for them. It was fun, it didn't feel like work."

"Good, I'm glad you got to enjoy the day a little bit," Mom said.

"And then next week, we're going to be on *Music After Dark*."

"Oh, that's a popular one with the kids."

"Exactly why we're doing it."

Chapter Four

A week later, Fate Struck arrived at the production studio to record their music segment for *Music After Dark*. Bailey and Scott had taken their equipment to the studio earlier in the day, so Kelly and the guys only had to sound check and get ready for their appearance.

The production assistant came out and led them back to the dressing rooms. They hung up their outfits for the show, got some water, and then followed the assistant out for sound check. They would perform their third single that had been released two months prior.

After sound check, a staff member took them to hair and make-up. As much as Kelly liked Jayna helping with her hair, she liked to be pampered by the stylists at the studios. The stylist did Kelly's hair and make-up along with the guys' then she dressed in her stage outfit.

Kelly watched the guys head to the restroom for their preshow pick-me-up while she opened her energy drink and drank half of it down. Despite what she told Ian about letting him know when and if she wanted it, she doubted she ever would. Then again, she broke down and used Ritalin on the tour, but cocaine was different. She could never see herself using that.

An hour later, the assistant came in and took them to the green room to await their time on the show. Also appearing that night were The Warning, who would go on last, and another up and coming heavy metal band, who went on first.

The show played on the TV in the green room. The heavy metal band was really good, and though Kelly wasn't a big fan of heavy metal, she did like some songs in that genre.

During a commercial break, the stage manager led Fate Struck out to the stage. The fans in the audience screamed and applauded as the band came out, then waited for the stage manager to give them the go-ahead. The show was recorded to be shown later in the night.

The show's host, Tom McDonald, came over and introduced himself and thanked them for coming on the show. He and the stage manager told them they'd go over to the couch once they were done with their song for a short interview.

Tom went back to his desk and the stage manager got the audience excited and applauding as they came back from the break. Tom introduced the band, and the audience screamed and applauded again as Isaac counted down the song and they started to play. Kelly stood at the mic at first, then took it off to move around the stage. They finished the song and the audience applauded louder than before. The band took off their instruments and bowed at the front of the stage, then went over to talk with Tom. Isaac sat closest to Tom, then Kelly, Ian, Paul, and Jake.

"Thank you so much for coming tonight," Tom said.

"We're happy to be here!" Isaac said.

"You've had a pretty quick rise to stardom," Tom said. "But you've also worked hard to get where you are, haven't you?"

"I think so," Isaac said. "I was out there getting us gigs anywhere I could—house parties, weddings, community gigs…"

"We were playing every weekend," Kelly said.

"And you managed yourselves for a while."

"Yeah, I did a lot of that," Isaac said. "But I was glad when Dean stepped in. He believed in us and really got us some great gigs."

"He's your uncle, right?"

"Yeah." Isaac nodded.

"And then that led to you getting a recording contract with Tyrian Records?"

"Dean worked his butt off to make that happen," Kelly said.

"There's been rumors, Kelly, that you and Ian are secretly dating," Tom said.

Kelly knew that Tom asked the hard questions, and had prepared for this.

"We are absolutely not dating," Kelly said with a laugh. "It's a rumor that was started by a disgruntled ex of Ian's."

"There seems to be a few rumors going around about you, Kelly," Tom said.

"Oh, God, what now?" she asked.

"You and Erik Dawson of The Disciples of Man?"

"Not true." Kelly shook her head. "We're good friends, but no, not dating. He's married and his wife is really nice." *Good friends, maybe, but he did kiss me and try to talk me into his bed last year. That's never gonna happen.*

"You and Toby Jensen of the boy band Then Suddenly."

"Where did that one come from?" Kelly asked.

"Man, Kelly, you get around," Ian joked.

"I've never even met him!" Kelly said incredulously.

"Jesse Taylor from Chellis," Tom said.

"Because we're from the same hometown?" Kelly asked.

"Most likely," Tom said.

"That's a nope," Kelly said. "Just how long is this list?"

Tom turned the paper to show her. Her eyes widened in surprise.

"I've been out with exactly two guys," Kelly said. "One was Greg, who you all know is wanted by the police, and the other I'd rather not say."

It was no one's business what she and Ian did, and she'd rather not have to explain it on TV.

"Was it a high school thing?" Tom asked.

"You could say that," Kelly said, which was true. She and Ian were friends in high school. "And my mom is probably having a heart attack about now."

"Why's that?" Tom asked.

"Kelly's the 'good girl' of the group," Jake said. "She is so un-rock and roll, it's funny."

"She's a rock and roll disgrace," Isaac said.

"But that's not to say that I haven't tried some things," Kelly said.

"She had a hangover once," Ian said.

"And the first time she dropped an F-bomb, it was like Mary Poppins swearing," Isaac said.

"You said it was like Sandra Bullock," Kelly corrected, laughing again.

"And then there's the gymnastics thing," Paul said.

"Yeah, that's very un-rock and roll," Tom agreed.

"But the fans like it," Kelly said.

"Okay, so one rumor shot down," Tom said, moving on. "How about you guys? Any rumors true?"

"Depends on what they are," Ian said.

"A girl in every port?"

"Absolutely not true," Isaac said. "In fact, I just got engaged to my girlfriend."

The audience applauded but some of the girls moaned at the loss of one of the guys being single.

"Congratulations! When's the big day?" Tom asked.

"No date yet, but sooner rather than later."

"Okay, Paul, how about you?"

Kelly knew that Paul had stayed faithful to Alexa. He didn't even look at other women in that way.

"Nope," Paul said. "Very faithful to my girlfriend."

"Not even a little deviation?"

"Not even interested," Paul said.

"Jake?"

"Still dating the same girl from high school," Jake told him.

Jake sometimes had a girl with him after the shows, but again, he didn't lie.

"Ian?"

"Ian's the only single guy here," Isaac said.

"I've had a bit of fun now and then," Ian said.

"Oooh," the audience chimed in.

"*You've* got the girl in every port," Tom hinted.

"No, not really," Ian said. "But women do tend to gravitate to me for some reason."

"It's been rumored, also, that you're dating Lena Hendricks of *All About Dad.* True?"

"I met her at a party. We exchanged phone numbers, and I took her out to dinner once, but that's been it. I went on tour soon after that. We've talked on the phone a couple times, but nothing else."

"Okay, we've got the sex out of the way," Tom continued. "How about drugs?"

"Nothing we can't get legally in certain states," Isaac said, ever the diplomat. "Nothing illegal on tour."

Kelly silently applauded Isaac for being tactful, but also for bending the truth a bit. He didn't outright lie, because they didn't have any illegal drugs *on tour*. The edibles were legal and Ritalin was legal, and they hadn't used coke while on tour.

"So that issue in Indonesia…"

"Was a farce. There was no way we'd be stupid enough to even bring caffeine tablets with us," Jake said.

"Does the self-professed 'good girl' have any vices?"

"Energy drinks," Kelly said. "Lady Grey tea."

"You're boring," Tom said, frowning, but his eyes twinkled. "Some rock star you are."

Kelly sat back on the couch, crossed her arms, and pretended to pout.

"She did need edibles once or twice to go to sleep," Isaac said, "but refused to eat them at first."

"Does 'mom' know about that?" Tom asked.

“She does, actually,” Kelly said.

“Okay, you’re redeemed,” Tom said, and Kelly uncrossed her arms and smiled. “Now, for the rock and roll. Your CD rocks! Have you got any other songs coming out?”

“I don’t know if there is another single coming out,” Isaac said, “or if we’re just going to concentrate on getting new material written for the next one.”

“And your tours of the U.S, Europe, and Asia were well-received.”

“They were! And we had a great time,” Ian said.

“Will you do one more song for us?” Tom asked, wrapping up the interview.

“Sure!” Isaac said, and they went over to the stage while Tom again thanked them for coming and mentioned the CD and video again.

When the band was in place, Isaac counted down a song and the band played their song.

Backstage, the band sat around the dressing room to relax and talk about the show.

“I loved how you skirted the questions about sex and drugs,” Dean said.

“Not lies, technically,” Isaac said.

“You’re right,” Dean said. “Well done! And Kelly, I didn’t even know half of those rumors.”

“I didn’t, either,” Kelly said. “That list was long.”

“Probably fueled by Jessica,” Ian said.

Back at home, Kelly warned her parents about what they talked about.

“There is no truth to any of the rumors going around about me,” Kelly said.

“We know,” Mom said. “If you were gone more often, then we might think they could be true, but you’re always home or at practice or with Jayna, so we know you don't have much time for dating."

"I just wanted to make sure you knew."

"We trust you, pumpkin," Dad said. "Besides, you're an adult, it's none of our business."

"Well, I still respect you guys, so I just wanted to let you know what we talked about."

The show was televised that night at midnight. Kelly stayed up to watch, and she thought they did well, though she still had a hard time watching and listening to herself. When their segment ended, she turned her TV off and went to bed.

First thing she did the next morning was check the band's Facebook and Instagram pages. Their friends and fans had made a lot of comments about the show, most of them positive, but of course, the doubters thought they just said what the fans wanted to hear.

There is no pleasing some people, Kelly thought. They would think what they wanted no matter what. The best thing she could do is just continue to be the person she was and hopefully the people who listened to Jessica and her gossip would come around.

It looked like the others had read the comments, too, because Isaac texted her.

"*Gotta hand it to Jessica. She sure can stir the shit around,"* he said.

"Yeah, she can. Not a lot we can do about it," Kelly replied.

"I can block her ass from the page," Isaac suggested.

"She'd just make another profile and come back."

"It'd sure be satisfying, though."

"Feel free to do it."

A few moments later, Isaac posted in the comments, warning Jessica to behave or she'd be banned. She replied that it was freedom of speech and it was her right to post what she wanted. A few moments later, Jessica had a gray circle with a line through it next to her name, indicating she'd been banned from the page.

"Nice job!" Kelly texted.

"Yeah, except I didn't do it," Isaac texted back.

A few moments later, Dean texted the group.

"I banned Jessica from the band page," he said.

"Kelly and I were just discussing that," Isaac replied.

"I'm tired of her shit. We'll keep watching for any new pages from her."

"Thanks, Dean," Kelly replied.

A few minutes later, Dean had posted on the band's page that while healthy discussions are encouraged, outright bashing and slander wouldn't be tolerated. Replies posted quickly after that, thanking Dean for taking out the garbage.

At least our friends and fans know us, Kelly thought.

A lot of things started happening for the band over the next several weeks. David got the gymnastic video done and it was already streaming online, to good reviews. For the preview of it with all the girls and Miss Suzy, Jessica didn't bother to show up. That was just fine with Kelly.

Their story in *Rockin' The Sport* came out, and Kelly, Jayna, and the guys bought several copies to give to family and friends.

"This is a really nice story," Mom said, as she finished reading the article. "You guys look like you had fun."

"We did," Kelly said.

"And I'm glad Jayna got to be in it, too."

"I know she's not part of the band, but she's a big help to us, plus I thought it'd be nice to have her there with us. They managed to get a picture of Dean in there, too."

The record company wanted a new album out later that year, and they didn't think the band would get enough songs written just meeting twice a week, so they rented an Airbnb in Malibu for them to spend two weeks in to write. It sounded like a good idea, being at the beach for all that time, but would they get any writing done? That remained to be seen. Jayna wouldn't be there, since she wasn't part of the writing team and would be at home with her husband, so Kelly would be there with just the guys.

"Jim wants you there, at the house, alone with four men?" Dad asked after Kelly told her parents.

"And Dean is okay with it?" Mom asked. "I'm not sure *I'm* okay with this, Kelly."

"It's not like I haven't lived with them all before," Kelly said. She trusted them, but she didn't trust other people to not read more into it than just a writing getaway.

"But Dean and Jayna were both there. I know you've known these young men for a long time, but they *are* young men."

"They respect me as their bandmate, Dad. How many times do I have to say that they treat me like their sister?"

"Feelings can change," Mom said. "I like the boys, Kelly, but it just makes me nervous."

"If anything was going to happen, it already would have," Kelly said. *And has*, she added in her head.

"I don't know about this," Dad said.

"I *am* an adult, you know," Kelly reminded them. "Weren't you just saying that after our appearance on *Music After Dark*?"

"Yes, but..." Mom started.

"I tell you what," Kelly said. "When I get there, I'll take some video of my room and send it to you, so you can see where I'm staying. I'm sure the door has a lock. Okay?"

Her parents looked at each other, and Mom nodded her head to her dad.

"Okay," Dad said.

"Cool beans!" Kelly said, giving her mom and then her dad a kiss on the cheek.

When it came time to pack, Kelly put in her swimsuit. Even if it was a writing getaway, she was going to spend some time on the beach. It couldn't be all work and no play, and maybe she'd be inspired to write something about the beach. A hard rock song about playing in the water—who knows?

Dean brought the van around to pick up everyone, then drove them two hours up the coast to the house, which was, as expected, right on the beach. The guys had brought their acoustic guitars with them, Isaac brought his cajon, a Peruvian percussion instrument, to keep the beat, and Paul brought his keyboard to write the songs with.

"Yeah, we'll get a lot of writing done here," Isaac said sarcastically.

"Jim is hoping a change of scenery will spark your imagination, and maybe get you relaxed enough to write," Dean said as he unlocked the front door. "The kitchen is fully stocked—food, water, beer, Mike's, Jack, Ritalin, energy drinks, coke…"

"Coke?" Ian asked.

"Well, the soda, anyway," Dean said, and pulled out a small plastic bag and tossed it to Ian. "Here."

"Excellent," Isaac said. "And I've got the doobage." He pulled out a bag with a small amount of marijuana in it.

"Hopefully it's not one big party here."

"I'll keep them in line," Kelly said, giving the guys a stern look.

"Yikes! Fear the Kelly," Jake said.

"Good. So, have fun—but not too much—and write the next big seller," Dean said, pumping his fist. With that, he left them to their writing.

They looked around the four-bedroom three-bath house. The living room looked comfortable with a big sofa and two matching chairs with a glass coffee table in the center of the room. A TV sat across from the sofa in an entertainment center, with a gaming console underneath the TV. After checking out all the bedrooms they all decided to let Kelly have the master bedroom with the *en suite* bathroom, and the others picked their rooms with an adjacent bathroom.

"Gotta keep our diva happy," Ian said.

"Oh, God, you guys," Kelly said.

Kelly got her phone out and did a quick tour of the house and her bedroom, giving a running commentary as she did.

"What are you doing?" Isaac asked.

"My parents weren't very excited about me being here with four guys," Kelly said when she finished. "So, I'm going to send this to them so they can see that my room has a lock on it. I trust you guys, and my parents like all of you, they're just concerned."

"I get it," Jake said. "But it does seem a little constraining."

"It is sometimes," Kelly said, putting her phone down after she sent the video to her parents.

"First thing I'm doing is hitting the beach," Isaac said.

"Same!" Ian said.

"You guys are incorrigible," Kelly said. "He's only been gone two minutes." She waited a beat. "I'm in!"

"Yes!" Isaac said.

They spent a few minutes taking their bags to their bedrooms and changing into their beachwear. They took a bottled water from the fridge, then Isaac grabbed the keys off the kitchen island and they walked out the back door and onto the beach. Beach chairs for their use lined the low wall in the backyard, and they each grabbed one and carried it down closer to the water. Kelly set up her chair and put on her sunblock, urging the guys to do the same.

"Or you'll be writing about how sunburned you got," she said.

The guys rubbed on their sunblock, then sat back in their chairs.

"If we want to be inspired," Jake said, "we need to relax."

"No argument from me," Kelly said, slipping on her sunglasses as she leaned back in her chair.

"God, Kelly," Isaac said. "Every time you take off your shirt, I get jealous of your abs."

"Oh, spare me," Kelly said, smiling. "You guys have abs way better than mine. I'm just glad that I have hips again. Not training three hours every day has given me a normal body."

"I'll say," Ian said, peering over the top of his sunglasses at her body.

"I walked into that one, didn't I?"

"Yep," Jake said, leaning back into his chair.

As they sat there, they did toss around some ideas for songs. They still had a couple partially finished songs already, and they each had an idea for a song or two.

"So, you know the person who is always cheering everyone else on," Isaac said, "but no one notices their achievements?"

"Kind of like the nerdy friend of the popular guy or girl?" Kelly asked.

"Yeah! The one who places first in the science fair, but everyone's more interested in the guy who sacked the quarterback," Jake said.

"Aw, how sad," Kelly said. "That's how I felt sometimes with Jessica in gymnastics."

"Oh, man, I'm sorry," Ian said. "I didn't realize she was like that."

"Jessica was good, I've got no problem with that. And I wasn't doing it for the recognition. It just would've been nice to have someone cheer me and Jayna on besides our parents."

They got ideas for a couple more songs while they sat there.

"So, see? This isn't a waste of time," Isaac said.

"Indeed," Ian said.

The guys had brought a Frisbee and they went out to throw that around while Kelly spread out her towel on the sand and lay on her stomach to watch. They did a few tricks with the Frisbee, throwing it behind their back, jumping to catch it, and Jake attempted a back flip in the sand. He made it around, but fell as he landed.

"Not quite as good as you," he said.

"Probably just as good as I could've done on the sand," she said as she applauded the effort.

They started to get hungry, so as the sun set, they walked back to the house. They brushed the sand off before they went inside, and headed into the kitchen to look at the possibilities for dinner. The fridge had the makings for sandwiches, and if they got really ambitious, there was ground beef and a roast. They checked the freezer, and found frozen pizzas, street tacos, and hamburger patties. Buns and other items were in the pantry.

"We can always call out for food, too," Jake said.

Since they didn't feel like cooking, they each pulled out something from the freezer to heat up in the microwave. When everyone had their food, they sat around the dining table with their beer and hard lemonade and ate.

***

After everyone went to bed, Ian thought about how this would work. With Kelly being a straight arrow, how would it be with all of them there for two weeks, drinking and using? Kelly never nagged them in the past, so he was pretty sure she wouldn't do it now, and she actually drank more than she used to. Would she feel left out? She knew where to get it if she wanted it, but it was her choice not to use and he respected it.

Ian awoke first the next morning. He went into the kitchen to find something for breakfast and found frozen pancakes in the freezer. He popped those into the toaster and found some precooked bacon in the deli drawer of the fridge, which he microwaved. Syrup from the pantry, and he was set.

Over the next hour the rest of the guys and Kelly woke up and came into the kitchen.

"What's for breakfast?" Kelly asked as she opened the fridge to look inside.

Even in her Star Wars pajamas, Winnie the Pooh slippers, and no make-up, she looked sexy as fuck. *Keep your mind where it belongs, Ian!*

"Frozen pancakes and waffles," Ian said, "eggs, bacon, I think there's cereal in the pantry, juice…"

"Awesome." Kelly grabbed the waffles and put two in the toaster. While she waited for that, she got out the bacon and put that on a plate and stuck it into the microwave. She poured herself some orange juice and by then the waffles had popped up. Kelly took out the plate of bacon, put the waffles on it, poured on the syrup, and sat across from Ian to eat.

"They really stocked this place pretty well," Ian said. "Everything we need."

The rest of the guys made their breakfast and came to sit at the table.

"We might have to do some cooking," Kelly said. "I wouldn't want that meat to go bad." She paused for a moment. "If there is a crockpot somewhere, I could throw the roast in it and it'd be ready whenever we want to eat for dinner."

Ian finished eating and put his plate in the dishwasher. He helped Kelly look for the crockpot when she finished eating and they found it in a cupboard. Kelly set it on the counter.

"I'll put the roast in after I change," she said, and she went to her room.

"We can't expect Kelly to do all the cooking," Ian said to the others.

"It wouldn't be fair," Isaac agreed.

"But we'll let her with this," Paul said. "I have no idea how to cook a roast."

"Neither do I," Kelly said, emerging from her room. "But I've seen my mom cook these in the crockpot."

With dinner figured out and cooking, they got ready to work on songwriting. Isaac did the honors of chopping out lines for them and they each took a turn, except for Kelly, who had her Rock Star energy drink.

"Do your girlfriends know about this?" Kelly asked, waving her hand over the table where the powdery residue remained.

"Hayley does," Isaac said. "I told her that night we tried it. She said, and I quote, 'Don't let that shit get out of hand.' I told her she has my permission to beat the shit out of me if it does."

"And she'll do it, too," Paul said.

"What about Alexa?" Isaac asked.

"I haven't told her yet," Paul said.

"Dude! You gotta tell her before she finds out."

"I know. She wasn't happy with me smoking weed, she really won't like this."

"Have you told Missy?" Kelly asked.

"I have," Jake said. "She wasn't happy about it, but also said she knew it came with the territory. I told her I'd keep it work related only."

They took a break after a couple hours to get the blood flowing again after sitting for so long. Isaac, Jake, and Paul went outside to smoke a joint. Ian stayed inside with Kelly.

"I think we're making good progress," Kelly said.

"I do, too," Ian said. "Even if we finish before the two weeks are up, we should stay here and enjoy the place."

"I'm down for that," Kelly said. "It's ours for that time, so no need to leave early."

The guys came back in and they all continued to work on songs until lunch time. They made sandwiches and opened the bag of chips. Kelly had a hard lemonade while the others drank beer with their lunch.

By dinner time, the band had finished one song and started another, but decided to call it a day.

"That roast is smelling really good!" Isaac said.

Kelly turned off the crockpot, then opened the pantry to find something to go with it. She found a couple cans of French-cut green beans, which she heated up on the stove, and five minutes later, dinner was ready.

"Just because I'm the girl doesn't mean I'm making dinner every day," Kelly said.

"Wouldn't dream of it," Isaac said.

"So then it's take out for the rest of the week?" Paul joked.

"I'll have you know that I *can* cook," Isaac said. "I just choose not to."

"Oh, okay," Jake said, rolling his eyes. "So that chicken you burned last week was just a fluke?"

"Of course," Isaac said with a wink.

"I can feel my cholesterol rising already," Ian said.

They managed to figure out something of a menu for the week, only factoring take-out in on a couple of days.

"We won't starve," Isaac said.

"That's encouraging," Kelly said.

Ian just hoped they didn't burn the house down with their cooking.

Chapter Five

By the end of the week the band had managed to come up with another three songs, which made nine total. To celebrate, they went to check out one of the nightclubs in the area. Isaac arranged for an Uber to come pick them up and take them into town to one of the better bars in the area.

They went inside and found a table that would seat all of them. A server came around and took their drink orders, checking all their IDs. She came back with the drinks a few minutes later. Since they were celebrating, Kelly ordered a Captain and coke instead of a hard lemonade. The guys ordered Jack and cokes.

"To our next album!" Isaac said, raising his glass. The others did the same. "May it be another bestseller."

"Hear, hear!" Ian said. They clinked their glasses and drank.

A local band had set up to play in the corner of the bar, and at 9 o'clock, they began their set, mostly country-rock with some pop rock.

After the first song, a man came over and tapped Kelly on the shoulder.

"Would you like to dance?" he asked.

"Oh, no, thank you," Kelly said. She didn't like to dance with people she didn't know, especially some random dude at a bar. Kelly smelled the alcohol in his breath and nearly passed out.

The guy took her left hand and gently pulled.

"Aw, come on, gorgeous," he said.

Kelly tried to pull her arm away, but the man had a good grip on it.

"The lady said 'no,'" Isaac said.

"You've got a lot of nerve coming up to a lady sitting with four guys," Paul said.

He let go of Kelly's arm.

"I don't see her dancing with any of you," the man said.

"Yeah?" Ian said. "What does this tell you?" Ian leaned over and kissed Kelly unreservedly, his hands in her hair.

"My apologies," the guy said, and he finally staggered off to another table.

"Thanks, guys," Kelly said. "Why can't people take 'no' for an answer?"

"Because he's an idiot," Jake said.

"A brave idiot," Ian said.

Kelly finished her drink and when the server came around, she ordered another one. As she waited for it, Ian asked her to dance, which she accepted.

When they got back to the table, the drinks had been brought over. Kelly also asked for a glass of water. She didn't want to be hungover tomorrow.

Two songs later, Isaac asked Kelly to dance while Ian found another partner to dance with, a cute blonde sitting with friends at another table.

As it got near closing time, Isaac called for another Uber to take them back to the Malibu house, and it arrived just as the band finished their set.

Back at the house, Kelly drank another full glass of water before heading to bed. She'd had three drinks and almost fell asleep on the ride back, and didn't bother even changing out of her clothes. She'd wanted to fit in a little better with the guys, even though she didn't use the drugs they used, but drinking seemed an acceptable way for her to join in with them.

Kelly awoke the next day slightly hungover, but not as bad as the guys, who clearly hadn't drunk enough water. They all sat around the kitchen table trying to drink their coffee. Kelly sat down with her tea, which was all she could drink at the moment. She did manage to eat a slice of toast. The others groaned at the thought.

"What's on the agenda for today?" Kelly asked.

"Recovery," Isaac said.

"Maybe the beach later on," Jake said.

"Taking the weekend off?" Kelly asked.

"Sure," Isaac said. "We've worked hard all week, I think we can take the weekend off."

"Sounds good to me." Kelly sipped her tea.

That afternoon, Dean stopped by to see how the writing was going. Isaac and Jake were playing a video game in the living room when Dean walked in.

"Hard at work, I see," he said.

"We've been working," Ian said. "We decided to take the weekend off."

"What have you got done?" Dean asked.

"We got three songs done, or mostly done," Kelly said. "And the beginning of at least one more."

"So this has been productive? Working here?"

"Absolutely," Isaac said, not taking his eyes off the game.

"We went out to celebrate last night," Paul said. "We took an Uber to a club in Thousand Oaks."

"Okay," Dean said. "You've all been eating? Is there enough food for you still?"

"Yeah, it's been great," Ian said. "And still a lot left."

Isaac and Jake stopped playing their game when Isaac lost.

"Do you want to hear what we've got so far?" Isaac set the controller on the table.

"Sure!"

Isaac turned on the computer and brought up the program with their recordings and played the rough versions of the songs for Dean. He sat and listened, tapping his foot along to the music.

"What do you think?" Isaac asked when the last song finished.

"I like 'em," Dean said. "Can't wait to hear the finished product."

"Once we get some crunchy guitar sounds in a couple of those, they'll sound really good," Jake said.

"I think we'll get another three done this week," Isaac said.

"Fantastic!" Dean said. "Well, I just wanted to see how things were going. I'll give you a call later in the week regarding when I'll pick you up."

"Sounds good," Isaac said.

With a wave goodbye, Dean left.

Two days later, while the band worked on a song, the doorbell rang.

"Who could that be?" Isaac asked. "We're not expecting anyone."

Ian went over to answer the door. When he opened the door, Lena stood there with a big smile.

"Hey," he said, trying to cover up his shock. "What a surprise! How did you find us?"

"When I found out you guys were holed up in a house to write, I asked a friend of a friend to find out where it was," she said. "I hope you're not mad."

"No! Not at all," Ian said. "Come on in."

Lena stepped inside and Ian shut the door. He wasn't mad, but he wasn't happy to see her right then. He and Kelly had had another play time that morning, and he couldn't remember what state he'd left his bed in. Plus, they were working, and working really well at the moment.

When they walked into the living room, the guys and Kelly didn't look happy to see her, either.

"Hey, look who's here," Ian said with more enthusiasm than he felt. "What a surprise, huh?"

"Hi, guys," Lena said with a wave.

"Hi," Isaac and Kelly said. Jake and Paul waved their hello.

"We weren't expecting anyone here," Isaac said, "since we're really busy working on new material."

"I know, but I thought maybe you could use a break and we could hang out for a bit," she said, pulling playfully on the front of Ian's shirt.

"Um, yeah, sure," Ian said. He turned to his bandmates. "Mind if I head out for a bit?"

"No, not at all," Isaac said, with a hint of sarcasm. "We'll just finish this without you while you have fun."

Ian got the point.

"I won't be long."

He took Lena's hand and then went out the back door to the beach.

***

"Well, I liked her up 'til now," Jake said.

"I thought they weren't seeing each other," Isaac said, looking at Kelly.

"They weren't," she said. "He called her a few times on tour, and he brought her to our party that one time, but that's been it. I figured they just couldn't make it work because of schedules."

"Obviously *she* didn't think that," Jake said.

It annoyed Kelly that Lena had dropped by to see Ian. Lena was beautiful, and funny, and much taller than she was. She and Ian weren't a couple, so she didn't have any reason to be jealous, and she *was* happy with their arrangement. But still, she couldn't help how she felt, but just pushed it out of her head. He was off limits to her to be anything other than what they were to each other. That had been the unwritten rule—no fraternizing with the band members, and they all had stuck to it, mostly because they all had girlfriends when she joined, and she was never interested in any of them. Until now.

What if he wasn't off-limits? He'd always been so kind to her, especially during their early days in the band. Ian didn't join the guys in smoking pot, so she and Ian talked a lot during those times, and they had bonded a little. He was good-looking, too. Kelly could see herself with him—if they weren't in a band together. If things didn't work out and they broke up, would it break up the band? She wasn't sure she wanted to find out.

Ian and Lena came back half an hour later, holding hands.

"I'm going to walk her out," Ian said.

"Nice to see all of you," Lena said with a wave.

"Same," Kelly said, smiling.

Ian disappeared out the front, returning a few minutes later.

"What the hell was that all about?" Jake asked.

"It's just like she said," Ian said, grabbing a beer from the fridge. "Friend of a friend gave her the address. I asked her to please not come back, though, since we *are* working. We'll talk again when we're done here."

Kelly silently cheered. Maybe they won't get together, she thought. *That's not like you, Kel. You want him to be happy. Could he be happy with me*?

By the end of the following week, the band had come up with another two songs, and part of a third, which, when finished, would make twelve songs, enough for another album.

Dean called to ask when he should come get them. They wanted to stay the weekend at the house, so he told them he'd come Sunday afternoon to pick them up.

With their work finished, they went out to a club again to relax. This time no one came over to bother Kelly, who danced with each of the guys. She was a safe partner for Jake, Paul, and Isaac, and Ian danced with a couple of girls there as well as dancing with Kelly.

By the time the club closed, they all had drunk more than they should have. They piled into the back of the Uber minivan, and the driver took them to the house. As soon as they got inside, Kelly started to unbutton Ian's shirt, kissing him as she did so.

"Hey, at least wait until you're in the bedroom," Isaac said.

"Okay," Kelly giggled and she pulled Ian to her room.

"Wait one little second," he told her as she sat on her bed.

He ran to his room for a moment, then came back to Kelly's room, locking the door behind him, wiping at his nose from the bump of cocaine he'd had, a condom in his hand. She hadn't moved from the end of the bed.

"Okay, *now* I'm ready," Ian said, and he kissed her eagerly.

She inched her way to the head of the bed, Ian crawling after her, kissing her as she did so. He lay on top of her, taking his weight on his forearms. Kelly looked into Ian's blue eyes. She could really get lost in those eyes, but needed to remember that they were not boyfriend and girlfriend. It was getting harder to keep what they were doing separated from love. His kisses made her tingle.

Ian sat up, straddling Kelly while he took off his shirt. Kelly started to slowly unbutton her blouse while Ian watched.

"God, you're sexy, Kelly," he said.

She smiled as she unbuttoned the last button, and Ian pushed the sides open. He ran his hands slowly up her body to her chest, then under her to unhook her bra. Kelly slipped her arms out of the blouse and bra and Ian bent down to take her nipple into his mouth, caressing the other with his fingers. Kelly sighed.

"You like that?" Ian asked.

"Yeah."

He ran his tongue around the pink center, then moved to her neck and back to her lips.

"Tell me what else you like," he whispered in her ear, then taking her earlobe between his teeth.

Kelly moved her hands to his fly, unsnapping and unzipping his pants. Ian smiled.

"I like the way you think," he said.

She pulled his pants over his butt, feeling the smoothness of his skin, then moved her hand to his erection. Ian quickly pulled off his pants, then Kelly's, revealing a purple thong.

"Jesus, Kelly," he said. He turned them over, and he ran his fingers under the string as she lay on top of him, alternately kneading and caressing her butt. She kissed his lips and moved to his face and down his neck. He smelled of sandalwood soap and shampoo. She breathed in deeply as she nuzzled his neck. Ian slipped the string of her thong down and she kicked it off.

"Sit up, I want to see you," he said.

Kelly sat up, straddling his waist, his erection pressing against her ass. He covered her breasts with his hands. Kelly moved her hands over his and squeezed.

"Oh my god," he said. "You are so beautiful." He felt around on the bed until he found the condom he'd brought in and Kelly moved so he could roll it on, then he guided his erection into her, and she settled onto him and started to move. He took her by her waist and thrust into her with each of her movements, Kelly feeling him fully inside her. Ian sat up and buried his face between her breasts, then flicked a nipple with his tongue. Kelly encircled his head with her arms as they continue to move together. Ian turned them over again, and he continued to drive into her.

"Fuck me, Ian," Kelly said breathlessly. "Fuck me. Don't stop."

"God, I love when you talk dirty."

He lay on her, his hips moving in rhythm to her movements. Kelly grabbed her breasts and squeezed, then pinched her nipple.

"Goddamn," Ian panted. He took a nipple between his thumb and forefinger and pinched and twisted, not too hard, just hard enough to make Kelly bite her lower lip and moan. "Oh, God, Kelly, I'm coming," he said, and they climaxed, and Ian collapsed onto her, his face buried in her hair. They lay on top of the wrinkled bedding, sweaty and breathless.

"That was fantastic," Ian whispered.

"It was," Kelly agreed.

They lay there silently in bed for a few minutes, Ian softly stroking Kelly's arm.

"You are so different in bed," Ian finally said. "Everyone thinks you're so innocent, but not here. But then again, we've kind of been a bad influence on you."

"I've had a sheltered life," Kelly said. "But I'm learning."

"You definitely are."

"And drinking alcohol tends to lower my inhibitions."

"I like it," Ian said.

Ian got out of bed and put his clothes back on.

"Remember to drink your water," Kelly reminded him, as she grabbed her own bottled water and took a long drink from it.

"Yes, ma'am," Ian said, and he kissed Kelly's cheek and left.

As she settled into bed, she could still smell Ian's scent on her bedding, and pulled the sheet up and breathed deeply as she fell asleep.

Once again in the morning, they all nursed their hangovers. Kelly didn't feel like even eating toast, but she did manage some water and green tea.

I really gotta stop doing this, she thought.

Isaac's phone *dinged.* He pulled it out and read the text message.

"Dean says he'll be here about 4 o'clock," Isaac said. "That gives us time to pack and get rid of our hangovers."

None of them did anything for the first couple of hours except drink water and coffee or tea and pop ibuprofen. Kelly felt better by lunch time, but only ate half a turkey sandwich. No one else wanted to eat until later in the afternoon, after they'd done their packing, and then it was only leftover cold chicken or vegetable soup.

"I'm glad I don't have to go home to my parents' house," Isaac said in between spoonfuls of soup. "I'd never hear the end of it for being hungover."

"My parents don't care as long as I don't drive under the influence," Ian said.

"My parents still worry about me," Kelly said. "So I need to not *look* hungover, even if I am."

"I guess they would, with you being their only daughter," Jake said.

Now that Kelly had sobered up, she started to think about her and Ian's activities last night. She'd thought that Ian and Lena weren't seeing each other, but with Lena coming over earlier in the week, maybe they were still willing to give it a go.

When Isaac, Jake, and Paul went outside to take their weed break, Kelly sat down next to Ian on the couch.

"What's the status with you and Lena?" she asked.

"Why?"

"Well, I'm feeling just a little guilty about last night."

"Don't worry about it, Kel," Ian said, placing his hand over hers on her leg. "We're both keeping our options open. We have a lot of fun together, but the dates are few and far between. That's what we talked about that day she came here. We're keeping it casual, nothing serious at the moment. If she finds someone that is better for her, I wish her all the best."

A weight lifted off Kelly as she smiled.

"I was really concerned when I woke up this morning," Kelly said. "I don't want to be the reason a relationship goes south."

"Kelly, you are one of a kind," he said, and he kissed her cheek.

"Hey, none of that," Jake said as he slid open the glass door as the guys came back in. "Thought you did that last night?"

"We did," Ian said. "Going for round two."

"Ian," Kelly said, playfully slapping his arm.

By the time Dean came to pick them up that afternoon, the queasiness and headache that Kelly had that morning had finally subsided, and the guys said their symptoms had eased up.

“I’m glad this was productive for you,” Dean said as he helped gather up their belongings. “This may be the way to go next time you need to write music.”

“We had a good time,” Isaac said. “And got some work done.”

“We’ve got a total of twelve songs now,” Kelly said.

“That’s great! Money well spent by the record company,” Dean said.

They walked through the house to make sure they hadn’t forgotten anything. Kelly grabbed the last three energy drinks and put them into her bag, drinking one while it was cold to help with her recovery.

The drive home took a little longer than the drive up, with people coming back from their weekend away. Dean dropped Ian off first, two and a half hours later. Dean opened the back of the van and Ian got his bag and guitar out.

“See you Wednesday,” Ian said, and with a wave he ran up to his house.

Next, Dean drove to Kelly’s house and helped her get her bags from the back.

“Thanks, Dean,” Kelly said. “See you guys!”

Kelly walked into her house and found her parents sitting at the kitchen table.

“Welcome home!” Mom said. She got up and helped Kelly with her bags, setting them on the floor, then she hugged her daughter. “We just finished dinner, but I can warm some up for you real quick.”

“That’d be great!” Kelly said, sliding into her chair at the table.

“You look nice and tanned,” Dad said. “Are you sure you did work there?” he joked.

“We got five or six songs done—I can’t remember if we finished that last one we were working on,” she told them. “But yeah, we did play a little bit, too. I mean, a beach house? We weren’t going to just sit inside all day.”

"Well, I'm glad you didn't," Mom said as she brought over the warmed up chicken enchiladas and seasoned rice to Kelly. "You can't be expected to not have fun."

"That's exactly what we thought," Kelly said. She blew on her food to cool it before she took a bite. "But we always did our work first."

"We'll let you eat, and then you can tell us all about it," Mom said.

They want to hear all about the song writing? Or the fun? Kelly wasn't going to tell them everything.

She finished eating and put the plate in the dishwasher, then went to sort through her clothes to do laundry. After she started a load, she went to talk to her parents.

"The house was fantastic!" Kelly told them. "You saw the pictures and video I sent you, right?"

"We did," Mom said. "It was a beautiful house."

"And right on the beach, so of course we had to go check out the beach that first day. We sat and tossed some ideas around, then the guys played Frisbee while I watched."

"You didn't want to play?" Dad asked.

"No, I'm not very good at Frisbee," Kelly said. "Each day we worked about eight hours total on songs. The guys had their guitars with them and a keyboard, so that made it easy to work out the melodies. Tyrian Records had a computer for us there with a recording program that we could record our songs on, and Isaac took the flash drive home with him."

"And where did the fun fall in all this?" Dad asked.

"Well, we'd take a lunch break to eat then go to the beach, then after dinner we'd do the same. At the end of the week we took an Uber to Thousand Oaks to a club to celebrate getting some songs done."

"Nothing too crazy, I hope," Mom said.

"No, just a couple of drinks, then we went home." *God, I'm lying to my parents* again. She purposely left out the part about the guy wanting to dance with her. Even though she was an adult, they'd still be concerned.

"How was the food?" Mom asked.

"It was good. We took turns making meals, though none of us can really cook. There was a crockpot we used a few times, and there was frozen food, too. It was okay."

"I can't wait to hear the new songs!" Dad said.

"Me, too! Right now they're just demos, but I think they'll sound really good once we get them all worked out."

Kelly went to her room and called Jayna. They had texted every day while Kelly was gone, but now she wanted to call and talk to her best friend.

"Hey, Kelly!" Jayna answered. "You must be home!"

"Yeah, I just got home a little while ago," Kelly said.

"Tell me all about it."

Kelly told Jayna everything she'd told her parents, but including what happened with the guy in the bar and everything else.

"I can just see the guys fighting that guy," Jayna said.

"I think Isaac was ready to," Kelly said.

"Do you want to go to the mall tomorrow?" Jayna asked.

"Oh my god, yes! I need some retail therapy!"

"Cool! 2 o'clock?"

"I'll be ready," Kelly said.

At the mall the next day, the young women went into Bath and Body Works where they both bought lotion and shower gel, then walked to Hot Topic, where the cashier recognized Kelly again, even with her hair pulled back into a clip and wearing jeans and a t-shirt, looking like every other twenty-something shopper.

"Back for more stage outfits?" he asked.

"Not this time," Kelly said. "Just buying some t-shirts for now."

Kelly and Jayna found what they came for and checked out, then walked up and down the length of the mall once more before stopping to get ice cream from Baskin Robbins. They sat at the tables nearby.

"I can't wait to hear the new songs," Jayna said.

"I think they're pretty good," Kelly said. "Once we get them sounding right, they'll be awesome."

As they ate their ice cream and talked, a couple of teenagers came over to them.

"Are you Kelly Brennen?" the blond young man asked.

"I am," Kelly said, smiling.

"I told you it was her!" the guy told his friend.

"I didn't think you'd be shopping at the mall," the friend said.

"I shop here a lot," Kelly told them. "What are your names?"

"I'm Anthony," the blond said.

"And I'm Nate."

"Nice to meet you," Kelly said, extending her hand, which the boys shook carefully.

"Can we get a selfie with you?" Anthony asked.

Kelly turned to Jayna.

"Would you take my picture with them?" Kelly asked.

"Of course," Jayna said.

"Oh my God, that's so awesome!" Nate said.

Kelly stood between the young men and threw up a peace sign while the boys made devil's horns. Jayna took a couple of photos for them.

"Thank you so much!" Anthony said. "You guys are awesome!"

"Thank *you*." Kelly sat down again. "You guys have a fantastic day!"

"We will!" Anthony said, and he and Nate walked away, looking back every so often, as if what just happened wasn't real.

"Thanks, Jayna," Kelly said.

"You're welcome," she said. "If it's okay with you, it's okay with me."

"I figure it's easier to just give them a photo and autograph if they ask than to tell them we're busy. I mean, it's because of them that we're where we are, so it's not a big deal."

After they finished their ice cream, they walked the mall a little more. They passed an earring kiosk and Kelly stopped for a moment.

"What do you think about me getting another ear piercing?" Kelly asked.

"Sure, why not? I'm surprised you haven't done it already."

Kelly stopped and spoke with the employee there, and she could do it right then. Kelly sat in the chair and the worker disinfected Kelly's earlobes and finished the process in under two minutes, purple studs now in Kelly's ears. Jayna got hers done, too. After that, Jayna took Kelly back home.

"I had fun today," Kelly said. "Just what I needed."

"I thought you might need it after being cooped up for so long," Jayna said. "I'll see you on Wednesday at rehearsal. I've got some stuff to show all of you."

"Awesome! See you then. Tell Marty I said 'Hi.'"

"Will do!" With that, Jayna drove away.

The band and Jayna congregated at Dean's house two days later to discuss business stuff and new show possibilities.

"Let's start with Jayna," Dean said.

"Okay," Jayna said as she passed out print-outs of merchandise: keyrings, stickers, T-shirts, and a new item—can coozies. "What do you think of the logo? And the new item?"

The new logo was similar to the old one, which was the band name with a lightning bolt and a sword incorporated into the words. This logo had a much bigger bolt and sword, and purples and reds instead of just black and gold.

"I like it!" Jake said. "The new colors really make it pop."

"That's what the artist thought, too," Jayna said.

"Sticks to our brand," Isaac said. "I say go with it."

"Awesome," Jayna said. "I'll get those things ordered this week."

"Thanks for handling that, Jayna," Dean said.

"No problem," she said, making notes in her phone.

"We've had a couple of new venues reach out to us for a show, which is really something out of the ordinary, so they must really like us, as well as the annual Taste of Long Beach thing," Dean said.

"No Taste of Lakewood?" Ian asked.

"They haven't reached out to me yet. I can call and ask," Dean said.

"Yeah, that was always a fun one to do," Isaac said.

"Do we want to up our asking price?" Dean asked.

The guys and Kelly talked it over before making a decision.

"Whatever we asked last time, just add a couple hundred to it," Isaac said. "I mean, it's our hometown, I don't want to gouge them, but I think we should get a little more, and I think they'll pay it."

"The only one we don't want to up is our dads' holiday parties," Kelly said.

"Though I think my dad's company could afford it," Isaac said. "But as I've said before, it doesn't come out of my dad's pocket."

"You *really* don't like your dad, do you?" Paul stated.

"I really don't." Isaac took a drink of his beer.

"So that's a yes for all of the above?" Dean asked.

"Yes," Isaac said.

Dean made notes in his phone.

"Okay, that's it!" Dean said after a half hour of talking with the band. "I'll leave you to your rehearsal."

The band went out to the garage studio to rehearse, with Jayna going, too, to hear the new songs, even in their primitive form. The guys indulged in their habit before starting to play.

"Do you want to try it?" Ian asked her.

"No, I'm good," Jayna said. "Besides, Marty would have a fit if I did."

"Fair enough," Jake said, wiping his nose. "Gotta keep the marriage happy."

They played the new songs a few times through for Jayna, then worked on them one at a time.

"That's my cue to leave," Jayna said.

"See you soon," Kelly said. Jayna waved to the guys as she left.

Half an hour into the rehearsal, Kelly got a call from Jayna.

"Something must be up," she said, and she hit *Accept*.

"Sorry to interrupt your practice," Jayna said, "but I thought you should see what Jessica is saying on socials."

"I'm afraid to ask."

"I don't know how she found out, but she knows you and the guys were away at a rented house, and she's posting under a new account all kinds of things about you, saying how fun it must be to do four guys every night."

"Jesus Christ," Kelly said.

"What happened?" Isaac asked. Kelly lowered her phone.

"Jessica is posting shit on socials about us being away together for two weeks," Kelly said.

"Are you fucking kidding me?" Jake exclaimed.

Kelly turned back to her call.

"She's a piece of work," Kelly said.

"I'm putting out the fires, but I might need you guys to post as well, though I doubt Jess will believe it, but everyone else should. I have to stay professional, but you guys don't. Some are kind of calling her out on it, anyway, but you know her little clique won't."

"We'll see what we can do," Kelly said with a long sigh. "Thanks for calling."

Kelly hit End, then went on the band's Facebook page. The guys were already there, reading on their phones. She read the post and then the comments. Jessica's posts were crude.

"How did she even find out?" Ian asked.

"Same way Lena did?" Paul asked.

"I guess she could have," Kelly said. "She probably had to bribe whoever it was."

"I'm taking care of it," Isaac said, tapping on his phone, "and I'm not being nice about it."

"I can't even with her," Kelly said, tossing her phone on couch.

"Dean's also taking care of it," Jake said. "He just texted us, saying he'll bring her up on harassment and slander charges if she continues."

They looked at their phones and read the text. Kelly picked up her phone again and looked at Facebook, and saw what Isaac had commented, then the other replies, sticking up for Kelly. She also went on Instagram to see what she'd said there, and Jessica was getting flamed there from Fate Struck's fans.

"We've got very loyal fans," Paul said.

A few moments later, a new name popped up in the comments on Facebook. Hayley.

"*You've got a lot of nerve posting what you have*," Hayley had replied. "*You're not only disrespecting the band, but me and the other ladies as well. I've never had any issue with you before, but this is low, Jessica. Shut the fuck up and crawl back into your little hellhole you call a life. You must live a sorry life to keep harassing Kelly, Isaac, and the other guys*."

"Bravo, Hays!" Isaac said, applauding.

"I love your fiancée," Jake said.

"Not too much, I hope." Isaac winked at him.

***

On his way home, Isaac thought about what Hayley said on the band's Facebook page. She loved him so much and loved the band enough to come to their defense, and he was damn lucky to be getting married to her. He loved her more than anything, and he really felt like a bastard sometimes for hooking up with fans and others while on the road. He didn't do it to spite Hayley—he'd never do that. While he liked the attention women gave him, he was lonely on the road, and missed Hayley so much. That's why he drank so much every time he left Hayley to go on the road. He loved her, but wasn't sure he deserved her.

Chapter Six

Over the next few weeks, Fate Struck worked on completely learning two of their new songs for the new shows coming up. Dean had booked them at three different places, and got the Taste of Long Beach booked, even with the higher price.

On the afternoon of the first gig, Scott and Bailey came over to take the equipment to the venue, The Grove of Anaheim. They and their crew had everything set up by the time the band and Jayna got there. While Jayna went to set up the merch table, Kelly and the guys did their sound check.

Backstage afterwards, the band piled food high on their plates and sat on the couches and chairs in the room to eat. The guys kept pouring drinks for themselves. Kelly stopped at one hard lemonade and one Captain and coke. She didn't want to be drunk for the show, and after she dressed, she drank her energy drink while the guys had their coke ritual, which had replaced their pot ritual. Just before the opener went on, a local band also, Fate Struck invited them into the dressing room for the pre-show shot of Fireball.

Kelly heard the opener start their last song, so she began to stretch her back and legs to practice her aerial walkover. She was ready to go when it was time for them to hit the stage.

Isaac got behind his drum kit and counted down the song and Jake, Paul, and Ian came in on their parts. Kelly grabbed the mic from the stand and went to the edge of center stage and began to sing.

***

The band finished their song and Ian went back to his amp to take a drink of his jack and coke, while Kelly thanked the crowd. He looked down at his set list taped to the floor by his mic stand, and knew that Jake needed to change his guitar before they played their next song. He took that moment to look over the sold-out crowd. There was a pretty good mix of old and young, men and women, but a lot of the guys stood in front of Kelly, and the girls were in front of Jake and himself.

Jake was ready, and Isaac counted down the song. Jake and Ian came in together in the song, along with Paul on rhythm. Two measures in and Kelly started to sing. Kelly always used the entire stage, making sure she sang to everyone, and when it was time for Jake's solo, she stepped back to let him take center stage. She was always good about sharing the stage with all of the band.

Ian walked toward center stage as he played, never missing a note, and when it was time for his backing vocals, he jogged back to his mic and sang his harmonies along with Jake.

At the next break, he took a long drink from his water bottle while Kelly introduced the band. After Kelly introduced him, Ian went to his mic.

"And this is Kelly, our lovely singer and the rock and roll gymnast," he said, using the phrase their record company had called her when they signed their contract. The fans cheered for Kelly and the guys, and the band started their next song.

***

The band finished their set two hours later to deafening applause and cheers. Kelly smiled as she and the guys went to the front of the stage and took a bow, then turned so Dean could take their picture with the fans in the background. She took off her shoes as the fans cheered even louder, if that was even possible, and she did a round-off into a backflip and an aerial walkover. She waved to the fans as she picked up her shoes and followed the others to their dressing room.

Kelly picked up a bottled water and drank a quarter of it down, dropping her shoes on the floor next to the couch.

"You know," Isaac said, "you're going to have to start doing that at every show now."

"The fans are starting to expect it," Jake said.

"I know," Kelly said. "I've created a monster."

"They sure like it, though," Dean said. "Just make sure you're okay to do it, and keep it simple if you have any doubts. They'll love anything you do."

"If you're going to do that," Ian said, "you'd better get some rock star socks."

Kelly looked down at her feet. She had on pink socks with purple flowers on them.

"I'm going to wear what I like," she said, "rock star or not. I like 'em."

She put her shoes back on and went to the food table and got a couple of sandwiches and a hard lemonade. She sat down next to Isaac on the couch.

"Friends and family backstage?" Dean asked.

"For a little while," Isaac said. "Are my parents here?"

"I don't think so," Dean said.

"Fantastic! I know Hayley's here, so she can come in."

"I'll make sure I check everyone before they come in," Dean said, looking at Kelly.

"Thanks, Dean," Kelly said.

Dean disappeared and a few minutes later he opened the door and led in family and friends, about ten people total. Hayley ran over to Isaac and hugged him, then Isaac pulled her onto his lap as he sat down. Missy and Alexa went over to Jake and Paul respectively, and Marty sat in a chair to wait for Jayna. Kelly's parents and brother came in, as well as Jake's parents. Lena Hendricks was also there, and she went over to see Ian, and Kelly watched as he kissed her eagerly. *Get over it, Kel.*

"It's been a while since we've seen a show," Mom said. "You all have really gotten so good!"

Kelly turned her attention back to her family.

"Hasn't Kelly just taken command of that stage?" David asked.

"You really have, sweetheart," Mom agreed. "But you make me nervous when you do your flips. Don't you want a mat, just in case?"

"What I'm doing is pretty simple," Kelly assured her mom, "and I've already told Dean that I won't do anything if I'm not feeling up to it."

"That's good," Dad said. "I'm glad Dean watches out for all of you."

The parents and friends didn't stay very long.

"We just wanted to say Hi and congratulate you on a great show," David said.

"I'm always happy to see you at our shows," Kelly said, giving her mom and dad a quick kiss on the cheek, and her brother a side hug.

After they left, Dean let in the fans and music reporters and photographers, making sure that Greg was not among them. Fifteen minutes later, Jayna came back in and ran over to Marty and greeted him with a kiss, then she asked Kelly if she needed anything.

"Not at the moment," Kelly said.

The photographers took several photos of the band and some of the fans there while the reporters asked each member of the band a few questions for their articles they were working on for the review of the show. Kelly and Jayna stood together talking as one of the photographers came around to them. He first took a candid photo of them, then they turned and smiled, both holding up a peace sign.

Kelly looked around at everyone there. She knew they'd been getting more popular, but having all the people backstage made it very real for her. The crowd had grown since their first days as a headliner, and they even had to turn people away who wanted to come backstage. She'd gotten much more comfortable with the people who came to talk to her, though the male fans still looked disappointed that she didn't ask them to make out with her. They always seemed a little surprised that she was just a regular person when she talked with them.

"What's with the Jessica person?" one of the young men asked Kelly.

"Ever since I joined the band in high school she's had it in for me," Kelly said. "She and Ian dated for a while but he broke up with her."

"I can see why," he said.

"She used to give me these snide remarks in gymnastics, too. I try not to let it bother me, but what she said on Facebook was just too much, and totally untrue."

"You had a lot of people sticking up for you," the guy said.

"We've got such great fans! You guys are the best."

Ian and Lena were nowhere to be seen, so Kelly figured he'd found a place to go for privacy. She tried to tell herself that she didn't care what they did. Ian wasn't hers and she had no claim on him. That was true, but man, it made her chest burn when she saw him with Lena. She poured herself another Captain and coke and drank it down.

Two hours and several bottles of alcohol later, the band wanted to wrap things up there. Kelly watched as Dean went around to thank everyone for coming and soon just the band and Jayna and Marty were left.

"I'm really glad none of us drove ourselves here," Jake said, barely able to stand.

Even Kelly had gotten caught up in all the excitement, not to mention her jealousy toward Lena, and drunk more than usual. Kelly hadn't noticed when Ian had come back, but he'd come back alone.

"Denny's?" Paul asked.

"Yaaasss!" Kelly said, turning to the others.

"Denny's! Denny's!" they chanted.

"Okay, we'll go to Denny's," Dean said. "But you'd better behave."

"Scout's honor," Isaac said, holding his hand up in the Scout Salute.

"You were never a Boy Scout," Ian said.

"I bet Kelly was a Girl Scout." Isaac winked at Kelly.

"I was, actually," Kelly told them.

"There ya go!" Isaac said. "On Kelly's Scout's Honor, we'll be good."

"Hey, don't put that pressure on me! I'm not in charge of you."

"Get your things and let's go," Dean said.

Jayna helped Kelly with her bags while the guys managed their own with help from Marty. They took everything to the van, putting the bags in the back, then got inside. Dean, who never drank at the shows, got into the driver's seat. Jayna and Marty followed in Marty's car and they found a 24-hour Denny's restaurant only a few miles away.

At two in the morning the restaurant was pretty deserted, only a couple of travelers in there. The hostess seated the group in the back of the restaurant and after the group read over the menu, they placed their orders when the server came around.

"So, are you and Lena together now?" Kelly asked as she stirred sugar into her iced tea, trying to be casual about it.

"I think we're going to give it a try," Ian said. "Are you okay with that?"

"You don't need my permission," Kelly said. "You're a big boy."

"It won't change anything between you and me, though."

"That's cool." She played it off, but it was a knife in her heart to hear him say that, but she and Ian couldn't be together if they wanted the band to keep going.

The band, Dean and Jayna talked over the show, mostly just how great it was to be performing again after a few months of not doing any gigs. Kelly talked excitedly about being onstage, but by the time the servers brought out the food, she'd grown quiet. Her stomach gurgled and churned. She thought it was just from not eating, so she ate a couple bites of her food. That was the wrong thing to do, as the churning intensified. She drank some water, but that didn't help any, and the nausea became worse.

"Kelly, are you okay?" Dean asked. "You're awfully quiet."

Kelly shook her head and stood up.

"Excuse me," she said, and she walked quickly to the ladies room, where she barely made it to the toilet to vomit. She kneeled on the floor in front of the toilet, not knowing if she was done, or if more was coming. The smell of alcohol-tinged vomit made her queasy again. Another wave of nausea and vomit came just as she heard someone come into the restroom.

"Kelly?" Jayna asked.

"I'm in here," she said hoarsely, waving her hand under the stall wall.

Jayne opened the door.

"Oh, honey," Jayna said. She stepped inside and gently pulled Kelly's hair back away from her face.

"I really don't feel good," Kelly said.

"I can see that," Jayna said, holding Kelly's hair as she vomited again. "You'll feel better once it's out."

Someone knocked on the door.

"Are you okay for a minute?" Jayna asked.

Kelly nodded, and Jayna went to see who knocked.

"Is everything okay?" Isaac asked.

"Kelly's not feeling too well," Jayna said. "But I think she's okay."

"I'm okay-ish," Kelly said from the stall.

"Okay, I just wanted to check," Isaac said. "I'll let the others know."

"Thanks," Jayna said, and she returned to Kelly.

Kelly hadn't vomited anymore after five minutes. She stood and Jayna backed out of the stall and let Kelly out. She went to the sink and splashed water on her face and rinsed her mouth out. Jayna got a paper towel ready for her, and Kelly blotted her face and mouth.

"Feel better?" Jayna asked.

"Loads," Kelly said.

"You look a little pale, but I guess that's to be expected."

"I feel kind of shaky, but otherwise much better."

"Ready to go back to the table?"

"Yeah, I think so."

Jayna held Kelly's arm for a moment to make sure she was steady, then they walked back to the group.

"As you like to say," Ian said, "very rock and roll."

"Zero stars, would not recommend." Kelly forced a smile as she picked at her pancakes with her fork.

"We've all been there at some point," Paul said.

"We can get that to go if you want," Dean said.

"I think I can eat a little now, but yeah, I'll take the rest home."

Kelly ate a quarter of her pancakes and a slice of bacon, and had the rest boxed up to go.

"We do not tell my mom about this," Kelly said.

"You're a singer in a rock band," Jake said. "What does she expect?"

"You don't think she's gonna know when you get up tomorrow, er, later today?" Ian asked.

Kelly thought about that. She'd definitely be hungover and her mom would know.

"Maybe she won't notice," Kelly said.

"Kelly, sweetheart, your mom's gonna know," Jake said gently.

"Well, I'll deal with it when the time comes,' Kelly said.

"Good luck," Ian said.

Kelly didn't wake up until almost 12:30 the next afternoon, having finally gotten into bed at 4AM. Her head hurt so much, and the queasiness rose again, but didn't need to run to the bathroom. Her tongue felt like sandpaper. At least she'd had the foresight to put a bottled water next to her bed. She took a long drink from that, and lay back down, pulling the blankets over her head.

I feel terrible, she thought.

She lay in bed for another half-hour, trying to get up the courage to get up and face her mom. Kelly thought maybe she'd be able to pull off not looking like death warmed over and got up and went to the bathroom. She looked in the mirror. Her pale face and dark circles under her eyes gave everything away. She'd also forgotten to take off her make-up before going to bed, and most of her eye make-up had smeared. Kelly took a few minutes to take care of that by washing her face and using her make-up remover.

There, somewhat better, she thought.

She went to the kitchen to make some tea and maybe some toast. Her mom was in the family room next to the kitchen, folding laundry.

"Good afternoon, sweetheart," Mom said.

"Good morning," she said.

Mom looked up from her folding.

"Are you okay, Kelly?" Mom asked, concern in her voice. "You don't look so great."

"I'm fine," Kelly said. Might as well get it over with. "I over-indulged last night."

"That's not like you, Kelly." Mom set down the shirt she was working on. "What were you thinking?"

"I really didn't drink that much," Kelly said, which was true, at least compared to the guys. "I'm just a lightweight and more than two drinks and I'm done for."

"You may be a popular rock star but you certainly don't have to live the rock star life."

"I'm really not, Mom. This rarely happens. I just did too much talking and not enough paying attention to what I was doing." *And too much thinking about Ian and Lena.*

"Well, make sure it doesn't happen again."

"I can't make any promises," Kelly said. "But I also won't make it a habit."

Mom took up the shirt she'd been working on and folded it.

"Just be careful," she said.

"I will."

Kelly took her tea and toast back to her room. As she sat on her bed and ate, she thought about her room. It still had the look of a teenager's room, with posters of Ed Sheerhan, Twenty-One Pilots, and The Beatles on the walls, and the walls themselves painted a dark pink with white trim. The only thing that said rock star was the gold record on the wall and the poster from one of the gigs on the door. At twenty-two years old, it may be time for her to get her own place, or at least a roommate. In high school, she thought that she and Jayna would share an apartment together, but with Jayna being married, that was out of the question. She didn't want to get a place with Ian or Paul; that would lead to too many rumors, but she also didn't relish the thought of getting a place on her own. She wasn't close enough to either Missy or Alexa to get a place with them, but she thought it'd be better than getting a place with someone she didn't know, especially now as a celebrity. She'd ask around and see if anyone had any ideas for her, maybe ask David if he had any friends who needed a roommate.

After Kelly finished her tea and toast, she went back to the kitchen to wash her mug, then took some ibuprofen to get rid of her headache, and drank it down with lots of water. She checked her phone when she got back to her room and saw she had quite a few texts from both Jayna and Ian, wanting to know how she was feeling. She texted Jayna first.

"I'm alive, but barely. My mom wasn't too happy with my state of being."

Jayna replied back a few minutes later.

"Glad you're doing OK. I was worried about you."

"Nothing a little rest and water won't cure," she tapped out.

*"*hearts*"*

Next, she texted Ian.

"Sorry, just got up a bit ago," Kelly texted. *"I'm good, just hungover."*

"OK. Just checking," Ian replied immediately.

She also let the others know she was okay, sending a group text to Dean, Isaac, Jake, and Paul.

Kelly got some clothes together and went to take a shower to see if that would help her headache and overall tiredness. She washed her hair, then let the water hit the back of her head where it hurt the most, and the pain started to fade. She finished the rest of her shower quickly, and did feel better.

Fate Struck's next show was a week later, at the House of Blues in Anaheim, and this time they had organized a meet and greet before the show for the fans who paid for the opportunity. Dean arranged for a driver for their van this time, so he didn't have to do the driving, as he was meeting a few people there as well. The driver picked up everyone by 2:30 on Thursday afternoon and drove them to the venue. With traffic it took nearly an hour to get to Anaheim.

By now, the band's merchandise had grown to several boxes of items and wire racks to hang the shirts on, so that was always taken to the venue with the equipment, and Jayna set it up when she arrived with the band.

Dean handed the band their All Access badges and went backstage to the dressing room to set their bags down and get some food and water before going out to do sound check. The fans had been brought in to watch them go through sound check and they applauded when the band came out. They all waved to the fans as they took their places with their instruments.

They went through getting the monitors set first, making sure they all worked, with Kelly walking around the stage to see where the sound dropped out, and the technicians taking care of everything. The guys didn't do as much roaming around the stage, and it was set up more quickly.

Next they moved to voices, Kelly going first. She said a few "check-one-two's" into the microphone then began a song a cappella, with Jake and Ian doing the same for their backing vocals. The fans applauded Kelly's unaccompanied song, and she made an elaborate curtsy, which made the fans laugh.

After they got all that done, the band played a song so they could check the balance of everything and the techs could get the mix right for in-house and in-ear. They finished the song and Jake got on his mic.

"Can I get more Kelly in my monitors, please?" he asked.

"Start the song again and we'll mix it in," one of the techs told him.

They played the song, and when Jake liked the mix in his ear, he gave a thumbs-up to the tech and they ended the song at the second verse.

The band went backstage to grab a bottled water before being led out to the floor area where a table had been set up for them to sit at while they talked with the fans and took photos with them all. Jayna came in to help with anything that needed to be done, which would most likely be taking care of any gifts the band received from the fans.

The friends took their places at the table with Kelly in the middle, while Dean went and spoke with the manager of the HOB for a moment and they led the fans in.

They had never done a meet and greet before, so Kelly didn't know what to expect. The first fan was a young man in his late twenties who came up with a photo of the band for all of them to sign. With Isaac being on the end of the table, he was the first to greet the man.

"Hey, how's it going?" Isaac asked.

"I'm good!" the guy said. "I'm a big fan of you all, especially you, Isaac. I'm a drummer, too, and I love to watch you play."

"Well, thank you very much!" Isaac said as he signed the photo. The band had black and silver Sharpies to sign the fan's item.

"I've seen you guys probably about five times on your tour."

"Wow, a super fan!" Kelly said, smiling.

After getting his photo signed and talking briefly with the rest of the band, he gave Jayna his phone and she took a photo of him and the band, the man standing just behind the band. They all made devil's horns except Kelly, who flashed a peace sign.

It took about an hour for all the fans to come through and get autographs and photos with the band, and the band had quite a collection of gifts from the fans, which Jayna had carefully placed in the box she'd brought out with her.

At the end of the meet and greet the fans all applauded as the band stood to go backstage.

"Thank you so much for coming!" Kelly shouted to the fans. The fans would be staying in the venue and have first pick at their place in front of the stage before the doors opened for rest of the fans.

"You guys are awesome!" Isaac said.

Once backstage, Kelly and the guys looked over their gifts again, Jayna remembering who received what from the fans.

"How do you even remember all that detail?" Isaac asked.

"It's sort of evolved over the years," Jayna said. "I've got a pretty good memory now."

They got their stage clothes out and got ready for the show. Since Jayna already had the merch table set up, she was available to help Kelly in case she needed anything. Kelly dressed in her new outfit, which was purple flared pants and a shiny black sleeveless blouse that fit her body really well. She laced on her purple Chucks and started on her make-up and hair. She'd gotten the colors touched up earlier in the week and her hair was once again highlighted with purples and pinks. She'd also had her hair trimmed and long layers cut in.

Kelly stood in the middle of the room, thinking.

"What's up?" Jayna asked.

"You know, that stage is kind of small," Kelly said.

"Are you thinking about doing a flip?" Jayna asked.

"I was thinking about it. Not sure I can, though."

"You could probably do a side aerial," Jayna suggested.

"Yeah, that doesn't take up much room," Kelly agreed. "I better practice it a couple times."

Jayna moved a table out of the way to make room for Kelly to practice. Kelly got into position, pointed her toe, hands up, and did the side aerial. She stumbled slightly as she landed, but the guys applauded.

"That was sloppy," Kelly said.

"It wasn't that bad," Jayna said.

Kelly did it a couple more times until it was to her liking.

"It doesn't have to be perfect," Jayna told her. "I think the fans are happy with anything."

"Yeah, but there will be the Jess followers who will cut it to shreds."

"They don't even matter, Kel," Jayna said. "Just ignore them."

"I try, but it's hard."

The opener for the night was another local rock band. Dean asked them to come join the band for a pre-show shot and they came in a few minutes later.

"We're so excited to open for you guys," the singer, Ella, said.

"Thanks for opening for us," Isaac said. "You come highly recommended."

"Awesome!" said the bass player, Eddie.

Isaac poured a shot of Fireball into the red cups and passed them out to everyone, then held his cup high for the toast.

"May we have a fantastic show tonight," he said.

"Cheers!" everyone shouted and they knocked cups before they drank.

"See ya after the show!" Isaac said to the band.

"Break a leg!" Kelly said as the opener went back to their dressing room. They'd be taking the stage in ten minutes.

After the show, Kelly was careful not to drink as much as she did after the previous show. She didn't particularly enjoy the queasiness of overindulging, and made sure she drank lots of water with what alcohol she *did* drink.

In the morning, she didn't feel nearly as bad as she had before, and in fact her mom didn't even notice anything out of the ordinary. *Yay!*

Chapter Seven

None of the band had heard of anyone needing a roommate, so Kelly called David to ask if he knew of anyone.

"Well, as a matter of fact," David said. "I'm actually losing my roommate in a couple weeks. Would you want to move in with me?"

"Really?" Kelly asked. "You'd want me to move in with you?"

"Sure, why not? We've both got weird hours we work, and I'm not going to hassle you about when you get home or what condition you come home in."

"What the heck does that mean?" Kelly asked.

"Mom told me how hungover you were a couple weeks ago and was concerned. I know you don't make a habit out of it, but I also know it can come with the territory. I've been around a lot of bands lately and seen how bad it can get. You guys aren't even close."

David had been making music videos for a lot of bands ever since he did Fate Struck's videos.

"Plus, I live in a gated community, so if I'm ever away, you'll feel safe being by yourself."

Kelly hadn't even thought of that. David was sometimes gone for a few days for location filming.

"Or, you could have Ian come stay with you while I'm gone, or…whoever. And, you'd have a private bathroom."

"Oh, that seals the deal right there!" Kelly said. "How much?"

"A thousand a month, plus utilities."

"Awesome! Yeah, I'll take it!"

"All righty! I'll let you know when you can move in. Like I said, he's leaving in two weeks and then I'll have it cleaned for you and you can move in."

"Thanks, Davy, I appreciate it."

"You're welcome, little sis."

Kelly hung up and went to tell her parents the news.

"You're moving out?" Mom asked.

"Yeah, it's time, I think," Kelly said.

"Is it because I gave you a hard time about being hungover?"

"Not really," Kelly said. "It was part of it, but I'd also been thinking about it for a while. I need to be out on my own, so to speak."

"Where are you moving to?" Dad asked.

"I'm actually moving in with David. He's losing his roommate at the end of the month so I can move in there."

"Oh, that's wonderful!" Mom said. "I was afraid you'd move into an apartment on your own. Not that that's an issue, I just feel better knowing you are living with someone you know and not alone. I don't trust some of the fans out there."

Kelly knew who she meant, and he wasn't a fan; Greg was obsessed.

"Well, you won't have to worry. It's perfect for me."

Kelly packed up her things over the course of the next two weeks, while also preparing for the band's last gig until the Taste of Long Beach in August. She ordered a new bed and dresser set and moved in the weekend before their show at the Troubadour on Wednesday.

"Are you sure you don't need any help?" Dad asked.

"No," she said. "Davy's helping me take stuff in, and Isaac and Jake are meeting me over there, too."

"Okay," Dad said, wiping his eyes.

"Oh, Daddy," Kelly said, and she hugged her dad. "I'm not very far, and I'll come over all the time."

"I know," he said. "It's just our last child is leaving the nest. Like I told David, though, this is still your home if you ever need or want to come back."

"Thanks, Dad," Kelly said, smiling.

Isaac and Jake were waiting for Kelly when she drove up and started to grab boxes from her car.

"I really appreciate the help," Kelly said.

"It's no problem," Jake said.

Kelly grabbed a box and led the way inside the house to her room.

"This is really nice," Isaac said, looking around. "Damn! Your own bathroom?"

"Yep!" Kelly said.

They made several more trips to the car along with David to bring in her stuff. Her bedroom set would be delivered in a couple hours.

"Thanks for the help, guys," Kelly said when they'd finished bringing in all her stuff.

"You're welcome." Isaac hugged her.

"Anytime," Jake said, also giving her a hug, and they both left.

She dug through one of her boxes which contained some of her music memorabilia, including her gold record.

"Do you want to hang that in here?" David asked, indicating the living room.

"Can I?" Kelly asked.

"Yeah, I think it's cool, and you probably want a lot of people to see it."

"I don't like to brag, but yeah, pretty damn proud of that."

Kelly got a couple of Command strips and hung the plaque on the wall.

"Looks great!" David said.

On Wednesday, Fate Struck's show at the Troubadour went off without any issues and the crowd loved it. Kelly ended up drinking a little too much again that night, but not to the point of throwing up, and was hungover the next day. She went in to take a shower to help the headache go away, then went to the kitchen and made some tea and toast. David was up and working in the family room, looking over the shots from the previous weeks' work.

"Hey, she lives," David said.

"Yeah," Kelly said. "We had some of our band friends come to the show last night and they hung out for a while."

"You don't owe me any explanations," David said. "I've over-indulged a time or two."

Kelly smiled. It'll be nice not having to explain everything to Mom and Dad, she thought. She made her tea and toast and sat at the kitchen table and ate while she watched David work.

"What are you working on?" she asked.

"It's a corporate video," David said. "Not as fun as a music video, but it pays well."

"Nice!" Kelly said.

Kelly didn't do much that day. She had nothing planned and nothing happening with the band, so she decided to go for a swim in the community pool that was near the house. She changed into her swimsuit then pulled on her shorts, grabbed her sunblock and a towel, and started out.

"Hey Davy, I'm going to the pool…" she said, but stopped when she saw he had company. "Oh, sorry, didn't mean to interrupt."

"*This* is your sister?" the woman asked, surprise in her voice.

"Yeah," David said.

"Your sister is Kelly Brennen from Fate Struck?"

"I guess you've heard of us," Kelly said with a smile.

"Uh, yeah!" the woman said. "When he said his sister had moved in, he never said your name."

Kelly went over and shook her hand.

"Kelly, this is Tessa," David finally said.

"Nice to meet you!" Kelly said.

"So nice to meet you, too! I knew he'd done music videos for several bands, but he never told me you were his sister!"

"Dude, I thought you were going to brag about me," Kelly said sarcastically.

"I was waiting for the right moment," David said. "I guess this is it."

"My younger sister and I went to one of your shows a few months ago," Tessa said. "Freakin' awesome!"

"Thank you so much!" Kelly said. "We try."

"Oh, you do more than try," Tessa gushed. "Phenomenal."

Kelly blushed.

"Thanks!" Kelly headed to the door. "Well, like I said, Davy, I'm going to the pool for a bit. I won't be long."

"Enjoy!" David said.

"Tessa, it was great to meet you," Kelly said.

"You, too," Tessa said.

Kelly walked half a block to the pool at the community center for the neighborhood. There were several people in the pool, and a lifeguard on duty, but no one recognized her. *Yay, I don't have to deal with pictures being taken.* While she liked the recognition, she did like to do things without the attention sometimes.

Several lounge chairs surrounded the pool. Kelly picked one close to the gate and put her things down. She took off her shorts, applied her sunblock, then spread out her towel on the chair, kicked off her flip-flops, and walked to the steps at the shallow end of the pool. She'd worked up a sweat on the short walk and was anxious to cool off. Kelly dipped her foot in carefully, and didn't shudder even though the water wasn't very warm. Gripping the handrail she continued in until she was all the way in the water, then crouched down until only her head stuck out.

Kelly mostly just wanted to relax in the water. She stayed by the side of the pool in the shallow end for a few minutes, then swam the length of it. The people in the pool floated out of her way as she swam the length several times, then she got out and sat on the lounge chair, put on her sunglasses, and watched the kids play.

After an hour, Kelly pulled her shorts back on, gathered up her belongings, and walked back home. David and Tessa were eating lunch in the kitchen.

"How was the pool?" David asked.

"It was fantastic," Kelly said. "I think my headache is gone."

"Good," David said. "I got an extra burger if you want it and are feeling up to it."

"Oh, no, are you sick?" Tessa asked.

"No, just a little hungover," Kelly said. "Yeah, I feel like I can eat now."

Kelly went to the table and took the burger from the bag and sat and ate with them, drinking water to rehydrate.

Later in the week, Isaac messaged the band and Dean, to get rehearsals set up for learning the new songs.

"Can we start tomorrow?" he asked.

"Absolutely," Kelly texted back.

The others replied in the affirmative.

Kelly and the guys met at Dean's house the next afternoon to work out the songs. They had already worked on two of them and had added them into their set, but needed to get the others ready to record.

"Jim is really anxious to get another record out soon," Dean said, "and then get another tour booked."

"Plus, it'd be cool to have more new songs for the Taste of Long Beach in two weeks," Isaac said.

They all headed out to the garage studio, where the guys took their hit of coke while Kelly got her mic set up and took a bottle of hard lemonade from the fridge.

Isaac put in the flash drive and with a few clicks brought up the songs. They listened to them a few times, then worked on one of them, Kelly bringing up the lyrics on her phone.

Three hours later, they had two songs worked out completely. Dean came out to give them a listen.

"They sound fantastic," Dean said when they'd finished playing. "I think Jim will be happy with them."

"We'll be back tomorrow to work on the others," Isaac said.

During the rehearsals through the rest of the week, the band got the rest of the songs worked out and recorded on the computer and copied to Isaac's flash drive. Dean told them he'd contact Jim to let him know they'd finished the songs.

"So expect to be in the recording studio soon," Dean told them.

The night before the Taste of Long Beach show, Kelly and the guys helped tear down the equipment with Scott and Bailey. The roadies would take the equipment to the park early the next day and get it set up. Fate Struck headlined that year, so they'd go on in the evening, with sound check in the late morning.

Dean drove the band and Jayna to the park in the van instead of renting a limo. Traffic control directed Dean to a parking lot closer to the stage, under the trees. Dean went to find out where the band would be getting ready for the show and came back a few minutes later.

"They've got a tent for you to get ready in," Dean said. "Back behind the stage area, kind of like last time, except it's a little more private."

"Fantastic," Isaac said, and they got out of the van, grabbed their bags from the back of the van, and followed Dean to the tent, which was a step up from the last time they played there. Being famous had its perks, and they didn't have to share the tent with anyone this time, and food and drink had been set out for them. There was a small lighted mirror area for them to do their make-up and a screen for Kelly to change behind. They had even put down a plywood floor with throw rugs everywhere.

"Definitely better than last year," Ian said.

"If you want to walk around before the show and enjoy the event," Dean said, "you can do that after sound check. I would suggest not traveling in one big group unless you want to be stopped by fans every ten feet."

"Good idea," Jake said.

They walked out to the stage for their sound check. The way the stage was set up, the sun would be directly in their faces for about fifteen minutes into their show as the sun set. Right now the sun was hot and bright, so they wore their sunglasses and Kelly had her baseball cap on still.

Afterwards, they split up into groups of two so they wouldn't draw attention to themselves. Isaac and Jake, Ian and Paul, and Kelly and Jayna went their separate ways into the crowd of people.

Kelly wore her sunglasses and had her hair pulled back into a ponytail with a baseball cap on, and Jayna had on a wide-brimmed straw hat, so neither of them would be noticed while they walked around. Since Jayna had been partly featured in the *Rockin' The Sport* article, she'd been getting recognized sometimes, too.

The ladies spent their time checking out all the booths and sampling foods and drinks. Kelly bought a rock singer figure made out of shells, and Jayna found a sundress to buy. At 3:45 they headed back to the tent and arrived at the same time as Isaac and Jake. Ian and Paul sat in the tent already, sampling the beer.

The first of three openers took the stage, so the band went out front to watch. Kelly enjoyed each band, all from the Lakewood/Long Beach area like them. Between bands, they went back to their tent to grab another water and something to eat.

They walked to their dressing room tent as the last opener started their set to get ready for the show. Southern California was in the middle of a massive heatwave, so they dressed accordingly for the show, while still trying to keep to their usual style. Isaac wore cargo shorts and a white T-shirt, Jake had on long pants and a dark blue cotton shirt, left unbuttoned, Paul wore denim shorts with a dark gray

Sweet band shirt. Ian had picked out jeans and a black tank top, and Kelly wore dark purple cotton pants and a sleeveless black Spandex crop top.

"Whoa! Showing some skin tonight," Jake said.

"For comfort, not anything else," Kelly said. "I tried to find something that wasn't low-cut but had to compromise the length."

"Well, it looks great," Isaac said.

Kelly took the ponytail elastic out of her hair and misted her hair with water to freshen it after being pulled back for most of the day. While her hair dried, she put on her make-up and hoped she didn't sweat it all off. She stretched her legs and back, then popped open her energy drink and took a long drink from it while the guys did their thing.

They heard the crowd cheer for the band as they finished their last song. That was Fate Struck's cue to gather up whatever they needed for the stage. The stage manager came in fifteen minutes later and led the band to the side of the stage where they'd wait for their time to go on. Kelly put on her sunglasses and did a few more stretches and walked around a little bit until show time.

Isaac went out first as usual and got the beat going while the others walked out onstage with their instruments and picked up the song. Kelly ran out last and grabbed the mic and got the crowd excited for the show and started to sing.

As Kelly walked across the front of the stage as she sang, she heard calls of "Kelly! Kelly!" She looked down and grinned broadly.

Our friends are here!

"Hi, guys!" Kelly said in between verses, and waved to them.

At the end of the song, Kelly pointed out their friends to the guys, who also waved and smiled at them.

It had been a long time since someone they knew had been at the front of the crowd, and it gave Kelly an extra boost of energy to have friends there that she could actually see.

By their third song, the sun had gone down below the horizon and the stage lighting took effect, so Kelly took off her glasses and put them on top of her head. Halfway through the set, Isaac and Jake took off their shirts because of the heat, much to the enjoyment of the ladies in the audience.

In between songs, Kelly made sure to drink her water. She didn't want to become dehydrated like the time they played in Arizona in the heat when she almost passed out. She left the alcohol drinking to the guys for this show.

During a song, Kelly forgot she had her sunglasses on top of her head and when she flipped her hair back, her glasses flew up in the air and landed behind her. Ian and Jake saw what happened and started busting up while they played. Kelly laughed, too, missing a couple of words, but picked up the song again as she also picked up her glasses so she wouldn't step on them, and hung them on her mic stand.

At the end of the set, the fans cheered loudly for Fate Struck as they came forward to take a bow, then take their customary photos with the fans, and their friends, in the background. The crowd had grown while each band before them played, and now it was massive, barely being contained within the event boundaries. Kelly was amazed at how many people had shown up for them.

Kelly had worn her Chucks onstage, so she didn't have to take off her shoes to do her now-expected flips for the fans. The fans cheered as she got into position, then did a cartwheel and a side aerial. She waved to the fans as she picked up her sunglasses and water bottle and ran offstage. Kelly grabbed a towel to wipe the sweat off her face and took a bottled water from the table and drank a quarter of it down.

"Hey, you made it through the set," Isaac said, popping open another beer.

"I didn't drink any alcohol today," Kelly said. "I didn't want a repeat of Tucson."

Dean came in and out of the tent several times while the band rehydrated and got something to eat. He came back in one time with a request.

"There are quite a few fans waiting along the fence," Dean said. "Would any of you want to go out and sign a few things for them?"

"Sure!" Kelly said right away.

"Yeah, I'll go," Ian said.

The others agreed to go, too. Dean led them out to the waiting fans, who cheered when they saw the band walk out. Kelly saw that their friends stood at the back of the crowd.

"How are you guys?" Isaac asked as the band got closer.

"We're great now!" one fan said.

Kelly and the guys talked with the fans and signed autographs for them for about half an hour.

"Your glasses flying off your head was the highlight of my day," another fan said.

"Yeah, I forgot they were there," Kelly said, laughing. "Next time I need to remember to just hang them on the mic stand."

"And deny everyone another comedic moment?" Ian asked.

"Ha ha, you're funny," Kelly said with a smile.

When the fans had gotten an autograph and photo, the band's friends came up to talk with them.

"It's been a while since we've seen you guys play," Emily said.

"We heard you were playing here again, so planned on coming," said Bobby.

"Are you still glad you punched out Dillon for me back in high school?" Kelly asked. Bobby had punched Dillon in the face after he had asked Kelly to the Prom. She turned him down and he'd called her some names, and Bobby had taken exception to that. He got suspended for a day for it, and so did Dillon.

"Oh, man, I'd forgotten about that," Bobby said with a smile. "I can say that I was Kelly Brennen's bodyguard in high school."

"I still remember that, and glad you did it, though I was sorry you got suspended because of me."

"He deserved it."

The band chatted with their friends until Dean called them over to gather their belongings.

"Thank you so much for your support," Ian told their friends, giving them a handshake or fist bump. The others chimed in their thanks, and they went back to the tent. They got their things together and walked out to the van. They made their usual stop at Denny's to eat before Dean drove each of them back home.

Chapter Eight

Isaac picked up Hayley and took her to dinner so they could discuss the wedding plans.

"We should probably pick a date," Isaac said, "so we don't have to do what Jayna and Marty did."

"Yeah, we don't want to have to cut the honeymoon short," Hayley agreed.

After they ordered their food, they each pulled up a calendar on their phones to pick a date.

"We're probably going into the studio in a month or so," Isaac told her. "But you probably don't want to have the wedding that early."

"That wouldn't give me much time to plan anything," Hayley said.

"We're probably going to have the next tour start early next year, since we're shooting to have the next album out by Christmas."

"So we could have the wedding sometime between October and January?"

"I think that would be ideal," Isaac said. "Unfortunately I'll have to run it past Dean for approval, just to make sure he doesn't have anything planned for us during that time. We're still at the mercy of TV show schedules."

"I've learned to deal with it." Hayley shrugged. "I know it's not your fault. It's not anyone's fault, it's just the way things have to be done."

They both looked at their calendars, scrolling back and forth through the next few months.

"How about—October 16th?" Hayley asked.

Isaac looked at the date.

"That's only seven weeks away," he noted. "Does that give you enough time to get things planned?"

"It does cut it kind of close," Hayley said.

"How about November 10th?"

Hayley looked at her calendar again.

"That—looks like it would work," she said. "Okay, run that by Dean and see what he says about it."

"I'll text him right now," Isaac said, and he tapped out a message to his manager, then put his phone away as the food was brought to their table.

After dessert, Isaac checked his messages. Dean had replied back.

"He says that day will work!" Isaac said.

"Yay! We have a date," Hayley said. "I've got so much to do! I gotta find a maid of honor, a dress, a place! What kind of wedding do we want?"

"I'll leave that up to you. If you pick some places we can check them out together, but I know I'll love anywhere you pick."

"You're too easy," Hayley said, laughing. "Okay, I'll let you know."

Isaac dropped Hayley off at her home later that night, after they spent some time at his apartment. He walked her up to her porch.

"Let me know if you need anything to help with the planning," Isaac said.

"I will," Hayley said.

"I love you, future Mrs. Landry."

"I like the sound of that," Hayley said.

Isaac kissed her softly on the lips, then made sure she got inside before he left.

At rehearsal three days later, Isaac told everyone the news.

"Save the date on November 10th," he said.

"You picked a date?" Kelly asked.

"Yep! Dean okayed it, so we're on our way."

"Fantastic!" Ian said.

Isaac texted the date to his parents, and his mom replied back.

"We can't wait! So happy for you and Hayley!"

His father texted back later in the evening after Isaac was home.

"You couldn't have told us this in person?"

Isaac sighed. *There's no pleasing that man.*

He didn't reply back. Right now, he needed to do his own planning, starting with his best man. With him living with Jake, that would be the natural choice. They'd been friends since middle school, and he was the first person he asked to form a band.

Jake came home and went to the kitchen to grab a beer. Isaac followed him in.

"Hey, man," Isaac said. "Do you have a minute?"

"Sure," Jake said, tossing the bottle opener back into the drawer.

"Would you do me the honor of being my Best Man?" Isaac asked.

Jake smiled broadly.

"Hell, yeah!" he said, holding out his hand to shake Isaac's then hugged him.

"Thanks," Isaac said. "I'm going to ask Paul and Ian to be the groomsmen, which is basically two more Best Men."

"Of course. It wouldn't be right for just me to be up there with you."

"You don't think Kelly will be upset about not being included, do you?"

"I doubt it," Jake said. "She was already in Jayna's; I think she'd be happy to be out of the spotlight."

Isaac called Paul and then Ian to ask them to be part of his wedding party, and they both accepted wholeheartedly.

They had a couple of TV appearances coming up in the meantime, so at the next rehearsal, they practiced their three singles, not knowing which one they'd be playing until the day of the show.

The first appearance was on *The Midnight Show*, which recorded in Los Angeles. A limo picked all of them up in the afternoon to take them to the studio, where they'd record their part for a later broadcast at midnight. Bailey and Scott had already taken their gear there and had it set up for sound check, which the band did when they arrived.

"Which song are we playing?" Isaac asked once they'd gotten their levels set in their monitors.

"Can you do 'The Lies That You Tell'?" the producer asked.

"Sure," Isaac said, and he counted down the song and they started to play while the sound engineer set the levels for the house.

When they finished with that, they went backstage and got dressed and did their make-up, then the Make-up Department came in to touch up any shiny spots. They waited in the green room until the stage manager came in to take them onstage.

The band gave their usual high-energy performance before going over to sit with the host for the interview.

"Thanks for coming to visit with us," the host, RJ, said.

"Happy to be here," Isaac said quickly, still trying to catch his breath after playing.

After quick introductions, RJ got into the interview.

"There's not too many bands your age playing hard rock," he said. "Who or what inspired you to play this, and not something like pop or dance music?"

"The Warning has really inspired us," Kelly said. "Along with other bands like Plush, and The Pretty Reckless, but also older Seventies bands like Sweet or Mott the Hoople."

"And The Beatles," Jake said.

"Some heavy hitters there," RJ said. "Is that why some of you go heavy on the make-up? Inspired by glam rock?"

"I've always had a soft spot for Steve Priest," Ian said. "Just no cape."

"How did you all meet?"

"We've known each other pretty much all through school," Isaac said. "Kelly, Jake, and I have known each other since Kindergarten."

"That's a really long time!" RJ remarked.

"I met Ian the first year of middle school," Kelly said, "and I met Paul when I joined the band. I'd seen him around school before, just never had any classes with him."

"So you all decided to just form a band together?"

"I got the idea of forming a band in our senior year of high school," Isaac said. "I talked to Jake, who I knew had been playing guitar for a while, and then we both talked to Ian, who played guitar but also kind of fiddled around on bass. We got Paul in as rhythm guitar to give Jake more freedom to play lead."

"And I just want to mention that I'm perfectly happy playing rhythm," Paul said with a laugh.

"How about Kelly?"

"We heard her sing in the school choir," Ian said. "We actually wanted her and her best friend Jayna to join, but Jayna wasn't into joining a band."

"So you're probably all very comfortable with each other, knowing each other for so long."

"It's kind of a family," Jake said. "And Isaac's uncle is our manager, so it really is a family atmosphere."

"Any squabbles?"

"Not really," Isaac said. "Minor ones that get worked out pretty quickly."

RJ asked a few more questions, then wrapped up the interview.

"I want to thank you for coming on our show tonight," RJ said.

"It's been a pleasure," Kelly said.

For their next appearance they had to fly to New York for *The Late Night Show.* The show went about the same as the previous one—play their song, sit for the interview, then they were done. Easy peasy for them—hardly seemed worth the effort, Isaac thought, but was happy to do the interview regardless. If it got them more fans, he was okay with the effort.

After the show, Isaac and the guys went out to a club, while Kelly and Jayna stayed at the hotel. The club was fairly new, and there looked to be a lot of celebrities there that night. The guys paid their cover fee and walked in. Music blasted from the sound system and dancers packed the floor, but the guys managed to work their way to the bar and order their drinks, then they stood and watched the people dance.

"I don't know about you guys," Ian said, "but I'm going to check the place out," and he walked out onto the floor and got swallowed up by the dancers.

"We won't see him until morning," Paul shouted over the music.

"I think I'm going out, too," Isaac said. "Cheers!"

Isaac wandered out onto the floor and made his way through the throng of dancers and went to the men's room. He saw Ian in there, snorting a couple of lines.

"I guess we had the same idea," Isaac said. The music wasn't as loud in there and they didn't have to shout to be heard.

"Where's Jake and Paul?" Ian asked, wiping his nose.

"I don't know; I left them at the bar."

Isaac got his vial of cocaine out and his spoon and took a hit.

They left the restroom and split up again.

***

Ian downed his drink and asked for another one. He didn't notice the dark-haired beauty next to him until she backed into him.

"Oh, I'm so sorry," the woman said, putting a hand on his shoulder.

"No apology necessary," Ian said. "I'm glad you bumped into me."

"You are, are you?" the woman asked, turning toward him. Her eyes looked him over quickly. "Well, I'm glad I bumped into you, too."

"I'm Ian," he said, holding out his right hand.

"Giselle," the woman said taking his hand. "Lovely to meet you."

"Would you like to dance?" he asked.

"Absolutely," Giselle said, and Ian led her to the floor where they danced to a fast-paced song.

They came back to the bar for another drink. Ian glanced up and saw that *The Late Night Show* played on the TV screens around the club, and Fate Struck had just started their song. Giselle looked at the screen and then turned and looked at Ian in surprise.

"That's *you* up there!" she said.

"Guilty," he said, raising his right hand.

"I thought I had seen you before, but I wasn't sure where. You opened for The Disciples of Man when they played here earlier this year."

"We did," Ian said. "That was part of our own headlining tour. We're friends of theirs and big fans, too."

"That's fantastic," she said, and she watched them perform. They couldn't hear the interview, but he knew it had gone well.

Later that evening, Ian and Giselle walked the half a block to the hotel where Fate Struck stayed. Ian hoped that Paul hadn't returned, because he really wanted to spend time with Giselle. There was no sign on the door, so he opened the door and when he saw no one in there, he gently pulled Giselle inside, putting the Do Not Disturb sign on the door.

Ian kissed Giselle greedily, and Giselle returned the kisses just as hungrily. He backed her into the wall, where he took her wrists and held her arms over her head as he ran his lips over her jaw line to her neck. She tipped her head to give him full access, whispering, "Just don't make any marks."

"I won't," Ian breathed, and he moved back to her mouth, his tongue tangling with her.

Ian slid his hands down her body over her dress, then back up, lifting her dress to caress her ass, slipping his fingers under the string of her thong.

He remembered the first time Kelly wore a thong, and it was such a turn-on for him, knowing that little Miss Innocent did something daring and sexy.

Getting his thoughts back into the moment, he gently tugged at the string and pulled Giselle's thong down. Giselle moved her hands down to his waistband, unbuttoning his jeans and sliding her hands inside.

Ian picked her up and carried her to his bed, and pulled her dress up over her head and found she had no bra on underneath. He tore off his shirt and pulled off his pants and crawled his way up to her. He stopped only long enough to take a hit of coke before he continued moving down her body, kissing her. He licked his fingers before putting them inside her as his tongue teased her clit. Her hands flew to his head, and her fingers tangled in his hair. She made a sound between a groan and a sigh, and he took that as encouragement to do more, putting in two fingers as his thumb apply pressure where his tongue had been.

He moved up her body and turned them over so Giselle was on top. She worked her way down and before she took him in her mouth Ian hurriedly rolled on a condom. She sucked and stroked him to hardness, and moved up and straddled him. They found a rhythm as he grabbed her ample breasts, then he flipped them over again and thrust into her, keeping up the rhythm.

"Fuck me, baby," Giselle whispered with a raspy voice. "I want you to come."

"Oh, god, yeah," Ian said, quickening the pace as he got close to orgasm. "I'm coming, Kelly."

Giselle stopped moving.

"Kelly?"

Fuck.

"Why did you call me Kelly?" Giselle asked.

Fuck, fuck, fuck. He had to think, quick.

"Would you rather me fuck you, and call you Kelly, or fuck someone else?"

"Depends on who Kelly is. Your singer?"

"Absolutely not," Ian said quickly.

Giselle pushed Ian off of her.

"I think you are thinking of your singer." She stood and pulled on her dress and thong, the mood gone. She slipped her feet back into her shoes. "You must want her if you're screaming out her name."

Ian sat on the edge of the bed.

"If you say anything to anyone, I'll fucking deny it."

"Your secret is safe with me," Giselle said. "Maybe next time, though, get your big head into what your little head is doing."

She patted his face, then quickly scratched his face with her long fingernail. She gave Ian a smirk as she left him holding his left cheek.

I guess I deserved that. He pulled on his shorts and looked in the mirror at his cheek. Her nail had left a raised red line, but thankfully not gushing blood. He washed his face as Paul came into the room.

"There you are," Paul said. "We'd hoped you weren't lost in that place."

"Yeah, I came back here."

"Not alone, I take it."

"Nope, but I wish I had."

"Why? What happened?"

"I called her Kelly while in the throes of passion."

"Oh, crap."

"She said she wouldn't say anything, but then she gave me a 'gift' as she left." Ian turned his face to show Paul.

"Ouch. Well, you can always deny it."

"Which I told her I would, and she said she'd keep the secret."

Ian slept in until 11AM, Dean having arranged a late check-out. Paul was already up and showered, so Ian hopped into the shower before they all met for brunch down in the hotel restaurant.

Ian was quiet during brunch, so much so that Dean asked if he was ill.

"No, I'm not sick," Ian said. "I made a huge mistake last night."

"What now?" Dean asked, holding his fork midway to his mouth.

"Let's just say I have a big mouth and don't know how to control it." Ian told him.

"That's nothing new," Dean said, then continued to eat.

"Well, I just hope the person keeps her promise to not say anything."

"Of course it's a 'her.'"

Ian thought he saw Kelly look at him sharply. He'd tell her later.

"I can always run interference for you, too," Jayna said.

That calmed Ian down a little bit, and he continued to eat.

At the airport, they got through TSA quickly and had a couple hours to kill before they had to board so they went to one of the bars in the airport and had a couple of drinks, Kelly ordering ginger ale. When it got close to boarding time, they gathered up their belongings and walked to their terminal and waited for their flight to be called.

Ian fell asleep on the flight home, only waking up as they descended into LAX. After the rest of the band had been dropped off, Kelly asked Ian what happened.

"I called out your name while having sex with someone," he said. His face burned with embarrassment.

"Oh," was all Kelly said.

"That's it? You're not mad?"

"We're not together," Kelly reminded him. "You can fuck whoever you want."

"And with that," Dean said, "you're home, Ian."

Chapter Nine

With the studio time coming up in the next week to record their second album, Fate Struck rehearsed every day the week prior to get the songs down before they had to pay for the studio time.

They had their last rehearsal the night before their recording sessions began, and Dean joined them in the garage studio to listen to the songs. Before they started, Ian pulled out his little bag of coke and cut out lines for them, minus Kelly and Dean.

At the end of each song, Dean gave them suggestions for the song, something he'd learned from watching and listening to them the first time they recorded. When they'd finished all the songs, they tore down the equipment and packed it up for Scott and Bailey to take to the recording studio the next day.

The band used a recording studio in Long Beach this time, so they would be able to stay at home while they recorded instead of having to live in a motel near the studio.

"I've had enough hotel and bus living for a while," Isaac said.

"It'll be nice to be able to sleep in my own bed at night," Kelly said.

Fate Struck had their instruments taken to the studio, Beach Ball Studios, in Long Beach, about a twenty minute drive from Lakewood. Kelly drove herself to the studio and met everyone there.

"Wow, we are almost literally on the beach!" Kelly said.

The studios were across the street from Long Beach City Beach, where they could go to take a break from recording.

"Hopefully that will keep you all nice and relaxed," the engineer, Alan, said. "We're also fully stocked with beer, hard lemonade, Fireball, etc."

"Nice!" Isaac said.

Alan gave them a quick tour of the place, ending up in the control room.

"This is where I'll be," Alan said. "This is my technician, Robbie."

"Hey," Robbie said with a wave.

"And that's the tour! If there's no questions," Alan said, pausing for a moment. No one said anything. "Great! Grab whatever you need and we'll start in ten minutes. We'll get the scratch tracks down first, then go from there."

Kelly and the guys went to the kitchen to get their drinks. Kelly heated some water for a cup of tea while the guys grabbed a bottle of beer each, and Isaac poured a shot of Fireball into cups for each of them, then raised his cup.

"May we have another best-seller," he said.

"Cheers!" Jake said, and they all touched cups and drank.

The tea kettle beeped, indicating the water was ready. Kelly made her cup of tea and went back to the studio with it.

They spent the rest of the day recording the scratch tracks that they'd follow when they did the real recording of the songs, taking a break for both lunch and dinner. After eating dinner Kelly, Jake, and Isaac walked across the street to the beach and sat on one of the low cement walls that separated the beach from the parking lot.

"Are you two my bodyguards for today?" Kelly asked with a smile.

"This isn't the best area for you to be alone in," Jake said.

"True," Kelly said.

"I just wanted to get out for a few minutes. I need the fresh air to clear my head," Isaac said.

"Same," Kelly said.

They sat silently watching the waves rolling in and the kids playing in the water for fifteen minutes. It had been a while since Kelly had gone to the beach just for the heck of it. The only times she'd been to the beach lately was for *Rockin' the Sport*, and then when they stayed in the house on the beach in Malibu to write. Sure, they'd had fun, but they *were* working. And then Lena showed up. *At least she won't show up here*, she thought.

Isaac checked his watch.

"Time to go back," he said, and the walked back across the street to the studio.

They finished the scratch tracks late that evening.

"Thanks, everyone," Alan said. "Ian and Isaac, we'll have you come in tomorrow to get your tracks recorded, so I'll see you at 9 o'clock."

"We'll be here," Isaac said, looking at Ian.

"Yeah, I'll be here," Ian said, rather grudgingly.

***

Ian woke up to the sound of his alarm going off. He rolled over and saw that it was thirty minutes past when the alarm was supposed to go off. *Shit! Damn Snooze button.* He definitely wasn't going to be on time to record today.

He jumped out of bed and threw some clothes on, but had trouble finding his shoes. He looked around and finally found them under his bed. *How the hell did they end up there?* Ian pulled them on, then grabbed his keys. He heard his mom in the kitchen, making coffee.

"Gotta run! See ya!" he shouted as he slammed the front door. He heard the windows vibrate. *Oops!*

Ian drove through Jack in the Box for breakfast, and nearly t-boned a car in his haste to get back on the street.

His tires squealed as he turned into the studio parking lot. Ian grabbed his coffee and shoved the rest of his breakfast sandwich into his mouth as he walked through the door and into the studio. Isaac played his drums while Dean and Alan sat in the booth.

"Hey, there he is," Isaac said, setting his sticks on the snare drum. "You're never late, so I sent you a text."

Ian pulled out his phone and saw the text.

"I guess I still had it on silent," Ian said. "Sorry I'm late."

"Are you ready to start?" Alan asked through the intercom.

Ian drank the rest of his coffee and tossed the cup in the trash.

"Yeah, I just need to limber up a bit," he said. He picked up his bass and after tuning it, warmed up for a few minutes before he was ready to go.

Isaac stepped back into the drum isolation booth and put on his headphones. Ian put on his headphones and stood where he could see Isaac. Alan started the playback of their scratch track and they played against it.

By the time they broke for lunch at 12:30, they'd managed to get two songs finished. Dean went to get lunch for everyone, and after taking an hour to eat they were ready to play again. Before they began, however, Ian and Isaac both went to the restroom for a quick snort of coke, and came back ready to play.

Ian and Isaac fell into a groove and they played the songs well together. Ian closed his eyes as he played to get more of a feel for the song. The music took him away and by the time they broke for dinner, they'd finished another two songs and had started the third.

"What do you say we take a quick dinner break and then finish that last song up before we take off for the night?" Alan asked.

"Sounds great," Isaac said. "I could use an early night."

"Me, too," Ian said. "I plan to stay home tonight."

Dean went and brought dinner back, and then they finished the song in a couple hours.

"Sounds great, guys," Alan said. He and Dean came into the studio.

"We'll come back again tomorrow morning, same time," Alan said

"Try to get here on time, Ian," Dean said, not unkindly, but firmly, his meaning clear—don't waste our studio time.

"I will," Ian said. "I got in early this morning and didn't get much sleep and kept snoozing my alarm."

"See you guys then," Alan said.

By the end of the week, Ian and Isaac had finished their tracks for all the songs. Next would be Paul's turn to do his rhythm guitar tracks, and when he finished, Jake came in to do the lead guitar tracks. They both finished their tracks in a few days, then it was Kelly's turn to come in and do the vocal tracks.

***

Kelly got to the studio a little before 9 o'clock so she'd have time to make herself a cup of tea. She greeted Dean and Alan before going to the kitchen to make her tea, doing her vocal warm-ups while she waited for the tea to brew, then went back to the control room.

"Ready to get started?" Dean asked.

"Absolutely," she said. She went into the studio and found the microphone set up for her and headphones hanging on the mic stand. She pulled a stool over next to the mic stand to set her cup of tea on, and was ready.

She'd forgotten how tedious doing the vocals was, although Alan didn't make her do as many takes as Johnnie had. Either she'd improved, or Alan wasn't as picky, but whatever it was, it made her happy not to have to sing the same line twenty times over. She was sure that Dean would say something if anything sounded off.

When she got to The Hunted, Kelly had a hard time finding the right voice for it. Singing it straight with a clear voice didn't do the job.

"Just remember how you felt that day, Kelly," Dean said, putting his hands on her shoulders. He'd come into the studio to talk with her instead of using the intercom. "I know you were upset, but remember how pissed off you were, having our stuff gone through and how that made you feel."

"Okay," Kelly said. "Give me a couple minutes to get in the right frame of mind for it."

"Do you want a shot of Fireball or anything?"

"Yeah, that might help."

Dean left the studio for a few moments, and came back with a red cup with the alcohol in it. Kelly downed it. She began to think of how angry and upset she'd been, being detained in Indonesia, because of Greg's phone call to the authorities there, saying they had cocaine in their luggage. This was before the guys had started using cocaine, and they'd spent a couple hours there, at first waiting for something to happen, and then having their luggage thoroughly checked, and nothing was found. She paced the floor for a moment, then turned to Dean.

"I'm ready," she said.

Dean smiled and went back to the control room. Kelly put on her headphones and heard the music play, and she sang the song with a little more edginess and grit, almost growling during the line, "We'll fucking hunt you down."

When she finished the song, both Dean and Alan stood and applauded.

"That was fucking perfect," Alan said. "I'd be afraid of you if I was Greg."

She needed another few minutes to calm down after that song, and drank another shot of Fireball before continuing.

Kelly finished her vocals in four days, and then Jake and Ian came in for the backing vocals. They finished their parts in two days.

Dean asked them all to come to the studio to listen to the final recordings and to pick the order in which the songs would be placed on the album.

"You've hit a new high with the vocals, Kelly," Isaac said.

"Hell yeah!" Jake agreed. "'The Hunted' and 'The Cheerleader' came out really well."

"You can thank Dean and Alan for 'The Hunted,'" Kelly said. "Dean reminded me how upset I was and made me think about being detained, and what Greg's done since—the harassing text messages and cyberstalking."

It took them half an hour to talk out which songs should go where on the album, but they finally came up with a list that they all agreed on.

"It should take me about a week to mix and then a few more days to master it all," Alan told them. "Then it's up to Tyrian to get everything else rolling. Do you have a release date?"

"Not yet," Dean said, "but probably soon."

"It's been a pleasure to work with all of you," Alan said, shaking everyone's hand.

"It's been great," Kelly said.

***

With the recording out of the way, Isaac could spend his time helping Hayley plan the wedding, coming up in just six weeks. After Isaac had done his studio work, he and Hayley had gone out to look at different places to hold the wedding, and found the perfect place for them.

They had chosen their invitations and got them sent out and they were already getting the RSVP cards back. Isaac found that Hayley had everything very organized for the wedding, having made a spread sheet for all the details.

"I guess you don't need me to do anything," Isaac joked as they updated the RSVPs.

"I need you to take care of the honeymoon," Hayley told him.

"Already taken care of," Isaac said. "I did that once we'd settled on a date."

"Good," Hayley said. "And we've already taken care of the food for the reception..." She looked over her chart. "It looks like we're on schedule with everything."

"Fantastic," he said. "And my parents want to host a rehearsal dinner. Is that okay?"

"As long as you and your dad don't fight," Hayley said.

"I'll be on my best behavior, but no promises on his behavior."

"As long as you don't argue with him, I think it'll be fine."

"I may need a few shots of Jack beforehand," Isaac joked.

"Whatever works," she said.

Two days later, Isaac took Hayley apartment-looking. While Hayley had said that she wouldn't mind staying temporarily in his and Jake's apartment, Isaac wanted a place they could call theirs from the start. He made appointments to visit several places, one of which was a slightly bigger apartment in the complex he already lived in.

After seeing all of them, they talked about which ones they liked.

Ever practical, Hayley said the one in his current complex made sense.

"They know you," she said. "They know you're always on time with your rent, and it's a nice place. I say we pick that one."

"Are you sure?" Isaac asked. "It was actually my first choice, but I didn't want to sway you."

"Yeah, I'm sure, and we don't have to rent a U-Haul to move there."

Isaac hugged Hayley tight.

"Have I mentioned how lucky I am to be getting married to you?" he whispered.

"Mm, once or twice," she said, and she kissed his lips.

Isaac moved most of his things to the new apartment once it was ready, leaving only his bed and a few clothes at his and Jake's place. He was leaving the bed there for Jake for when he found someone else to share the apartment with, and he and Hayley bought a new Queen Size bed for them.

A week before the wedding, Jake held the bachelor party at a rented house on Sunset Beach. The house had a pool table and Jake made sure there was lots of booze for all of them. Isaac's father and Hayley's father both came, and after an hour they both were about to head out.

"You gotta stay for the stripper," Jake told them both.

"Stripper?" Isaac asked, surprised.

"Yeah, not sure I'm into seeing a stripper," Hayley's father said. Isaac knew his father's feelings on it.

"You'll all like it, I promise," Jake assured them. The music was loud as was the spirited game of pool. Half an hour later, someone rang the doorbell. Jake answered, and an old lady stood at the door.

"You fellas are being a bit loud," she said, cane and large purse in hand.

"Well, it IS a bachelor party," Jake told her.

"You men are all alike, aren't you?" she said, stepping into the room. Jake shut the door. "All you young men here, boozing it up and waiting for a stripper to come over. What would your mothers think of this?"

"Lady, you need to leave," Jake said.

"I didn't think we were that loud," Isaac said, stepping over to the lady and Jake. "We can't be any louder than people on the beach."

"It's past my bedtime, sonny," the lady said, tapping Isaac with her cane. "I need my sleep, and you people are just making it too hard to sleep. I'm calling the police!"

"No! Come on, ma'am, please don't call the police," Ian said from the pool table.

The lady became angry.

"I'm telling you all right now that I'm calling the police and I hope they arrest every one of you!"

The rest of the young men, and Isaac's and Hayley's dads shouted at the lady, and Jake grabbed the lady's cane. She fell over, then did a roll and pressed a button on her bag. The room filled with music and the lady started to dance, or rather, hobble to the music, shaking her ample butt as she took off her shawl and swung it around. All the guys stopped what they were doing to gather around to watch this old lady bump and grind. She bent over once and pretended she couldn't straighten back up. Isaac stepped over to her and helped her, and the lady kissed him on the cheek, then continued her routine, the guys clapping and laughing. Isaac had tears in his eyes from laughter, and even his father was laughing and clapping along. Jake had his phone out to capture the moment.

The dance lasted about three minutes, and at the end, the lady pulled her wig and glasses off with a flourish, and a much younger woman stood there in a fat suit. The men applauded as she bowed.

"Thank you so much!" she said with a deep bow. "I'm Valerie, and I hope you enjoyed the show. I specialize in clean, wholesome bachelor and birthday parties. Where's Isaac?"

"Yo!" Isaac stepped forward next to her.

"Congratulations on your wedding," Valerie said.

"Thank you," he said, still wiping his eyes.

"This is for you," she said, and she handed him a plush doll, dressed up as herself, with an attached cane in her hand, and a sash across saying *Congrats!*

"This is great," Isaac said.

"Jake has business cards if you'd like to book me. Have a good day," and with that, Valerie gathered up her things and left.

"That was awesome!" Isaac said. "I'm glad it wasn't a real stripper."

"Yeah, I knew that wasn't you, so I had to go with this."

Isaac shook Jake's hand, then hugged him.

Isaac's and Hayley's fathers left after that, and the guys began drinking and playing pool again.

By the end of the night, only Isaac, Jake, Ian, and Paul were left. They all stayed the night at the house in order to recover from the party.

The night before the wedding, Isaac and the wedding party went to the wedding rehearsal. While Hayley's sister and her maid of honor were used to being around the guys from the band, her two other friends were not. They got a little star-struck for a few minutes, giggling as they got paired up with the guys. It took a little while but they eventually relaxed, though both were clearly excited to be close to someone in a rock band. After the rehearsal, they gathered at the rehearsal dinner. The families of the bride and groom had met several times before at the various band functions, but at the request of both Hayley and Isaac, they kept dinner less formal. Isaac's parents held the dinner at Tokyo Hibachi. The parents sat together on one end and Isaac had his mom and Hayley between him and his father, but the parents mostly talked among themselves while Isaac and Hayley spoke with their friends.

Hayley's father stood up to make a toast to the couple near the end of dinner.

"May Isaac and Hayley have many long years together," he said, holding up his bottle of Kirin beer. "And welcome to the family, Isaac, though you've been 'family' for a few years already."

Everyone held up what they were drinking and shouted "cheers!" and drank.

Isaac's father stood up to also make a toast. Isaac cringed at the thought of what he might way, and hoped he kept it short.

"To Hayley and Isaac," his father said. "May you have a long and happy marriage." He held up his bottle of O'Doul's non-alcoholic beer.

"Cheers!" everyone said, and they drank again.

After everyone had gone, Isaac drove Hayley to her home for the last time.

“We’ll be living under the same roof very soon,” he said.

“I can’t wait!”

The big day came and Isaac rode with Jake to The Queen Mary in Long Beach, where the wedding and reception would take place. Paul and Ian would meet them at 2PM so they could all get ready together. A limo had already brought Hayley and her attendants there to get ready.

“Are you nervous?” Jake asked.

“Not in the least,” Isaac said. “But I can’t wait to get it over with.”

At 3:45, the director came and told the men it was time, and led them out to the deck next to the gazebo, where the wedding would take place. Luckily the weather cooperated and they had a beautiful November afternoon for the wedding, though they had a back-up plan in case of bad weather. Isaac smiled as he took his place in the gazebo and waited for the wedding music to start.

The harpist began to play at 4PM and Isaac turned to watch for Hayley to walk with her father. Hayley’s sister Jenna came out first as her junior bridesmaid, then her bridesmaids, walking with Ian and Paul, then her maid of honor, her best friend Anna, with Jake. The harpist then changed to playing The Wedding March, and Hayley stepped out into the aisle with her father. Isaac caught his breath when he saw how beautiful Hayley looked in her white dress. The unadorned bodice of her dress had a boat neckline and long fitted sleeves, and floor-length skirt had an off-white lace overskirt with pearl beads and silver thread running through it. Her sheer veil with lace around the bottom and a simple wreath of flowers to hold it in place completed the look.

She and her father walked up the aisle and when they reached Isaac he smiled broadly. The clergyman stood and began the ceremony. Hayley’s father lifted her veil to kiss her cheek, then gave her hand to Isaac.

“Wow, you look stunning,” Isaac whispered to Hayley.

The ceremony lasted just over half an hour. The ceremony ended just as the sun set over the ocean.

"I now present to you Mr. and Mrs. Isaac Landry," the clergyman said and as Hayley and Isaac turned to their guests, the guests applauded. The harpist played their recessional music and they walked down the aisle, followed by the attendants and then the clergyman.

The reception was held indoors in one of the banquet rooms. Everyone filed in while the photographer took photos of the couple with the sunset in the background.

The photographer finished taking pictures, and the wedding party went inside. The attendants walked in first, then Isaac and Hayley entered with much fanfare. The guests applauded and Isaac and Hayley made their way to their seats at the main table where the wedding party sat.

Dinner was served and the cake was cut, then the DJ called the wedding couple up for their first dance. Isaac led Hayley out to the dance floor and they danced to their wedding song, and part way through the wedding party came out to dance with them.

Isaac and Hayley spent their first night as husband and wife in the wedding suite aboard The Queen Mary. Hayley went into the bathroom to change, and when she came out, Isaac had thought she couldn't look more beautiful than she had in her wedding dress. He was wrong. She spun around, her white lace nightgown flowing around her.

"You are so beautiful," he said, and he walked over to her and kissed her passionately on the lips.

Before they made love, he pulled on a condom, because getting pregnant now wouldn't be the best thing for either one of them. The CD was about to be released and then the band would go out on tour, leaving Hayley home on her own. Isaac wanted to be part of every aspect of any pregnancies, and he couldn't be if he was gone.

Chapter Ten

With Isaac gone on his honeymoon for two weeks, there was nothing happening with the band. Kelly spent the time catching up on her reading and hanging out with Jayna. Even in the middle of November it was still warm enough to swim in the community pool, and on the days it wasn't, the pool was heated. She and Jayna worked out together at the community college, where they'd both enrolled earlier in the semester in the gymnastics class to just work out with the team.

A week before Isaac and Hayley were due back from their honeymoon, Dean asked everyone to meet at his house for an update.

"Thanks for coming on short notice," Dean said.

"Nothing really going on right now," Ian said.

"Just a couple of things that I didn't want to text out because I suck at texting," Dean said. "The first single from your next CD is going to be 'It's All On You.'"

"Woo hoo!" Kelly and the guys cheered.

"Now, this next thing—I'm not sure how you guys will react to it, but," he paused for a moment, "*Stripped* magazine wants to feature you guys in the magazine in a couple months."

"I've never heard of it," Kelly said.

"Oh, Kelly, bless your heart," Jake said. "It's a magazine for women, if you get my meaning."

"Oooohhh," Kelly said, getting the drift.

"Well, they want to write about the band, so you'd be involved, too, but they'd like the guys to—ahem—*appear* in the magazine."

"Since I won't be *appearing* in the magazine like the guys would, it's up to them," she said, looking to Ian.

"I'm down," Ian said with a mischievous smile.

"Oh course you are," Kelly said, laughing.

"I'm down if I don't have to appear fully stripped," Paul said. "I couldn't do that to Alexa, or my mom."

"Hell, yeah," Jake said. "I'll run it past Missy, but I'll do it."

"As long as I don't have to take my clothes off, I'll do it," Kelly joked.

"One hundred percent guarantee you won't have to," Dean said. "Okay, when Isaac gets back, I'll ask him about it. We have a couple weeks to make the decision, since I told them Isaac was unavailable at the moment."

"Have they talked about the next tour?" Jake asked.

"Yes! Thank you," Dean said, scrolling through his notes. "I almost forgot about that! We're looking at February for the start of the US tour. That gets us through the holidays before we have to leave. We're going to do more of Europe this time, too, and not so much Asia right now."

"That's fine with me," Kelly said. "I didn't like that long flight there."

"You'll go there eventually, just not with this next tour," Dean said.

Dean didn't have anything else for the band, so the guys stayed to play video games while Kelly left.

The newly married couple returned from Hawaii, tanned and relaxed. Kelly met up with the guys at Dean's for a rehearsal and Dean let Isaac know what they'd already talked about.

"I'll have to ask Hayley if she's okay with it," Isaac said. "I'll go full Monty if she's okay with it, but I doubt she will be, but I'll do it." He looked at the others. "What are you guys doing?"

"You know me," Ian said.

"Yeah, stupid question," Isaac said. "What about you two?"

"I'm not going fully stripped, for Alexa's sake and my mom's," Paul said.

"Missy is okay with me going nude," Jake said.

"I'm staying fully clothed," Kelly joked.

"Okay, I'll let the editors know," Dean said.

With business finished, they walked out to the garage to rehearse. Ian, Paul, and Jake did their thing, and asked Isaac if he was joining them.

"Naw, not right now," he said.

"You on the wagon, dude?" Jake asked.

"Not really," Isaac said. "I just went without while on my honeymoon and I really don't need it right now." He got a bottle of beer from the fridge and popped it open. "But I'll definitely need it on tour."

They worked on their new songs and a longer concert version for a couple of them. They decided which old songs to play, and made out a set list for the holiday parties for Isaac's father's company and Kelly's.

"Oh, I almost forgot!" Isaac said, taking off his shirt. "Look what I got in Hawaii."

Isaac had a small heart tattoo with Hayley's name and their wedding date on it on the left side of his chest.

"Hayley got one, too," he said.

"Awesome!" Jake said. "Did it hurt?"

"Not as much as you'd think," Isaac said, pulling his shirt back on.

"I've been thinking about getting one or two," Jake said.

"Same," said Ian.

"Ooh, sexy," Kelly said.

"You think?" Ian raised an eyebrow.

"Oh, did I say that out loud?"

"You did," Isaac said, smiling.

Kelly knew she said it out loud. She meant for Ian to hear, but said nothing more on the subject as they got to work.

They felt like they were still stuffed from all the food at Thanksgiving when the holiday parties began, both for Fate Struck to play at and to be invited to. Kelly's father's company holiday party was the first weekend, then the next weekend Isaac's father's party, using the same set list for both parties. Kelly kept it professional and didn't do any gymnastics at either party, though a couple of people asked if she would.

"Not in this dress," she joked. The band had decided to dress it up a bit, and the guys wore tuxedos and Kelly wore a red knee-length dress. She could move in it, but wasn't about to try doing an aerial walkover in it.

They were invited to the band Chellis's Christmas party in Lakewood. Chellis had been around for a few years and were very well known. Isaac said that Fate Struck was excited to be invited to the party.

"Fate Struck is getting really popular, so we wanted to see what the competition was like," Evan, Chellis's lead singer said.

"He's joking!" Jesse the band's guitar player said, seeing Isaac's surprised face. "Since you're in the area, we wanted to invite you because we think you're pretty cool."

"Well, thanks!" Kelly said. "I listened to Chellis in high school all the time. Still do."

"Does that mean we're old?" Evan asked with a wink.

"No! High school was only four years ago, so not old," Kelly assured him.

Fate Struck reciprocated the invitation a week later when they had a Christmas party and combined birthday party for Isaac and Ian at Dean's house. Evan, Jesse, and Sean from Chellis, all the members of The Disciples of Man, and Maggie, Melanie, and Nick from MagNetic were invited along with their friends from high school they still kept in touch with. Hayley and Missy had helped Dean's fiancée Rosa decorate the house and backyard, and then the two of them carried out the cake with Isaac's and Ian's names on it.

"Wow, that thing is huge!" Isaac said as the girls put it on the table.

"That's what she said," Ian said.

"You're funny," Hayley said, smacking him on the arm. She turned to Kelly. "How do you put up with these guys on the road?"

Kelly laughed.

"I tune out a lot," she said.

After the cake had been served and everyone had eaten, all the musicians got up to play. They decided on a song to play and then started to jam, each of the four singers taking a different part.

An hour later, Isaac and Ian talked Kelly into singing a few Christmas songs.

"But it's your birthday party," Kelly protested.

"We wouldn't ask if we didn't want to hear it," Ian said.

"Okay, but I'm going to ask Jayna and Maggie to sing with me," Kelly said.

"Maggie sings?"

"She's in a band, maybe you've heard of them…" Kelly joked.

"I mean, I know she's in a band, but she sings stuff other than rock?" Isaac asked.

"She was in her high school choir, too."

"Wow, okay, then," Isaac said. "Get everyone together!"

Kelly went to ask Jayna if she'd sing with her.

"Of course," Jayna said. "I love to sing with you."

"We're going to get Maggie, too," Kelly said.

"What?"

"Maggie sang in school like we did," Kelly told her.

"No pressure or anything," Jayna said.

"You'll be fine," Kelly assured her, and they both went to ask Maggie.

"Sure, though it's been a while," Maggie said.

"For us, too," Kelly said. "But I think it'll all come back to us."

They went over to Isaac, who told them he'd introduce them.

"Now, for a special Christmas treat," Isaac said at the mic. "We're fortunate to have a few singers that know some Christmas songs, so please welcome Kelly, Jayna, and Maggie."

The ladies stepped up to the mics and Kelly spoke for a moment.

"Well, none of us have actually sung said Christmas songs for a while," Kelly said, "but we'll give it a go."

They started off singing "O Holy Night," with Kelly and Maggie singing soprano and Jayna doing the alto part. It was like being back in high school again, singing in the holiday concert they'd done every year. She missed singing those songs with her best friend.

When they finished, the crowd exploded with applause, and the young women smiled at each other.

"I guess we can still sing!" Maggie said.

"Looks like it," Kelly said, smiling.

They did "Carol of the Bells," "Silent Night," and "Away in a Manger" before they had to stop as Maggie's voice started to sound a little rough.

"Sorry, ladies," Maggie told them.

"No worries! I think we've done more than we probably should have," Kelly said, her own throat a little raw from those high notes she hasn't sung since high school.

The guests applauded as the ladies left the stage. Before they got too far, though, several people came up to them to tell them how good they were.

"You never cease to amaze me," Erik said. "Why are you singing rock music with a voice like that?"

"This voice is what got me into the band," she said. "Jayna and I sang a duet in our Spring Concert and Isaac asked us to join the band. Jayna wasn't into joining a band, but it's what I've wanted to do for a long time."

"All three of you sounded fantastic."

"Thank you!" Kelly said, smiling. "Maybe we'll do a Christmas album sometime."

Dean came up to them.

"That's not a bad idea," he said, having overheard Kelly.

"Good luck selling that to my manager," Maggie said. "She doesn't like me doing extra stuff. She'd probably scold me for singing today like we did."

"It'd be great marketing," Dean said. "We'll talk about it sometime."

At one in the morning, Kelly was ready to leave. Jayna and Marty had left earlier, and Maggie had gone too. She went to say goodbye to Isaac and Hayley.

"This was a fantastic party," Kelly told them.

"Yeah, it turned out really well," Hayley said. "You, Jayna, and Maggie were great!"

"Not too bad for no warm-up," Kelly said.

"You and Jayna always sounded great in school."

"Thank you! All three of us were a bit rusty, though, trying to hit those high notes."

Kelly hugged Hayley, then turned and hugged Isaac.

"See you at rehearsal. Merry Christmas!" Kelly said, and with a wave she left.

The band had their photo shoot for *Stripped* magazine shortly before New Years. Kelly had a few butterflies fluttering inside, not knowing how it was going to turn out. She'd definitely seen Ian and had even seen the rest of the guys in the literal flesh once, but it felt weird to her to be doing this.

She had picked out her black flared pants and her blue sequined blouse to wear, and her platform shoes. Kelly would get dressed at the studio for her part of the photo shoot.

They all met at Dean's house where the limo would pick them up and drive them to the studio. Kelly drank a couple shots of Fireball on the way to get over the nerves. The guys on the other hand, were very calm about the whole thing.

"So, what did Hayley say about this?" Jake asked.

"She was going to be a good sport and give the okay for full-frontal," Isaac said. "But I know my dad wouldn't like it and as tempting as it is to stick it to him, I'm sure we'd also lose out on going back for the holiday parties. So, going as far as I can without showing anything."

They arrived at the office building and a staff member took them upstairs to the studio where they'd do the photo shoot. A woman came in from the offices and introduced herself to them all.

"I'm Amanda," she said, extending her hand to everyone. "I'm the editor-in-chief of *Stripped*. I'm so glad you agreed to do this."

"We're happy to be here," Isaac said.

Dean introduced them all to Amanda.

"We'll take you all to Hair and Make-up to get you looking fabulous," Amanda told them, and she led them down the hallway to another studio with several mirrors and three women talking to each other. When Kelly and the guys entered, the women jumped up to get to work on them.

Two hours later, they all looked great after having their hair washed and styled and make-up applied. They all were made up like they were going onstage, to give the women a real look at them. That meant heavy eye make-up for both Ian and Jake, some on Isaac, and Paul hardly wore any. Kelly was also made up for stage—her purple eye make-up and dark pink lips, with her hair curled and left loose around her shoulders.

"What I'm going to have you do, Kelly," Amanda said, "is sit in this chair here." She pointed to an ornate chair in the middle of the room. "The guys are going to stand around it, with their clothes on," Amanda added quickly, noting Kelly's look of panic. "We'll take a couple of photos that way, and then you'll be done with your part of the shoot."

Jayna gave Kelly's hand an encouraging squeeze before Kelly walked over and sat in the chair. The guys' had been asked to bring their stage clothes with them also, and that's what they wore for this first set of photos. Jake had left his shirt unbuttoned to the waist, Ian wore a leather vest and jeans. Paul wore a black t-shirt with his pants, and Isaac had on jeans and a white t-shirt. They gathered around Kelly in the chair, who tried to relax but was still shaking.

"Red or white?" Amanda asked.

"Red or white what?" Kelly asked.

"Wine," Amanda said. "We need to get you relaxed, girl!"

"Uh, red, I guess," Kelly said.

A few moments later an assistant brought a glass of red wine to Amanda, who gave it to Kelly. Kelly drank half the glass down.

"I don't know why I'm so nervous," Kelly said. "I've done photo shoots before."

"This one *is* a little different," Amanda said. "Even though you're not disrobing, it can be a little overwhelming."

Kelly finished the glass and someone came to refill it.

"It looks good in the photo," Amanda said.

Kelly finally relaxed, and they got the photos done. She sat in the chair with her legs crossed, and they took a few with her holding the glass of wine and smiling, then without the glass, then with Kelly gesturing with her hands to the guys around her.

"All right, we've got what we need for that," Amanda said. "Kelly, thank you so much! You're a doll!"

"No problem," Kelly said, and she got up from the chair. She stumbled a little and Isaac caught her.

"I guess a little too relaxed now," Kelly said. She caught her balance and was okay to walk on her own.

An assistant led the guys to the dressing rooms where they would get ready for their individual photos. Jake came out first, dressed in a white bathrobe. He had grown back the stubble on his face after the movie premiere, and his long brown hair, usually brushed smooth, had been tousled to look like he'd just gotten out of bed. *He looks hot!* Kelly thought, finally seeing what fans saw about him.

Amanda directed him to the bed, having him lay across it with the robe covering everything, while he read the morning paper. After a few shots of that, she had him move the robe back to show his body in all its glory. Kelly turned away, red-faced.

"It's nothing you haven't seen before," Jayna reminded her.

"Yeah, but this is different," Kelly said. "This is meant to be sexy and I usually don't see them that way."

"Except for Ian," Jayna whispered.

"I know, but the rest are like my brothers. It's just weird."

"I get it," Jayna said, watching as Amanda directed Jake to a different pose. Kelly took a quick glimpse, then turned away again.

When Jake was done, he pulled his robe on and went back to the dressing room.

Ian came out next. Kelly watched as Ian sat in the same chair Kelly had sat in, with his robe covering everything. After a few photos, he took off his robe. This time Kelly didn't turn away, watching as he turned on the seductive look he always had onstage and after the show. Out of all the guys, Ian was the sexiest. She'd seen first-hand what the look could do. Kelly wasn't in love with him, as she kept telling herself, but he could make a woman do anything with that look. Watching him do the shoot really turned her on. She may have to have him over later.

Isaac came out next, dressed in just his jeans and a white shirt, unbuttoned and loose. They took a few photos of him in that outfit, running his hand through his short blond hair. Amanda then had him take off his shirt and had him unzip his pants and show as much as he was comfortable with.

"Ooh, a tattoo," Amanda said. "Let's make sure to get that in the picture."

As Isaac pulled the opening of his pants apart, the photographer took many shots, getting photos from the front to get the tattoo in frame. He stopped short of showing his genitalia, but only just. Kelly thought it was incredibly sexy. The next few photos were of him undressed standing at a prop window with his back to the camera, looking through the window. She thought it was a very tasteful photo.

Paul came out last, and did several similar poses, not going as far with his pants as Isaac did. Though none of them were shy, Paul was the most reserved. He never looked at any of the girls backstage in such a way that made them think he wanted them. Always respectful to them, he only kissed them on the cheek if they asked for a kiss. Reserved onstage as well, he left the antics to Jake and Ian, but always looked like he was having fun.

When Paul had finished his photos, he went back to change, then they all came out to meet with the interviewer, Mara.

"I'm just going to do a quick interview with all of you," she said. "Kelly will join us for that."

The interview went well. Mara asked them great question that had substance, not the usual band-related questions, but general life questions.

When they finished, both Mara and Amanda thanked all of them for doing the photo shoot and interview.

"It was really fun," Jake said.

"I'll let Dean know when the issue comes out," Amanda said.

"Fantastic," Isaac said.

They shook hands with Amanda and Mara, and headed back to the limo waiting in front of the building.

The driver took them back to Dean's house, where they talk about a few things.

"Hey," Kelly said as she and Ian walked to their cars later. "Want to come over for a bit?"

"Hell yeah," Ian said. "I'll follow you there."

Kelly got into her car and drove off. She parked in the driveway and Ian pulled up in front of the house. She waited for him at the porch and unlocked the door.

"It looks like Davy's not here," Kelly said, unlocking the door.

"Better for us," Ian said, nuzzling her neck as they went inside. Kelly locked the door again and led Ian to her room.

Inside her room, Kelly dropped her bag to the floor and locked her bedroom door. Neither of them had washed their make-up off, and Kelly always liked Ian in his make-up.

They lay in bed afterwards, catching their breath.

"God, that was amazing," Ian said.

"Fantastic," Kelly said. "You looked great at the photo shoot, and I just wanted to fuck you then and there."

Ian laughed.

"I was hoping you would," he said. "I like it."

Kelly heard David moving through the house.

"I guess Davy's home," Kelly said.

"He won't…"

"No, he won't care. He knows about us, remember?"

"Oh, yeah, I forgot." He looked at his watch. "I better get going, though. I told my mom I'd be home for dinner tonight."

They both got dressed and Kelly walked Ian out.

"Hey, David," Ian said as he and Kelly walked through the living room.

"Hey, how was the photo shoot?" David asked.

"It went really well," Kelly said. "I was a little nervous, but after a couple glasses of wine, I was better."

"It was fun," Ian said.

Kelly and Ian said their goodbyes at the door. Ian got in his car and drove away.

"What are you working on today?" Kelly asked. David was always busy working on a video for either a corporation or a band.

"I'm working on The Disciples of Man's music video," David said. "It's going to look really cool when we're done with it."

Kelly went to the kitchen to get a bottled water and warm up some leftovers for dinner. When that was ready, she sat back on the couch to watch David work.

"Right now, I'm going over all the footage, to see which shots are the best," David explained. "Once that's done, I'll get my editor working on it, syncing it up to the music. When *that's* done, I'll look it over once more and make any adjustments, then send it to their record company, where they'll check it over and make any changes. If there's none, then I make the final copy. If there's any changes, the editor and I work on it more, then send it out again for approval."

"That sounds like an awful lot of work and then waiting around," Kelly said.

"I work on other stuff like preproduction for another video while I wait."

"Was it like that for our videos, too?"

"Yep!"

"Wow, I had no idea so much work went into it. I hope you get paid well for it."

"I do, actually. The record companies want it to look good so they pay well. Thanks to you, little sis, I get lots of work."

"Always happy to help!"

Chapter Eleven

The New Year started off with a bang as David finished The Disciples of Man's video and they had their premiere of it at a party. They invited Fate Struck and a few other musician friends of theirs to the party, held at a hotel in one of the ballrooms. David brought Tessa, and while she'd gotten used to being around Kelly now, she seemed a little nervous to be around all the other celebrities there.

"I'm sorry Davy's got to schmooze with the musicians," Kelly said as they hung out by the bar. "But you can hang out with me."

"I've met Erik and Will," Tessa said, "and they seem really nice, but it is a little overwhelming."

Kelly took her around and introduced her to Jayna, and then the rest of Fate Struck.

"We love David," Jake said. "He's taken really good care of us and our videos."

"Yes, he has," Kelly said.

Tessa stayed and talked to Jayna while Kelly went to the restroom, which was directly across the hall from the men's room. As Kelly came out, Erik, Stevie, Ian, and David went into the men's room together.

That can't be good, Kelly thought. *Would David do that? Only one way to find out*, and she pushed the door open into the men's room.

Stevie was already making lines for them when Kelly came in.

"What the hell, Davy?" Kelly exclaimed. "You, too?"

David froze where he sat. Ian looked at Kelly.

"You *do* know you're in the men's room, don't you?" he asked.

"Yes, I know," Kelly said. "I was just surprised to see Davy walking in with you guys so I came to investigate. You know what? I don't care. It just surprised me, is all."

"Don't you use?" David asked.

"No!" Erik, Stevie, and Ian said.

"She doesn't." Ian shook his head.

"Why am I not surprised," David said. "Kelly's a good girl."

"She's very un-rock and roll," Ian said with a smirk.

"Well, you guys carry on, then," Kelly said, and she left.

David found Kelly later, talking to Tessa with Jayna, Marty, and Isaac.

"Can I talk to you for a minute?" David asked.

"Sure," Kelly said. She turned to the others. "Excuse me for a minute."

Kelly followed David to a corner of the room.

"That was a bit awkward," David said.

"You're telling me," Kelly said.

"I probably should've let you know, but it just never came up. I just use it when I'm out."

Kelly put her hands up to stop him.

"You don't owe me any explanations, Davy," Kelly told him. "I don't care as long as it doesn't affect your work or my work. I take it Tessa doesn't know?"

"She knows, but she'd rather not know about it," David said.

"Gotcha. Well, I'm used to being around it because the guys use it. Whatever floats your boat."

"Thanks, sis," David said.

***

Fate Struck's next tour would start at the beginning of February, and rehearsals were daily. They worked out longer versions of some of their songs and made their set list with mostly new songs, but also playing the singles and a couple other popular songs from their first album. They had enough songs to play for nearly two hours.

"The fans will like that," Dean said, after watching a complete rehearsal.

"We thought so, too," Isaac said. "I've always liked going to concerts where the band played for a couple hours."

"Give 'em their money's worth," Jake said.

Isaac looked at his watch.

"Hey, I gotta get going if we're done," he said.

"What's your rush?" Ian asked.

"Hayley and I are going to my parents' house for dinner."

"Oh crap," Jake said.

"Yeah, and it's already tense between me and my dad. Hayley doesn't take my dad's shit, though. She'll call him out on stuff."

"Does he like her?" Dean asked.

"He does, and so does my mom. She's a good go-between for us, though I don't like her getting in the middle of our arguments."

Isaac told them goodbye and drove home to shower quickly before he and Hayley drove over to see his parents.

Dinner went smoothly, but Isaac needed to tell him about the magazine he and the other guys would appear in, just so there weren't any surprises. As they sat down in the family room for dessert, Isaac decided to tell him.

"I wanted to let you both know," Isaac started, "that in a few weeks, the guys and I are going to appear in *Stripped* magazine."

"What's that?" his mom asked.

"It's a magazine for, um, women, to look at men."

"Like nude pictures?" his father asked.

"Yes," Isaac said. He waited a moment for maximum effect. "I don't appear full frontal nude, however."

"And you gave him permission to do that?" his father asked Hayley.

"I don't need to give him *permission* for anything," Hayley said, her tone even. "But we *agreed* that he could do it, and go as far as he felt comfortable with."

"Which was me covered in front, out of respect for Hayley, Mom, and you," Isaac said. "But there is a photo showing my backside."

"How is that respectful?" his father asked.

"It's better than Jake and Ian did. They both went *au naturel* for their photos. Kelly is fully clothed."

"Kelly took part in that?" his mom asked.

"For the cover photo. It's very nicely done, and there's a great interview in the magazine."

"I thought she was better than that," his dad said.

"She turned down Playboy," Isaac shrugged.

"That was smart of her," his father said.

"It's good publicity for us."

His father shook his head.

"Not the kind of publicity you should want."

"Look," Isaac said, modulating his voice. "I only let you know so you're not surprised when it comes out and people say anything to you. It's a done-deal. My part in it is not that bad."

"And if I'm okay with it," Hayley interjected, "it shouldn't bother you. I'm smart enough to realize that women look at Isaac 'in that way.' He's good-looking, and women want to see him. Hopefully this will give them what they want and they'll leave him alone when he's on tour."

Isaac doubted that it would, but it sounded logical, and if Hayley believed it, then that's all that mattered. He didn't go looking for it, but he knew that women would find him out on the road after the shows.

His father conceded the argument. He didn't say anything else regarding the magazine.

"Steven," his mom said. "We've got to trust that his wife knows better and it's really not our business what Isaac does."

"If he wants his band to continue doing the holiday parties for the company, he won't do anything like that again," his father said.

"Yep, I see how it is," Isaac said, his voice rising.

"Isaac," Hayley said, shaking her head. "Leave it." She picked up her purse and stood up. "It was nice having dinner with you."

Isaac's parents stood and Hayley gave them both a hug. Isaac sat for a moment longer, then stood. He kissed his mom on the cheek, but bypassed his father's outstretched hand.

"Any time, dear," his mom said, walking them to the front door. "We'll see you later."

Once inside the car, Isaac let it out.

"That man drives me insane!" he said. "He's got some fucking nerve to threaten me like that. I don't fucking care about the holiday party. We do it as a courtesy to his company. If we didn't do it again, we'd be just fine. I might turn him down this year if he's going to be like that. And he's got no say in what I do anyway. God!"

"I know, Isaac," Hayley said gently. "But you had to know how he'd react."

"I did, but I thought it'd be better for me to tell him than have him find out from someone."

"It was better you told him. You can't control his reaction, though. He'll get over it."

Isaac started the car and drove off toward home.

As it got closer to when the band would leave for their tour, Isaac and Hayley planned out how she'd live on her own for those five months.

"At least we live in a gated apartment complex," Isaac said. "I don't feel so bad leaving you on your own."

"I can always get someone to come stay with me, too," she said. "Or I can go stay with my parents at night."

“I know you’ll be safe,” Isaac said. “But I do worry about you.”

The night before Fate Struck planned to leave, Isaac and Hayley went out to dinner at a nice restaurant in Long Beach. Isaac had booked a table in the corner for them, so they’d be out of sight of most diners.

After dinner, Isaac drove to the beach and they walked along the beach as the sun set.

“When I get back, we’ll do this again,” Isaac said.

“I can’t wait,” Hayley whispered.

When they got home, Isaac and Hayley headed to the bedroom, where they made love and he held her until she fell asleep.

***

The band met at Dean’s house early the next day to get everything loaded onto the bus. Scott and Bailey would again be joining them on this tour, taking care of their equipment, and they loaded the equipment onto the trailer. Dean also hired a guitar tech for both Jake and Paul, since they each had several guitars to change out for different songs. When everything had been loaded, the guys said tearful goodbyes to their significant others, then got onto the bus and their driver, Artie, pulled away.

Dean connected his phone to the speakers to play music and the first song he played was Willie Nelson’s “On the Road Again”.

“You’re a funny guy, Uncle Dean,” Isaac said.

“I try,” Dean said.

Their first stop on the tour would be in Santa Barbara, and in fact, David and Marty were driving up together later in the day to watch the show.

The band arrived in Santa Barbara early so Scott and Bailey could get the equipment set up.

The day was sunny and beautiful, so while the roadies did that, Artie drove the band to the beach. Kelly, Jayna, and the guys got out and played on the beach for a couple hours, until Dean called them back so they could go get lunch, then Artie drove them back to the venue, where Jayna went to set up the merchandise and Kelly and the guys went to the dressing room to shower and relax before the show.

After the show, David came backstage to congratulate the band on another great concert.

"As usual, your performance was fantastic," he told his sister.

"Thanks," Kelly said. "I felt a little rusty, though, after not being onstage like that for so long."

"You certainly didn't look rusty."

"Well, thank you." Kelly hugged her brother. "Where's Marty?"

"He went to help at the merchandise table," David said.

Dean let the backstage pass holders in and the band mingled with them, taking photos with the fans and talking with them. Ian found a cute blonde to hook up with, while Jake found a girl to make-out with. Paul stayed true to himself and Alexa and just talked with the fans, as Kelly did. Isaac, as was his usual after leaving Hayley, drank quite a bit while he talked with the fans, but didn't hook up with anyone.

David took photos backstage for the band, as he usually did, to give them to use for whatever they needed.

"We should probably put you on our payroll," Dean said.

"Nah, I like doing this for you guys," David said. "I'm here anyway, so I might as well make myself useful."

"We appreciate all you do for us, Davy," Kelly said as she hugged her brother.

A couple hours later, Dean made his rounds, thanking everyone for coming, essentially kicking them out. Marty and Jayna had returned backstage to spend some time together before he had to leave. David hugged his sister.

"Take care, Kel, and I guess we'll see you back in about four or five months?" David asked.

"Yep," Kelly said. "I'll miss you!"

Kelly watched as Jayna gave Marty a tearful kiss and they hugged each other tight for a few moments before he quickly kissed her head and walked to the door and waited for David.

David shook hands with all the guys and then he and Marty left.

"Marty's gonna try and meet up with us at some point during the tour," Jayna said, still staring at the door Marty had just gone through.

"I hope he can," Kelly said.

They gathered up all their belongings and headed back out to the bus to start their drive to the next venue in San Jose, about six hours up the coast.

Artie got them there later that morning, so they had a lot of time to kill.

"Why don't we take a tour of the Bewilderment House?" Dean suggested.

"I do love a good puzzle," Jake said.

Artie drove to the venue first to get the equipment unloaded so Bailey, Scott, and Sam could set up, then drove to the Bewilderment House and parked at the back of the parking lot. Dean went in and bought their tickets as they looked around the grounds.

"The tour starts in twenty minutes," Dean said when he returned. "We meet in the gift shop for the tour."

The group met up with the tour guide at the indicated time and they followed her as she talked about the house and its many quirks and mysteries. Kelly took pictures of everything that she'd post later to the band's social media. She was fascinated by the tour and the stories behind everything.

After the tour, Artie first drove them to get lunch, then back to the venue. Dean walked with them to the dressing room. After bringing in their bags packed with their stage clothes, the guys went back out to the bus to play video games while Kelly and Jayna stayed and watched the crew set up.

Just before sound check, Kelly went to the dressing room to get her in-ear monitors and Jayna left to set up the merch table in the lobby. Kelly and the guys went onstage and did their sound check, which took an hour, and afterwards, they went backstage to relax and prepare for the show.

Kelly wore one of her new stage outfits. Once she was dressed, she went out where Jayna gave her a once-over.

"You look fantastic," she said.

"It's not too much?" Kelly asked.

"No, it's perfect for the music you guys play. It's different, but still you."

Kelly stepped out and asked the guys and Dean what they thought.

"Wow!" Jake said. "Are those leather pants?"

"Faux leather," Kelly said. "I wouldn't wear the real thing."

"It looks like the real thing," Isaac said.

"It looks really good with your sparkly top," Ian said.

She'd put on her blue sequined sleeveless blouse with the black pants, which had Spandex along the seams, so she could still move in them.

"As you like to say, very rock and roll," Dean said.

"I thought I'd try to dress more like you guys do," Kelly said.

"You look great in whatever you wear onstage," Paul said.

"Don't try to be too much like us," Ian said with a wink.

"I won't," Kelly said. She still had no desire to try cocaine.

When it got close to the time for the opener to go on, Dean invited them over for a shot of Fireball with Fate Struck. After they drank, the opener went out to wait for their time to go onstage.

Kelly did her stretches as she heard the opener began to play. Her new pants moved with her like she'd hoped, making it easy to stretch in them. She then warmed up her voice, doing scales and then singing a song a cappella. The guys warmed up, too, running scales on their acoustic guitars, and Ian and Jake warmed up their voices.

After the opener finished, their roadies cleared their equipment from the stage and Scott and Bailey got everything ready for Fate Struck to take the stage. As they came offstage, Bailey stopped to talk to the band.

"Do you want us to take your drinks out there for you?" he asked.

"That'd be great!" Isaac said, handing Bailey his bottled water and beer bottle. Bailey and Scott got all the drinks put in place for the band—Isaac's on a small table next to his computer, Ian's, Jake's, and Paul's on their amps, and Kelly's on the drum riser.

They went out onstage in their usual order—Isaac first, to make sure his drums were ready, then as he played the beat for the first song, Ian came out, followed by Paul and then Jake. Once they started the song, Kelly came out. She grabbed the mic and stand and began to sing.

The crowd sang along and jumped around to the songs. Kelly stepped to the front of the stage and bounced along with the fans, then skipped back to the drum riser and stood on that while Jake stepped forward to do his solo.

As Kelly jumped down from the riser, she thought she saw Greg out of the corner of her eye in the audience. She looked again, and saw him straight away. She ran offstage to Dean while Jake continued his solo.

"Greg is here!" she panted.

"What?" Dean asked. "Are you sure?"

"I'm positive," Kelly said. "Ian's side, four people back, purple hoodie. It's him!"

Dean got on his radio and talked to security to go check it out. Kelly ran back onstage and continued to sing her part. She watched security go over to that area while she sang. She didn't see Greg anymore. Security looked all through the crowd, but couldn't find him. She glanced over at Dean, who shook his head.

Damn it, she thought. *He knows I saw him and reported him.*

They finished the song and they all met briefly at the drums.

"What happened?" Isaac asked.

"Greg was here," Kelly said. "I saw him in front of Ian."

"I thought I saw him, too," Ian said. "But I wasn't sure. The lights only hit him briefly."

"Are we continuing?" Jake asked.

Kelly knew Jake was asking her specifically.

"Yes," Kelly said.

They went back to their positions. Kelly took a drink from her hard lemonade, then from her water bottle. Just what she needed, having Greg there. She had to put that out of her mind for now to get through the set.

The rest of the show went without a hitch, and at the end of the set, Kelly took off her shoes and did her flips, then waved as she picked up her shoes and ran offstage.

In the dressing room, Dean told Kelly security was looking at the security recordings to see if Greg had come in.

"I know it was him," Kelly said confidently.

"We'll know shortly," Dean said. "In the meantime, guests backstage?"

"Yes," Isaac said.

"Just make sure *he's* not among them," Kelly said.

"Absolutely," Dean said.

A few minutes later Dean opened the door and let in the fans and others who had a backstage pass. Kelly's shoulder muscles tightened and her hands shook as the fans came in, and she went and tossed back a couple shots of Fireball to calm her nerves. She relaxed somewhat once Dean shut the door and Kelly didn't see Greg anywhere. Several guys and some girls came over to talk with her.

"What was the deal with security?" one of the girls asked.

"Oh, just a problem with one of the fans," Kelly said. "The guy took off, though, and they couldn't find him."

"Glad it wasn't something major," said the tall blond guy.

"Me, too," Kelly said. "I don't like it when things like that happen. It kills the vibe."

Dean came over to Kelly.

"We need you to come to the security office," he said.

"Okay," she said, and turned to the fans. "I'll be back in a few."

She followed Dean to the office where they had the recording from that day pulled up, watching the fans come through the door.

"Is this who you saw?" the head of security, Tony, asked.

Kelly looked carefully at the image on the screen. Purple hoodie, but hard to see his face, though the rest of it looked similar to Greg.

"I can't see his face," Kelly said. "But that's who I saw."

Tony fast-forwarded the recording to about the time when Kelly had noticed him and security went looking for him. They saw the guy in the hoodie run out of the building.

"Well, whoever it was, he got spooked when you noticed him," Dean said.

"I'm positive it was Greg," Kelly said.

"We'll have to keep our eyes peeled for him," Dean said. He stood up. "Thank you for checking for us."

"No problem," Tony said. "We don't want any trouble happening with the artists."

Dean and Kelly walked back to the dressing room. Kelly got a text message as she walked inside. She pulled out her phone and saw the message from Greg.

"You looked hot tonight in those pants."

"Ugh," Kelly said, and she shoved her phone back into her back pocket.

"What was that?" Dean asked.

"A message from Greg, saying how good I looked in the pants. He's creeping me out."

"We'll up security at the next venue," Dean said.

"Thanks," Kelly said.

"I thought he'd left the country," Isaac said, walking over to them.

"I thought so, too," Dean said.

After the fans left and the band and roadies got back on the bus, Kelly, Jayna, Ian, and Isaac had a few more shots of Fireball. Kelly just wanted to forget about seeing Greg and tried to get the image out of her head, but unfortunately, even getting drunk didn't help her stop thinking about it, though she didn't feel as stressed about it anymore.

"I'm going to bed," Kelly said, standing up.

"Do you want some company?" Ian asked.

Kelly thought for a split second.

"Sure," she said.

Ian stood and followed her to the back of the bus and shut the door.

***

Isaac watched as Ian followed Kelly to the back of the bus. He knew he'd help her forgot what happened that night. On that note, he decided to call Hayley. Even though he'd only been gone for 48 hours, he missed her.

He punched in her number, even though it was early morning, and waited for her to answer.

"Isaac," she said sleepily. "I was hoping you'd call tonight."

"Yeah, I'm sorry I didn't call last night," he said. "We hit the hotel and crashed, we were so tired. It's gonna take a bit to get used to being up late."

"I bet," Hayley said, more awake now. "How did the show go?"

"It was great, except when Kelly saw Greg in the audience."

"Are you kidding? How does he get in with the police looking for him?"

"I don't know," Isaac said. "It spooked Kelly a bit. We're beefing up security at our next show."

"Good! That's all you guys need is more drama."

"Yeah, we've had enough to last quite a while."

They talked until Isaac felt like he could finally go to sleep.

"I'll call you again soon," Isaac said.

"I love you," Hayley said.

"I love you, too," Isaac said, and he disconnected.

Chapter Twelve

The next two shows went well, Dean had security beefed up, and Greg didn't show up. What did show up were fans bringing *Stripped* magazine to the meet and greets for the band to sign. Their pictorial had come out and a lot of the female fans had bought it. They also asked Kelly to sign the group photo, and some of the male fans expressed their disappointment that Kelly didn't have a pictorial.

"When are we gonna see you in *Playboy*?" one fan asked.

"When Hell freezes over," Kelly said. "It would kill my parents if I did anything like this."

"Kelly's too smart to do that," Ian said. "Some of us did it for the shock value."

Isaac laughed.

"And some of us chickened out," he said.

During the show, the women held the magazines up, and Kelly had to stop looking at the fans in front as she'd seen enough of the magazine. She still wasn't comfortable seeing Jake, Paul, and Isaac in the magazine.

Kelly noticed that the female contingency came on to the guys a little harder than they had previously, the opposite of what Hayley had hoped for. Ian, Jake, and Isaac didn't seem to mind, but it was difficult on Paul, who never looked at other girls. She didn't judge the guys, but she did know that Paul tried very hard to not fall into that practice. Usually Isaac or Ian saved Paul from the women and took them to the bus or another area of the venue.

Someone had the idea to take photos backstage with the fans holding their copies of *Stripped* with the guys for their social media pages. Jayna was roped into taking the photos.

"You know the drill—no compromising photos," Isaac said.

"I know," Jayna said, pulling out her phone.

She got photos of the guys surrounded by some of the fans, mostly women, and took several photos of the band and the fans. She got one of Kelly standing next to Ian, covering her eyes while Ian smiled with a fan holding the magazine open to his page. Jake, Isaac, and Ian had a few taken with the girls kissing their cheeks, which the guys deemed okay to use. Paul asked Jayna to not take any photos of the girls kissing him. The band and the fans had a good time with the photos.

"I'll have to do a little editing," Jayna said when they finished. "Can't post nude photos on Facebook."

"We trust you'll make us look good," Jake said.

Back on the bus on the way to New Mexico, Paul thanked the guys for helping out with the women backstage.

"I know you can only say 'No' so many time before it wears on you," Isaac said.

"And these women are relentless," Paul said. "I didn't even take off my clothes! I might just start going to the bus when they come in."

"Do what you gotta do," Ian said. "We're here to take up the slack."

"I appreciate that," Paul said, and he and Ian clinked their beer bottles together.

They got into Albuquerque that afternoon. They were only two weeks into their tour and Kelly already felt worn out. She tried drinking more energy drinks, but it just gave her a headache, and the same with popping No Doz tablets. Kelly needed Ritalin again to get her going for the shows, but the guys had moved on from that. She asked Dean to get her some and at the next show he had them for her.

Also in that two weeks, all their belongings had migrated all over the bus. Kelly found one of her books under a pile of quickly discarded t-shirts, Jake found the belt he'd been missing for over a week wedged into the couch cushions, and Bailey found a pair of his work shorts under the bottom bunk.

"You guys will really have fun finding your stuff when we get home," Dean said. "Maybe you all can pick up a little bit when you get up tomorrow?"

"We'll see," Isaac said with a wink.

Kelly and the guys checked out their social media pages, to see any photos that fans had taken and posted. The female fans had made a lot of comments about Isaac's tattoo. Some didn't like it, mostly because it had Hayley's name on it, but most of the fans thought it looked cool.

"It's nice to not be on the receiving end of comments for once," Kelly said as they all read the comments.

"At least they're not calling me names," Isaac said, referring to Jessica and her followers.

Kelly thought she saw Greg at every other show. He'd just make his presence known to her, then he'd leave. She began to think either she was hallucinating, because no one else saw him except for Ian one time, or he was very good at ditching the authorities. Whatever it was, it was affecting her job, and she didn't look forward to taking the stage.

She started to drink more during and after the shows, especially when she thought she'd seen Greg in the audience. She needed some way to destress after the shows and alcohol was the preferred method, but sometimes she'd eat a couple of CBD gummies to help her sleep. Her morning routine of drinking Lady Grey tea became more of a necessity now, to get caffeine in her to start the day.

Artie pulled the bus into the parking area in Texas, at the music festival Fate Struck would perform at for the next two days. They had a co-headlining spot on one of the smaller stages with MagNetic. After several openers, Fate Struck would play for 90 minutes, then Maggie's band would play for the same amount of time.

Since Fate Struck wouldn't be playing until later that evening, they walked around to check out some of the other bands with their

All Access pass. Kelly, Jayna, and Ian stayed together and Isaac, Jake, and Paul went out among the people together.

"Do you feel okay, walking with all these people around?" Ian asked.

"I actually feel safer with so many people," Kelly said. "I'm pretty sure if anyone did anything to me, they'd have all these people all over them."

"True," Ian said.

They walked around for a couple hours before returning to their bus to cool off and eat their lunch they'd bought at one of the vendors. Jake, Isaac, and Paul came in a few minutes later.

"We had the same idea," Jake said as they all sat down with their lunch.

"I'm kind of bummed that we won't be able to see The Disciples of Man's show tonight," Kelly said.

"They know we would if we could," Dean said.

"You could visit them at their bus before sound check," Isaac said.

"Not by myself," Kelly said.

"We'll go with you," Jake said.

"Cool beans!" Kelly said.

After lunch, Kelly, Ian, Jake, and Isaac walked over to The Disciples of Man's bus and knocked on the door. One of their roadies opened the door, and recognized them.

"Come on in!" he told them, stepping aside while he held the door open.

They stepped inside and found the band in the middle of their lunch.

"Oh, sorry," Isaac said. "We'll come back later."

"Nonsense," Erik said, motioning them over. "We can eat and talk at the same time."

"Don't talk with your mouth full, Erik," Stevie joked.

Erik took a bite of his sandwich and then stuck out his tongue at Stevie.

"Yummy," Stevie said, washing his own bite down with his beer.

"We just wanted to say 'Hi' since we won't be able to catch your show tonight," Kelly said.

"That's right, you've got the co-headliner with MagNetic!" Erik said. "Congrats!"

"Thanks," Isaac said. "Maybe someday we'll get to the stage *you're* on," Ian said.

"Probably very soon," Stevie said.

Erik got them all a beer, except for Kelly, for whom he poured a rum and coke. She took a sip and pulled a face.

"Damn, that's strong," she said.

"Sorry, I made it how I like it," Erik said, and he poured more coke into her glass. She took another sip and deemed it much better. "I forget you're a lightweight when it comes to drinking."

"She's catching up, though," Ian said.

"We'll make a proper rock star out of you yet," Stevie said.

Kelly and the guys stayed for an hour, then needed to get back to the bus to get their stuff together.

"Break a leg tonight!" Kelly told them as they stepped out the door

"You guys, too," Erik said.

As they walked back to the bus, Kelly got a text message. She pulled out her phone and saw it was from Maggie. She opened it and read it quickly.

"Hey, Maggie wants me to come see her for a minute," Kelly told them. "I'll meet you back at the bus in a little while."

Kelly walked around until she found Maggie's bus, parked a few aisles over from Fate Struck's. She knocked on the door and Nick opened the door.

"Come on in," he said.

Kelly stepped inside.

"Maggie's in there," Nick said, pointing to the back of the bus. Kelly walked down the narrow corridor and knocked softly.

"Come in," Maggie said.

Kelly opened the door and saw Maggie sitting on the bed, a tissue in her hand. She shut the door and walked over and sat next to her on the bed.

"What's wrong?" Kelly asked.

Maggie sniffled.

"Mel broke up with me," she said quietly.

"What?" Kelly put her hand on Maggie's arm. "What happened?"

"We've been together for a long time," Maggie said. "She knew what she was getting into. She didn't like me being on the road for so long."

"I'm so sorry," Kelly said, rubbing Maggie's arm.

"I've told her she could come with me—with us—but she didn't like living on a bus for part of the year. I even suggested just coming on part of the tour, but she said no."

"She's just telling you this now? After being with you for three tours?"

"Yeah, strange, huh? I think it's something else, and this was just a convenient excuse."

"That really sucks," Kelly said.

"Anyway, I just wanted someone to talk to that wasn't male, you know? I mean, they understand, but it's not like talking to a friend."

"I'm glad you think of me as a friend."

"Are you kidding? Besides Mel, you're the closest thing I have to a best friend."

Kelly stayed and talked with Maggie until Kelly had to leave to get ready.

"Thanks for coming over," Maggie said as they walked to the front.

"Of course! Any time, sweetie," Kelly said.

"Here," Nick said, handing something to Maggie.

"Thanks," Maggie said, and she popped what Nick had given her into her mouth and washed it down with water.

"Uppers," Maggie said, noticing Kelly's questioning look. "To get me out of my funk."

"Oh," Kelly said. "Well, I hope it helps. I'll see you after the show."

"Will you come over after?"

"If you want me to, sure."

"Okay, I'll see you then."

Kelly walked back to her bus.

"What did Maggie want?" Jayna asked.

"Melanie broke up with her," Kelly said, as she sat down on the couch.

"Ah, man," Jayna said. "That sucks."

"Yeah. Anyway, she just wanted to vent. I'm going to see her later so we can talk more."

"You're such a good friend to have," Jayna said.

"Aw, thanks, Jayna. I just try to be kind to people."

"That, you are," Ian said.

As it got closer to show time, the guys had their pick-me-up while Kelly popped a Ritalin, then they had their shot of Fireball. They all grabbed a bottled water and their alcoholic drink of choice and made their way to the side of the stage, where the third opener's roadies were tearing down their equipment and Scott, Bailey, and Sam would get Fate Struck's equipment in place, Sam making sure the guitars were all tuned correctly.

The band walked out onstage and started to play, and Kelly realized that this was probably the only place where she couldn't see any individual faces in the crowd, except for those in the first few feet behind the barrier separating the fans from the stage, so she really didn't worry about seeing Greg, or what she thought was Greg, in this audience. She smiled more while she sang, and was having fun again as she entertained the fans.

The crowd had doubled in size since that morning, and before it got too dark she saw signs with the band's name, with their logo of a lightning bolt and sword, and also with the name of individual band members being held up. Their popularity had grown, with radio airplay and being on so many TV shows over the last few months. It overwhelmed her at times, but most of the time she just took it all in. She quite enjoyed the band's popularity now. It excited her to know that their fans liked their music so much, and she poured her energy into her performance.

Kelly stepped back to the drum riser and took a sip of her water while Jake stepped up to play his guitar solo. He leaned over his guitar as he played, then flipped his hair back as he looked over the audience. Kelly knew he was checking out the women there, hoping to maybe see some later.

When he finished his solo, Jake stood at the edge of the stage, arms hanging by his sides, looking very sexy. Kelly walked over to him and put her arm around his shoulders as she started to sing again. He kissed her cheek as he went back to his spot at his mic.

Later in the show, Ian pointed out a sign to Kelly. It read "Kelly, will you marry me?" in bright yellow letters.

"Oh my god," Kelly said, feeling her face flush.

It grew too dark to see any more signs, but as they started their power ballad "No Words" from their first album, hundreds of phone lights came on and the fans waved them back and forth in time with the music, Kelly leading them from the stage.

When they'd finished their last song, they got into position for their picture that Dean took, then Kelly took off her shoes and did a round off-backflip-aerial for the fans, who cheered loudly for her as she waved and ran off stage.

They decided to all go to MagNetic's bus to hang out with them after MagNetic's set. Nick let them in and brought out bottles of vodka, rum, and tequila for them with various mixers. Kelly grabbed a rum and coke and sat next to Maggie.

"You had a fantastic show," Kelly told her.

"I certainly didn't feel fantastic," Maggie said.

"I know," Kelly said, putting her arm around her. "It's gotta be hard to go through this and still go out and look like you're having fun."

"That's why I'm drowning my sorrows now." Maggie held up her glass of vodka and juice.

An hour and three drinks later, Maggie wanted to get away from the liveliness of the others. Some of the guys in both bands had gone out to find girls and had brought them onto the bus.

"Y'all are just too fucking cheerful," Maggie said as she stood up.

"Sorry, Mags," Jimmy said.

She softened her stance.

"It's okay. I can't expect everyone to be depressed just because I am," she said. She turned to Kelly. "I'm going to the back lounge. You wanna come with me? I could use your ear again."

"Sure," Kelly said, and after filling her cup again, she followed Maggie down the hall and shut the door.

Maggie turned on a lamp which gave off a red glow and sat on the bed, crossing her legs in front of her. Kelly sat across from her and did the same.

"I know they care about me," Maggie said. "But I don't need to see them making out while I'm hurting."

"Of course," Kelly agreed. "I'm sorry we're not helping matters."

"No! You're fine! It's my issue, not yours or theirs. It just gets to me."

Kelly shifted on the bed until she was next to Maggie. She put her arm around her again and hugged her.

"You should've brought Jayna with you," Maggie said.

"I asked her if she wanted to come, but she wanted to call her husband." Kelly felt her slump. "Oh, God, I'm sorry."

"You can't stop living because of me. I'll be okay, it just…hurts."

Maggie lay her head on Kelly's shoulder, and Kelly stroked her hair.

"Vent all you want. I'm a good listener," Kelly whispered.

"Thanks."

They talked for an hour, with Kelly mostly listening as Maggie did do some venting, but mostly she just cried.

Kelly could hear all the guys talking and laughing, including Ian, Isaac, and Jake, so she knew the party hadn't died down yet. Maggie texted one of her guys to bring the bottle of vodka and another rum and coke to the bedroom. Nick softly knocked and Maggie opened the door.

"Are you okay?" he asked.

"Yeah," Maggie said.

"Let us know if you need anything else."

"I will."

The young women drank and Kelly got pretty drunk. She wasn't sure if she could even walk at that moment, but had to use the bathroom. She went out and staggered to the bathroom, bracing herself on the walls for balance. When she finished, she went back to the bedroom and closed the door.

"Are you okay?" Maggie asked. "I know you don't drink much."

"I'm getting better at it," Kelly giggled. "But yeah, I'm okay. I just need water."

Maggie reached over and got a water from the mini fridge in the room and handed it to her.

"Thanks," Kelly said. She unscrewed the cap and drank.

Maggie started to softly cry again. Kelly moved her hair from her face, gently smoothing it down her back, then rubbed her back. Maggie looked up at Kelly, and then leaned over and kissed her softly on the lips, which surprised Kelly.

"I'm sorry," Maggie said, pulling back. "I shouldn't have done that."

"It's okay," Kelly said quietly, and kissed Maggie back.

Kelly lay back on the bed as Maggie continued to kiss her; soft, sensual kisses that made Kelly's body tingle and her stomach flutter. Not thinking of anything but the moment, Kelly reached under Maggie's blouse, hesitated, then reached again and caressed her breast through her bra. She had touched herself when she'd had her playtime with Ian, but this was different. It was exciting and felt somehow forbidden, in the sense that she'd never thought she'd ever do this, growing up as sheltered as she was.

Maggie sat up for a moment to take off her blouse and reached behind her to unhook her bra. Maggie had several more tattoos on her stomach and back other than the few on her arms that Kelly hadn't seen before. Kelly took off her blouse, and Maggie reached underneath her to unhook her bra. Maggie leaned down again and touched Kelly's breast gently, barely even touching, like a breeze blowing past. Kelly grabbed her hand and squeezed, making Maggie squeeze her breast.

Their kisses deepened, and Maggie kissed her way down to Kelly's breast, running her tongue around the nipple, then taking the nipple in her mouth. Kelly softly moaned involuntarily.

God, this feels good, she thought. *And very different from being with Ian.*

Maggie nuzzled Kelly's neck, kissing her, finding her way back to her mouth. Maggie turned them over until Kelly was on top, and she did the same for Maggie, kissing her all over, caressing her. Maggie unbuttoned Kelly's pants, slipping them over her hips.

"Ooh, a thong," Maggie said breathlessly. "Never pictured this."

Kelly kicked off her pants then lay down again, facing Maggie, who had taken her pants off. Maggie moved her hand to Kelly's vagina, covering it over the silky fabric. She caressed it over the fabric, then slipped her fingers inside, pressing her middle finger inside Kelly.

Maggie pulled Kelly to her until they touched, breasts against breasts, as Kelly stroked Maggie's back, running her hand down to her butt. Maggie took Kelly's hand and brought it back to her vagina. Kelly hesitated again. This had gone farther than she had intended. Maggie shifted and Kelly realized what was about to happen, and her head started to spin.

"Maggie," she whispered.

"What?" Maggie asked, kissing Kelly's face again.

"I-I'm not ready for this. I can't do this."

Maggie pulled back to look at Kelly's face.

"What do you mean?"

"I've never been with a girl before. I'm not ready to go further. I can't."

Maggie sighed.

"You did seem a little reluctant," Maggie said. "I thought it was just the booze."

Kelly shook her head.

"It's the booze that had me go this far. I'm sorry. I really should've stopped this before now, but God, it felt so good. Mel's an idiot to leave you."

***

Ian sat on the couch at the front of the bus making out with a woman he'd brought onto Maggie's bus, as were all the others. But he also realized that Kelly had been in there with Maggie for a very long time, coming out only once to use the bathroom.

"Should we check on Maggie?" Ian asked.

"No," Nick said. "She's in there with Kelly. They'll be fine."

"Very fine," said Jimmy.

"What's that mean?"

"Maggie likes girls, man," Nick said.

"Kelly wouldn't do that," Ian said firmly.

"If you say so," Jimmy said.

Would she?

The thought of it made him excited, yet concerned. Kelly was still fairly inexperienced when it came to sex. She was a quick study but also didn't want to try new things.

A couple hours later, Kelly and Maggie came out, and Ian stopped kissing the woman for a few moments. Kelly looked really drunk and staggered down the narrow hallway, a water in her hand, and she just fell onto the couch next to Ian and the woman he was with.

"Hey," Ian said.

"Hey," Kelly replied. "Sorry to interrupt. I just needed to sit."

"Yeah, I can tell."

"Hey, the back room's free now," the woman said, kissing Ian's neck. "Can we take advantage of it?"

"Probably not," Ian said. He wondered what just happened in there.

"I'm going back to the bus," Kelly said, standing up and swaying on the spot.

Ian grabbed hold of her arm.

"Not by yourself, you're not," he said. He turned to the woman. "I'm going to walk her back. Stay here and I'll be back."

"Promise?" the dark-haired woman asked.

"Yep," Ian said.

Ian put his arm around Kelly and held her up as they walked to their bus a couple aisles over.

“Thanks, Ian,” Kelly said as they walked.

“No problem,” he said.

“I hope I didn’t fuck up your night.”

“You didn’t,” he said. “She’ll either be there when I get back or she won’t, it’s not a big deal.”

“Okay,” Kelly said.

They got to their bus and went inside.

“What the hell happened?” Dean asked.

“Oh, it’s Party Central over at Maggie’s,” Ian said, making sure Kelly sat down before she fell down. “I think she’s had enough for the night.”

“And the week,” Jayna said.

“I’m going back over there,” Ian said. “Make sure she drinks water before going to bed.”

“We will,” Jayna said.

***

Kelly sat on the couch in the bus, but it felt like it was spinning. She put her hands out on both sides of her to stop the dizziness.

“Just how much did you drink over there?” Paul asked.

“I don’t know,” Kelly said, shaking her head.

“That’s not a good sign,” Jayna said, sitting next to Kelly.

“I need a bucket,” Kelly said suddenly. “Now!”

Dean grabbed a large bowl from the counter into which Kelly threw up. Jayna held back Kelly’s hair as she puked.

“Let it out,” Jayna said.

Kelly threw up a couple more times, then Jayna walked her to the bathroom so she could wash her face and rinse her mouth out.

“Thanks,” Kelly managed to say.

"You're welcome," Jayna said as they walked back to the front, where Kelly sat down again.

"I think you need to get into bed," Dean said softly but firmly.

"I need to drink more water," Kelly said.

"Can you keep it down?" he asked.

"I think so," she said.

Dean brought over a bottled water, and Kelly drank half of it down, and she did manage to not throw it up again.

When she'd finished the bottle, she stood up, Jayna by her side.

"Okay, I'm going to bed," she said.

Jayna helped her to her bed. Kelly didn't even undress, just crawled into the bunk with everything on. Jayna took off Kelly's shoes and covered her up.

"See you in the morning," Jayna said.

"Thanks, sweetie," Kelly said, and she fell asleep quickly.

Chapter Thirteen

Kelly awoke with the most God-awful taste in her mouth. She looked around her bunk and found her water bottle and drank from it. That made her mouth not taste as bad, but it still felt nasty.

What the hell did I do last night? Or is it still last night?

She looked at her phone, which barely had any power left. 12:04 PM. *Nothing like sleeping the morning away.*

Kelly plugged her phone into the charger and opened the curtain to her bunk and saw that Jayna was already up, as was Dean, of course. Kelly rolled out of her bunk and shuffled first to the bathroom, then to the kitchen area.

"Good morning," Jayna greeted softly. "How do you feel?"

"Like shite," Kelly said, sitting down at the table. "What the hell did I do last night?"

"I'm not sure?" Jayna said. "Ian brought you back from Maggie's bus early this morning and you were totally wasted."

"I think I had a few rum-and-cokes," Kelly remembered.

"Maybe more than a few?" Dean asked.

"Probably. I was talking to Maggie again, letting her vent…" Kelly stopped talking and started to remember what happened. She stood up quickly and grabbed Jayna's hand. "I need to talk to you, right now!"

Jayna went with Kelly to the back room and Kelly shut the door.

"What's wrong?" Jayna asked.

Kelly held her hands up to her head and paced back and forth.

"Oh my God!" Kelly exclaimed.

"What, Kelly? You're scaring me."

Kelly finally stopped pacing and sat down on the bed. Jayna sat in the chair across from her.

"I went over there to talk with Maggie," Kelly began. "She is really upset about Melanie breaking up with her."

"Go on."

"We drank a lot. I mean, I must have had four or five drinks," Kelly said.

"Holy shit," Jayna said. "No wonder you were sick."

"Yeah. So anyway, I was letting her vent and just put my arm around her, or was brushing her hair back or something, I don't exactly remember," Kelly said "but then…she kissed me."

"She kissed you?"

"Yes, and I didn't stop her, and actually kissed her back. One thing led to another and we made out on the bed and almost had sex."

"Almost?"

"I panicked when she—sorry if this is TMI—started to touch me…down there…and I stopped us."

Jayna sat silent for a moment, taking in what Kelly had said.

"Well," Jayna said, breaking the silence. "Not to brush it off, but it happens."

"You're not surprised?"

"I'm surprised because it's *you*, but it's not an end-all event."

"Does that mean I'm bisexual?"

"I wouldn't say that with this happening just one time. If it happens again, you might be. Which isn't a bad thing, by the way."

"I know, it just—took me by surprise, is all."

"I wouldn't worry about it, Kel," Jayna said.

Kelly relaxed. It wasn't that she was worried about it, it was just something new and something she never thought would happen.

"Thanks for listening."

The girls stood and Kelly hugged Jayna.

"Any time," Jayna said.

They walked back to the dining table and sat down.

"Everything okay?" Dean asked.

"Yes," Kelly said. "It is now."

"Great," Dean said. "We've got line check in about an hour. If the guys aren't up in half an hour, I'm gonna have to wake them, and it won't be pretty."

Kelly made herself a cup of tea, then showered to get last night's make-up off. By the time she was dried and dressed, the guys were all up, looking the worse for wear.

"How late were you guys out?" Kelly asked.

"I think we came in at 5 AM," Jake said with a yawn.

"We'll be pulling out a couple hours after the show tonight," Dean said. "So party fast if you're going to."

"Not me tonight," Kelly said. "I feel awful right now."

When it was time for sound check, Kelly grabbed her cup of tea and a water bottle to take with her. The guys had their coffee and water and they walked slowly to the stage and got ready to do their line check. Kelly only did the minimum around the stage to make sure the entire stage was covered for her mic and in-ear monitors. The whole thing took less than five minutes. The festival would start at three o'clock, and they only needed to do line checks since everything was still pretty much set from the night before.

As she and the guys walked back to their bus, Kelly saw Maggie and her band heading to the stage. Kelly stopped for a moment.

"Hey," Maggie said.

"Hi," Kelly said.

"I, um, just wanted to apologize for last night." Maggie looked down at her foot scuffing the dirt.

"It's okay," Kelly told her. "Nothing to apologize for."

"You don't hate me?"

"No! Why would I?"

"Well, I came on really strong last night and…"

Kelly held up her hands.

“I was a willing participant. It’s okay. I was a little freaked out about it this morning, but I talked to Jayna and she helped me come to terms with it.”

“Well, I’m glad you were there for me. I appreciate it. Still friends?”

“Absolutely!”

“Will Mags please get her ass to the stage?” Nick said from the stage.

The young women laughed.

“I guess I better go. Thank you for being such a cool chick.”

Maggie gave Kelly a quick hug, then ran to the stage.

Kelly returned to the bus and fell onto the couch.

“I can’t do these extended nights,” she said, resting her head on the back of the couch.

“We’ll turn you into a proper rock and roller yet,” Isaac said.

“What did Maggie want?” Ian asked.

“First of all,” Kelly began. “Thanks for bringing me back here last night. I was really out of it.”

“You’re welcome,” Ian said.

“Maggie was just making sure we were still friends, after last night.”

“Did you two have a fight?” Paul asked.

“Just the opposite. This may get out somehow so you might as well hear it from me.” She took a deep breath and let it out quickly. “I was ‘with’ Maggie last night.”

“We know that, we saw you with her,” Jake said.

“That’s not what she means,” Ian said, smiling. “She was with her in the biblical sense.”

“Except it didn’t get quite that far,” Kelly said, feeling her face turn red.

“Oh my God!” Isaac said.

“That’s hot!” Ian said.

“Whoa!” Jake said.

“Wait. What?” Paul asked.

Dean didn’t say anything, and it was hard to read his expression. He didn’t look disappointed, but there was something Kelly couldn’t quite put her finger on. Concern? She wasn’t sure.

“Anyway,” Kelly continued, “we’re still friends and it won’t happen again.”

“Damn,” Ian said. “I would totally watch that.”

“Jesus Christ, Ian,” Kelly said. “Horn-dog.”

“You know it, babe.”

“I’m just worried about my parents finding out,” Kelly said.

“Kelly honey,” Jake said. “You’re 23 years old. You gotta live your own life. If you want to have sex with a girl, or fuck Ian, that’s up to you.”

“I know, but…”

“No buts,” Isaac said. “You gotta do what you want to do. It’s no one else’s business, not even ours unless you want to tell us.”

“I appreciate that,” Kelly said softly.

“You’re a big girl,” Dean said, “and you can do whatever you want, of course, but just remember that some things have a tendency to get out, so I want you *all* to remember that your actions will have consequences eventually, and you will need to deal with those consequences.”

“Message received,” Isaac said.

The guys went to the back room to play video games, while Jayna and Dean worked on their tablets. That gave Kelly time to think about things while she made and sipped her tea. She had never had any thoughts about Jayna other than friendship, and the same with the girls on the gymnastic team. But Kelly had sometimes thought about girls in the past. She was attracted to boys, but something about girls intrigued her sexually. Being brought up as she was, not experiencing a lot of life, had made her ashamed of those thoughts, and she never told anyone about them, not even Jayna. Kelly wasn’t sure how to feel about everything at the moment. She loved Maggie as a friend, and had never thought of Maggie "in that way" before last night, but obviously Maggie thought of her that way. She wasn't going to worry about it right now. Whatever happens, happens.

When it was time to get ready for the show, Kelly and Jayna went to the back bedroom and kicked out the guys so Kelly could get ready. Kelly dressed in her black flared pants with the small flowers on them, her short, black knit top that showed off her gymnast body well, and her purple Chucks. Kelly put on her make-up while Jayna touched up her hair with the curling iron. When they finished, Kelly stood and turned around.

"Looking fabulous as usual," Jayna said with a smile.

"Thank you for your help," Kelly said. "I just wish I felt fabulous."

"Well, after the show, we can rest while we drive to the next city," Jayna suggested.

"I hope so," Kelly said. "No more drama."

Jayna left the room so Kelly could try to rest a little more. She was so exhausted.

Instead of resting, she went out and dug around in her bags for the bottle of Ritalin and found it in the bag with her hair supplies. Kelly opened the bottle and shook out one tablet. She put the bottle back and got a cup of water to take it with.

It was nearly time for Fate Struck to take the stage, so Kelly did her stretches and vocal warm-ups. She didn't feel any more energetic than she did before taking the medication, but hoped it would kick in soon, plus the adrenaline usually kicked in once she hit the stage.

Dean walked with them across the bus parking lot to the side of the stage, where the roadies were making the changeover for Fate Struck. When it was time, Isaac went out first, followed by Ian, Paul, and Jake, with Kelly coming out last. She set her water bottle and her energy drink on the drum riser, then grabbed the mic and began to sing.

While her voice was 100% on the money, she still felt tired. She walked onstage instead of running, and jumping felt impossible. After the second song, she took a long drink of her energy drink, and a drink from her water bottle and continued on.

The energy drink kicked in a bit, and she was finally able move around more onstage, though still not as much as she usually did. She finished the rest of her drink and by the last four songs, she had found the energy to jump around again.

At the end of the show, the band came to the front of the stage to bow and Dean took some photos of them. Kelly then got into position on the side of the stage to do her usual skill set. She took a running start like she always did and performed the round-off into a backflip, but when her hands hit the stage for the backflip her left wrist buckled. She cried out in pain and couldn't get much air to do the aerial, and aborted it, landing with a bounce as she grabbed her wrist.

Kelly fought the tears as she waved to the fans as she left the stage, Dean and the guys meeting her at the side.

"Oh my God, Kelly," Dean said. "What happened?"

"My wrist gave out," she said, tears streaming down her face.

Dean got on his radio and called for the medical team to meet them at the stage. They walked down the steps and the medical team came around the corner, one of the four-person team carrying a bag. Maggie and her band, and a few other performers had gathered around once they found out what happened.

Kelly and Dean told the medical team what happened. The doctor examined it, then said it should be X-rayed.

"You guys wait here," Dean told Isaac, Ian, Paul, and Jake. "I'll go with her. I'll call you when I have information."

"Okay," Isaac said, the blood drained from his face.

"Hang in there, Kelly," Jake said.

"Love ya, Kel," Paul said.

"Thanks, guys," Kelly said.

One of the medical team had gone to get the Cushman electric cart to transport Kelly, Dean, and the doctor. They arrived at the building of the festival grounds and one of the assistants brought a car around. Dean and Kelly stepped in and the assistant drove them to the hospital, Kelly wiping the tears from her face.

Three hours later, after icing the wrist and putting it in a brace, Kelly was released and she and Dean were taken back to the festival grounds to their bus. Dean had called to give the guys and Jayna an update and they greeted her when she walked in.

"How are you feeling?" Jayna asked.

"Better," Kelly said, sitting down on the couch. "It feels much better now that it's immobilized."

"Did they give good drugs for it?" Isaac asked.

"No, just ibuprofen," Kelly said, "and ice every couple of hours while awake for the first 24 hours."

"Damn it," Isaac said.

"It's a good thing we have a couple days off," Ian said.

"Yeah, but I'll have to find something different to do after the shows now."

"You're not doing any gymnastics on stage," Dean said.

"Come on, Dean," Kelly said. "There's other things I can do besides flips. I can do a Wolf turn, or the splits, or a side aerial. Those are easy."

"Well, not for a few days or even a couple of weeks," Dean said. "I don't need another heart attack like you gave me tonight."

"Sorry about that," Kelly said. "I must have been too tired to do that tonight, but didn't realize it."

"Yeah, you did seem a little lackluster tonight," Dean said.

"The Ritalin didn't help?" Isaac asked.

Kelly shook her head.

"No, not really. The combo with the energy drink helped a little, but not much."

"You can get lots of rest now, then," Isaac said. "We need you rested and back to your energetic self for the next show."

"Yeah, I'm just going to take it easy on this drive," Kelly agreed.

She'd been tired in general and the anxiety from being with Maggie didn't help. She needed the time to recuperate from the injury and rest. Kelly's phone dinged, indicating a text. She looked and saw a message from Maggie.

"I hope U R OK," Maggie wrote.

Kelly tapped out a reply.

"I'm OK now. Wrist is braced and it feels better."

"Glad 2 hear!" came the reply.

"*Sry I can't party 2nite. Need to rest."*

"I understand. Feel better!"

"Thx."

She silenced her phone after that.

"I'm going to change and go to bed. It's been a draining couple of days." Kelly said, and she walked to the bathroom to change.

She crawled onto her bunk with a sigh. It had been a long day. She plugged her phone into the charger, turned out her light and fell asleep with her left hand propped up slightly on her pillow.

Kelly called her mom the next day to let her know what happened.

"I was hoping nothing would happen," Mom said. "But I did mention doing it on a mat."

"I think it would've happened anyway," Kelly said. "The way I landed with my hands, my wrist just gave out. I was too tired and didn't realize."

"Well, don't do anymore if you're tired."

"I'm going to find something else to do that's easier but still entertaining. But we've got two days off, so I should get plenty of rest before the next show."

"Just be careful, sweetie," Mom said. "We want you back in one piece."

"I will," Kelly said. "Love you, Mom."

"Love you, too, buh-bye."

Kelly hit *End* and put her phone on the table.

I can't be the "rock and roll gymnast" without the gymnastics, she thought. *I'll come up with something.*

Chapter Fourteen

Each time Artie stopped to get gas or food, Kelly walked outside to get some kind of exercise. She still felt tired, but figured walking would help combat some of that. On the bus, she rested and did some light exercises, like sit-ups and squats, anything to try to get some of her energy back before the next show, but nothing too strenuous that would make her more tired.

While Kelly went on her walks, she did some thinking. The guys had been using cocaine for a while, and it seemed like they had boundless energy onstage. But she had always been anti-drug. She caved into using Ritalin, but she'd been desperate and it was legal, even though they didn't use it for its intended purpose. No, she wasn't going to start using illicit drugs. She'd stick with her energy drinks and Ritalin.

By the time they got to their next venue, Kelly felt rested and ready to go. She'd tried to eat better while on the road, eating fresh fruits and veggies and ordering something with fish or chicken when she could.

Fate Struck waited on the side of the stage while the roadies made the changeover for their set, and Kelly drank down a 5-hour energy drink.

"We'll see how it goes with that," she said, tossing the bottle into the trash can.

"You've certainly taken better care of yourself these past couple of days," Dean said. "I hope it pays off tonight."

"I feel better at least," Kelly said.

They started their show and Kelly ran out to the mic and got the crowd going, and they went right into their first song. Kelly still felt somewhat tired, but she didn't feel the exhaustion that she'd had their previous two shows at the festival. She stood on the drum riser during one of Jake's solos, then jumped down and ran over to Jake and stood back to back with him while she sang a few lines of the verse, then went to the front of the stage again. She didn't see as many copies of *Stripped* this time, though a few fans still waved them around. Kelly pointed them out to Ian, who smiled broadly at the women who held them.

Kelly only dropped the mic once, when she held it in her splinted hand. She laughed at herself for dropping it, but also cringed at the *thud!* it made on the stage. She still hadn't figured out what she'd do at the end of the set, but decided that a Wolf turn was probably the safest, and added in an Illusion turn after it, which got cheers from everyone.

"That was a cool thing you did at the end," Isaac said.

"What was that?" Dean asked.

"I did a Wolf turn, then an Illusion turn," Kelly said.

"It looked like a flip!" Ian said.

"That's the illusion," Kelly grinned.

Tiredness hit Kelly fast. She sat on the couch backstage and talked with the fans, only getting up to get another hard lemonade and some crackers from the table. There wasn't supposed to be a crash from the 5-hour energy drink, but there was this time. She looked around the room and saw that Ian didn't seem to be having a good time with the fans. She texted him to meet her at the bus in a few minutes. He replied that he'd be there.

Kelly went out to the bus and waited for Ian in the back room. He came in a few minutes later and locked the door.

"Pretty presumptuous of you," Kelly joked.

"Isn't that why you asked me here?" Ian asked.

"Of course it is," she said.

She stood and walked over to him and kissed him hungrily. He picked her up and carried her back to the bed, laying her down gently, kissing her as he did so. He straightened up and took off his shirt, then lay down on top of Kelly, his hands in her hair as he kissed her again.

Half an hour later, they lay on the bed, Ian stroking her arm as they lay facing each other.

"You didn't seem too tired to me," Ian said, referring to her text she'd sent him.

"I was hoping this might get my energy up," she said. "I also wanted to make sure I still liked guys."

"And what's the verdict?"

"I do." Kelly giggled.

"That's *very* good to hear," he said. "But it's okay if you like girls, too."

Their phones dinged, indicating a text.

"Probably Dean," Ian said. He pulled his phone from his pants that lay on the floor and looked at the message. "Yep. Dean wants us back to get our stuff. We're leaving soon."

They gathered up their clothes and put them back on, remade the bed, then walked back into the backstage area to get their belongings.

***

As they drove to their next city, Ian lay in his bed, trying to sleep, but sleep wasn't coming, even after eating two of Kelly's CBD gummies. What kept him awake was the fact that he couldn't stop thinking about Kelly and her recent adventure with Maggie. Ian hadn't really had much time to think about it before, with sound check, gig, and partying. He never would've thought Kelly would have sex with a woman. She hadn't, but almost, and it both excited and troubled him. She was such a good girl, but being around all of them had changed her to a certain extent, getting into one aspect of the rock star image. He just hoped Kelly stayed as kind as she was and not turn into a bitch. She didn't *seem* the type. They joked about turning her into a "proper rock and roller" but he didn't care if she did. He liked her the way she was. Not in love with her, as he kept telling himself, but truly liked her as a person and as their singer.

He thought back to the first time he heard her sing, in their junior year of high school, again at the Christmas concert the choir and the band did together. She had a beautiful voice then, and still did now.

Ian knew he couldn't control what happened to her, how she might change, but he just hoped it didn't go too far. He knew he was part of the problem, but what was done was done. He finally drifted off to sleep, and ended up dreaming about Kelly. He'd done that before, ever since they started being friends with benefits, but this time, he told her he loved her.

The bus jolted him out of his dream. A little light came in from the gap between the curtain and the wall. Ian pulled it open and saw that it was daytime and they must have pulled off to get gas. He heard Kelly get out of bed, pull her shoes on, and leave the bus, most likely to do some walking. It seemed to have helped her with the last gig. He looked at his phone and saw he'd been asleep for roughly four hours. He'd try to go back to sleep, maybe pick up the dream where he left off. Even if he couldn't tell her in real life, he could still tell her he loved her in his dreams.

***

Isaac called Hayley the next day. He hadn't called her for a couple days and wanted to know her opinion on the pictorial the guys had done for *Stripped* magazine.

"Hey, stud," Hayley answered.

"So you've seen the magazine?" he asked.

"Yes, I have," she said. "I thought you looked awesome!"

"Really?"

"Yeah. It was very sexy."

"Have you heard from my parents about it?" he asked.

"Actually, yeah," Hayley said. "Your dad asked me how I could let you do that. I told him, again, that I didn't *let* you do it, we decided you *could* do it."

"What did he say to that?"

"Not a whole lot. Just that he was disappointed that you did it. He doesn't think too highly of Jake and Ian, either."

Isaac scoffed.

"Yeah, we're all low-life drug-using rock and rollers, and Kelly is stupid to be in the group with us."

"The pictures on Facebook were kinda cool, too," Hayley said.

"I don't know whose idea it was, so I hope you're not mad."

"The photos were fine. I know girls kiss you on the cheek and vice versa. The one of Kelly was hilarious."

"I wonder if my dad has seen those."

"He hasn't mentioned it if he has. I also talked to Alexa," Hayley continued. "She liked the pictorial, also, and was glad Paul didn't bare it all."

"There was never any doubt that Paul was keeping his clothes on." Isaac chuckled. "Has Missy said anything?"

Jake had gone *au naturel* along with Ian.

"She liked it, but was concerned that girls would throw themselves at you guys now."

"They do that anyway," Isaac said. "But we don't encourage it. Well, Ian might, but the rest of us don't."

Which was true, they didn't encourage it, but they didn't turn the women down, either, except for Paul. Was it really a lie if it was just an omission?

"Well, you know how I feel about that," Hayley said.

"Yes, I do."

Hayley didn't want to know if anything happened backstage with him or any of the guys.

"I love and miss you so much," Isaac said.

"I love you, too," Hayley said. "Call me soon."

"I will," he said, and they disconnected.

***

Kelly came back in from her walk around the parking lot of the gas station. She wanted to keep up the workouts since they seemed to work at the last show. She'd done four laps around the lot while Artie gassed up the bus, walking at a steady pace.

Just before the next show, Kelly got a text from Greg, saying he was watching her and knew where she was.

"How the hell is he getting around without anyone seeing him?" Kelly asked. That made her more nervous about the situation, not knowing if or when he'd show up.

"I don't know," Dean said, "and that concerns me. But that also means that he's throwing caution to the wind, and may make a mistake. I think the best thing to do is to stay vigilant and keep security increased at our shows, and you are not allowed to go anywhere alone outside of the venue or bus."

"Greg's more unstable than Jessica ever was," Ian said.

"And that's saying something," Jake said.

"Great, he's holding me hostage and he's not even here," Kelly said.

"Better than him really being here," Dean said.

"I know, but it sucks."

When the house opened that night, security made everyone take off their hats and hoods so their faces could be seen on the cameras. Security later commented that someone wearing a dark hoodie got out of line once they saw what was happening at the entrance.

"I'll bet it was Greg," Kelly said. "God, he was soo close…"

"The next step we can do is send his photo to the venues and they can keep a look out for him," Dean said. "If he's going to be stupid enough to come to a show, we can catch him that way."

"I hope so," Kelly said.

Fate Struck had their pre-show drink with the opener and after the opener went onstage, Kelly knocked back a couple more shots of Fireball. It made her nervous thinking that Greg could somehow be out there, watching her. Would he try to sneak in? Could he even *do* that? Did she have to have someone with her everywhere she went?

Kelly drank one more shot, and stopped at that. She already felt dizzy but didn't want to be sick on top of that and try to sing. She drank some water and then drank her energy shot, and as it got closer to their show time, she stretched her legs and back and did her vocal warm-ups.

By the time Fate Struck took the stage, Kelly was somewhat better, even though she still felt a little dizzy. She brought her water bottle out with her and set that on the drum riser before she took the mic and started to sing. Kelly held it together onstage to get through the set, but was very wary of everything and, backstage after the show, she sat on the couch and drank a hard lemonade.

"Kelly, are you okay?" Dean asked. "You really didn't seem like yourself onstage."

"I'm just really nervous about this Greg situation," she said. "I'm honestly nervous to get onstage or go anywhere."

"You know you're safe back here," Isaac said. "And Dean and security are diligent about screening the fans before they're let back here."

"I know," Kelly said. "It's just nerve-wracking, and frustrating, and I want to smash his face in."

She got a text on her phone. She looked and it was from Greg.

"Fuck," she said, holding her phone up to Isaac.

"You seemed a little drunk tonight," the message read.

"Shit," Isaac said. "He was here. Again."

"I thought he'd left when they made everyone take off their hats and hoods," Kelly said.

"So much for beefing up security," Ian said, sitting down next to Kelly.

"I've about had it with stalkers," Kelly said. "First that whacko that followed us around after we opened for the Disciples of Man, then Jess, now Greg."

"At least Jess didn't torment us by following us," Ian said.

"There is that," Kelly said, gesturing with her bottle.

"Are you okay with the backstage pass holders coming in?" Dean asked. "I can turn them away, no problem."

"No, don't do that," Kelly said. "Just make sure Greg isn't with them."

"I'll check them one by one," Dean said, and he left.

Fifteen minutes later, Dean came in with the group of fans and others who had backstage passes. It looked as though some hesitated to come over to Kelly and Ian, so Kelly motioned them over.

"Come on over!" Kelly said. "We won't bite."

"Too hard," Ian added.

A couple of guys and several girls came over and sat down on the floor or they dragged some chairs over to sit on.

"Fantastic show tonight!" one of the guys said, looking at Kelly.

"Thank you!" she said. "Not too bad for being a nervous wreck."

"You were nervous?" a blonde girl asked.

"A little," Kelly said. "There's some drama behind the scenes that's getting a little out of hand, but we think security is on top of it."

Kelly didn't really feel like that, but wanted to brush it off so the fans didn't worry.

"We're glad it's nothing serious," another girl said.

Not serious. Ha, that's a laugh.

“Nothing we can’t handle,” Ian said, stroking the arm of the girl closest to him.

“That’s why I’m drinking,” Kelly said. “Nerves.”

“You’ve always said you’re not much of a drinker,” another guy said.

“I’m not,” Kelly said, taking a long drink of her bottle.

“That’s why she’s sitting down,” Ian joked. “She can’t hold her liquor.”

Dean came over a minute later and brought Kelly a bottled water.

“Thanks, Dean,” Kelly said, taking a long drink of the water. “Can you walk me to the bathroom?” she asked.

“Sure,” Dean said, and steadied Kelly as she walked to the bathroom. He waited for her and walked her back a few minutes later. In that time, Ian had taken one of the girls to the corner of the room. Kelly sat down on the couch again. The guy who had spoken with Kelly earlier sat down next to her.

“Are you okay?” he asked.

“Oh, yeah, I’m fine,” Kelly said. “I’ll be better once I drink more water.”

“You *are* fine,” the guy said.

Kelly giggled.

“So, do you have a name?” she asked.

“Bryce,” he said, holding out his hand.

“Nice to meet you, Bryce,” Kelly said, shaking his hand. “Have you been to any of our shows before?”

“I saw you guys last year on your tour,” Bryce said.

“You must have liked us if you’re back again,” Kelly said.

“I love you guys! And I love that you do flips after the shows.”

Kelly held up her left arm.

“That won’t be happening for a while, since I hurt myself at the last show,” she said.

“Those turn things you did were pretty cool, too.”

"It's about all I can do right now," Kelly said.

Kelly and Bryce talked for about twenty minutes before he picked up her right hand and brought it to his lips.

"You are really beautiful," Bryce said softly.

"Thank you," Kelly said, smiling shyly.

"Can I kiss you?"

Kelly had always said she'd never make out with fans. It wasn't in her nature to just make out with a guy, though lately she'd been doing things she'd never imagine—like making out with Maggie. Should she try it, maybe try to fit in more with the crowd and their expectations? Bryce was pretty hot, with his short dark brown hair and brown eyes.

"Yes, you can," she said.

Bryce leaned over and kissed her gently on the lips, pulled back and looked into her eyes, then kissed her again, a little more eagerly. Kelly shifted on the couch to face Bryce, returning the kisses, her hand in his hair. He guided Kelly back onto the couch, and she felt his hand slide under her blouse to her breast. He deepened the kiss, his tongue stroking hers. Kelly felt light-headed as she kissed Bryce, and she reached under his shirt and ran her hands over his back.

What the hell was she doing? It felt good, but this wasn't her. She didn't make-out with random guys, and was still a little leery about guys in general thanks to Greg. She turned her head away from Bryce's kisses.

"Bryce," she said softly. "We gotta stop."

"Why?" Bryce asked, as he continued to kiss her neck. He gently caressed her breast through her bra.

"Really, we need to stop," Kelly said again, more firmly that time, her hands pushing lightly on his chest.

Bryce pulled back and sighed.

"What gives?" he asked, irritated. "Isn't that what you all do? Hook up with different people in every city?"

"I don't," she said, sitting up as Bryce backed off her. "I've actually never done this before with a fan, and my ex hasn't really helped matters. I'm sorry."

"Maybe next time, then," Bryce said. He kissed her hand again and walked off to talk to Isaac.

Kelly sat up and put her face in her hands and blew out her breath slowly.

"Here."

Kelly looked up and saw Ian holding out a cup to her. She looked in it and smelled it. Fireball.

"I thought you might need it after that," Ian said.

"Thanks," she said, and she drank it down in one.

"Are you okay? Do I need to punch him?"

Kelly snickered.

"No, I'm okay. I just drank too much and let things go too far." She looked around while she played with the buttons on his shirt. "Where's your friend?"

"She didn't want to go to the bus, she just wanted to make out." Ian shrugged. "It happens." He looked Kelly in the face. "Do *you* want to go to the bus?"

"Absolutely," Kelly said.

Ian texted Dean to let him know he and Kelly were going out to the bus, so he didn't worry when he couldn't find Kelly backstage.

In the back room, Ian had a bump of coke before they took off their clothes and got into the bed. Neither of them needed much foreplay to have sex that night since they'd nearly got there with the fans they'd made-out with.

As they got dressed, Ian got a text. He looked at it and put his phone back in his pocket.

"Time's up," he said with a laugh.

"Dean?"

"Yeah."

They finished dressing, and as Ian opened the door, he stopped and turned to Kelly.

"Are you okay still with this arrangement?" he asked.

"Yeah," she said. "Why?"

"I just wanted to make sure. I don't want you to feel like you're being used or, I don't know, feel bad."

"I don't feel used or anything. I don't have feelings for you other than friendship." *Liar*. "But I do think you're sex personified. You take care of my needs, and I hope you don't feel used, either."

"Use me all you want! Guys are wired differently—we can have sex without attachment. I know women sometimes need that emotional attachment." He chuckled as they walked down the hallway to the front of the bus. "'Sex personified.' I like that."

Everyone had gone by the time they got back to the dressing room. They gathered up their belongings and went back to the bus with the others. On to the next city.

Chapter Fifteen

At the next venue, more security had been brought in. The band had to foot the bill, but it was to keep Kelly safe and hopefully catch Greg. Fortunately, or maybe unfortunately, with all the added security, Greg didn't even make an attempt to see the show.

"I guess that's a good thing," Kelly said, after doors had opened and they'd scanned every person and saw every face. Dean had emailed a photo of Greg to the rest of the venues and security had his picture right at the door to look for him.

"I'd love to catch him, though," Dean said.

"So would I, and then punch him in the face," Kelly said.

"Hopefully you'll get the chance," Isaac said. "The rest of us will be standing in line to do the same."

Kelly took a drink from her second hard lemonade. She'd finally built up a tolerance for them and two barely made her tipsy. Anything else, though, and she'd be wasted, so she tried to be careful. She didn't want to ruin the band's performance by being out of it onstage.

When it was time for Fate Struck to go out, Kelly and the guys headed out onstage in their usual order. Kelly set her drinks on the drum riser, grabbed the mic off the stand and got the crowd going before she began to sing.

As usual, Kelly stepped back while Jake did one of his solos, and as he neared the end of it, Ian called over to Paul.

"Let's go to the front," he said.

Paul grinned. He rarely ever went to the front of the stage, preferring to stay back behind the lead and the bassist, but he walked up next to Jake with Ian, and as they played, they synced up their moves, swinging their guitars with the music. Kelly smiled and applauded as she stepped back up to the mic. The guys laughed as they walked back to their spots onstage.

In the middle of the set, both Isaac and Jake took off their shirts, and the women in the audience cheered. Jake almost threw his shirt into the fans, but decided against it when all the women in the front started clamoring for it.

"Maybe next time, ladies," he said, and Isaac got the beat going for the next song.

Kelly kept the drinking to a minimum after the show, since she wasn't a fan of the hangovers she'd been getting for the last week. She drank a hard lemonade and when she finished with that, only drank water. Kelly picked at the food that Hospitality had laid out for them, eating mostly the veggies and cheese.

"I wish he'd get a life," Kelly said, after receiving another text from Greg. "Maybe he and Jessica could get together."

"They're perfect for each other," Ian said.

"Why don't you block him?" Paul asked.

"I have, twice," Kelly said. "He either gets a new phone or finds a way to text me anyway. The phone numbers are different, but I know it's him just by what he says."

"How many times does he text you?" Dean asked.

"A lot, like five times a day. Sometimes more."

"What does he say?"

Kelly pulled her phone out and went to her text messages, then showed Dean.

"Jesus, Kelly," Dean said as he scrolled through. "This is harassment. This is something else we can add to the list to have him arrested."

"If we can find him," Isaac said.

"We don't need to find him to add this, though," Dean said, handing Kelly's phone back to her. "I'll make some calls."

Dean went to the back room to make his calls.

"No wonder you've been drinking more lately," Ian said.

"Yeah, it hasn't been a pleasant experience," Kelly said.

"He can't be flying," Isaac said. "He can't board a plane with being wanted by the police. He's gotta be driving, so how do we catch him?"

"I wish I knew," Kelly said, setting her phone on the table.

Kelly had a hard time getting into the right frame of mind at the next show. She'd tried to put Greg out of her mind, but his constant texting began to wear on her. She called her brother.

"What's going on?" David asked.

"I can't talk to Mom about this," Kelly said. "Greg is really starting to bug me."

Kelly told him everything that had been going on with Greg and what the police have done.

"They just can't find him," Kelly said. "But yet he manages to get in to see some of the shows. It's really making this tour not very fun."

"Maybe it's time to just come home," David suggested.

"No way. I'm not cancelling the rest of the tour. I just need to find a way to cope with this."

"Maybe exercise will help."

"Maybe," Kelly said. "I mean, I walk when I can, but maybe it's not enough. I don't know, Davy. I just want it to stop."

"I know. I think talking will help, so maybe talk with your bandmates or Jayna or Maggie, or even me. We may not have any advice, but we can listen."

"Yeah," Kelly said, drawing circles on the table with her fingers. "I may do that. I know we're all frustrated with him and the situation. Anyway, thanks for listening, Davy."

"You're welcome, little sis," Davy said. "Let me know how the show goes."

"Will do!"

She disconnected and set her phone down again. Maybe she needed to talk to her bandmates more about this. She knew they had to be angry about this, too, though the guys never looked upset. Right now, however, she needed to get ready for their show. While Kelly showered, Jayna went out to set up the merch table, then came back to help Kelly get ready, using the diffuser on the hair dryer to make waves in Kelly's hair.

"It's almost time for a touch-up," Jayna said.

"Yeah," Kelly said. "I'm trying to decide if I want to keep these colors or do something else."

"You could go all purple," Jayna said.

"I might do that."

When Jayna finished with her hair, Kelly put on her make-up, using metallic purple eye shadow on her eyes, and dark pink on her lips. She wore her black flared pants with a dark red short-sleeved blouse. She would put on her platform ankle boots after she'd stretched.

Right before the opener went on, they all had their shot of Fireball together. Kelly did her vocal warm-ups, then stretched her back and legs. With Jayna close-by just in case she needed spotting, she attempted an aerial and was able to do it, to do at the end of the show.

"Just be careful," Dean said. "I know that's an easy skill for you, but just don't give me a heart attack."

Kelly smiled as she put on her shoes, then opened a bottle of hard lemonade to take out onstage with her as well as a bottle of water.

When it got close to show time, the guys had their snort of cocaine just before they and Kelly went out to wait on the side of the stage as the roadies finished the changeover. Isaac went out amidst cheers from the fans. He sat at his drum kit, checked that everything was to his liking, and started pounding out the beat to their first song. Kelly came out to the loudest cheers. She took a drink of her hard lemonade, then went to the mic to sing.

At the end of the show, Kelly took off her shoes and the fans cheered, knowing what was coming up. She got into position to do the aerial, then executed it flawlessly and the fans cheered even louder than before. Kelly picked up her shoes and with a wave she left the stage.

"You always give them what they want," Jake said when they got back to the dressing room.

"I have fun doing it," Kelly said. "I may not be able to compete anymore, but I can do this every so often. I'd love for Miss Suzy to do another exhibition."

A couple days later, Kelly received a phone call from David.

"I've got a letter here from your high school," he said.

"Ooh," Kelly said. "I wonder if they *are* having another exhibition. I was just talking about that the other day. Can you open it and see what it is?"

"Sure," David said. Kelly heard him tearing the envelope open and pull out the contents. "Oh! Your five year high school reunion is coming up this year. They're having it at the Senior Class President's house."

"Oh, cool!" Kelly said. "Though I don't relish the thought of seeing Jessica, but other than that, it could be fun."

David told her the date, which was September 12th. Kelly realized they'd be finished with the tour by then.

"I'll talk to the others and see if they're going," Kelly said.

Kelly mentioned it to the guys and Jayna, and they called their families to find out if they'd received an invitation. They had.

"What do you think?" Kelly asked them.

"It could be fun," Paul said. "It'd be cool to see our friends we haven't seen since we graduated."

"You know Jess will be there," Ian said.

"I don't care," Kelly said. "I can steer clear of her. Besides, most of our friends are on our band page. I think they'll keep her in check."

They all decided to go, and told their families to send the RSVP with the money.

That cheered Kelly up for a few days, then the gloom of the Greg ordeal crept in again. She did a lot of thinking while they drove between cities to the next venues. She hadn't heard from Greg in a few days, but not knowing when or even if he'd show up at a show had Kelly being very cautious all the time, not to mention nervous. Every time she thought about it she'd hyperventilate, and had to take a few minutes to calm down again, pushing the thought out of her head. She again thought about what the guys used, but she stuck to her guns and just asked Dean to get her Ritalin again, to help ward off the anxiety. That helped.

A week later they arrived in Texas for a couple of shows. Kelly still hadn't heard from Greg and hoped he'd finally given up on her.

No such luck. The day of their first show, Greg texted her, telling her she'd better watch her back while there. It made her and everyone else nervous enough to not go out to explore the city. There's no way Greg could know what they were going to do, but if he was watching them, he could follow and cause issues. No, Kelly was staying out of sight until show time. The thought of even seeing Greg in the audience made her light-headed and Dean had to bring her a bag to get her breathing back to normal.

With her wrist brace on Kelly still couldn't do any proper flips, but she stuck with the aerial and the Illusion turn. It'd been three weeks since she'd hurt her wrist and it still hurt sometimes when she had the brace off and moved it wrong. She called her doctor who told her to leave it on another week and then check it.

Nothing happened while in Texas, and after a few more threats and nothing happening in another city, Dean figured the Greg was just messing with them and wouldn't do anything. That didn't make Kelly feel any better. Greg was a loose cannon and would strike if they let their guard down, so Dean kept the extra security at the venues, and Kelly stayed inside.

The band had two shows to do in Detroit so they stayed in a hotel. The guys wanted to go check out the city and asked Kelly and Jayna if they wanted to go.

"No way," Kelly said. "I don't want to chance Greg showing up."

"You can't stay inside the whole time," Isaac said.

"He's keeping you prisoner and he's not even here," Jake said.

Kelly thought about that, but she was still nervous about leaving.

"We'll all stay with you," Paul said.

"No one will get near you with us around," Isaac said.

They finally convinced her to go with them. She put on her jeans and a T-shirt, laced on her Chucks, grabbed her sunglasses and was ready to go. Jayna and the guys had dressed the same, trying to be inconspicuous. Although they weren't a household name yet, they'd been noticed quite a few times while out and about.

They ate lunch at a burger place, then walked around and hit a couple of bars. No one bothered any of them, and Kelly started to relax a little. It felt really good to get out and walk around and be in the sunshine and fresh air. She almost forgot about Greg. Almost.

As the group walked back to the bus, Kelly got a text message.

"Well, this can't be good," she said, pulling out her phone. It was from Greg.

"Don't get too complacent," the message read.

"How the hell does he know?" Jake asked.

"He's got to be watching us," Isaac said.

"That's creepy," Paul said.

"Yeah, it is," Kelly said, her hands shaking as she tamped down another anxiety attack. "Now you know why I didn't want to go."

They stepped into the bus and Kelly told Dean about the text.

"He's got to be around here somewhere," Dean said, picking up his phone to call the police.

"He's probably long gone by now," Kelly said.

Dean spoke with the police for a few minutes, then hung up.

"They said they'd look around," Dean said. "But they don't know what car he's driving or anything like that, so chances are slim he'll be found right now."

"Damn it," Kelly said.

Kelly didn't venture outside for the rest of the day, only leaving the bus when they all went inside to get ready for the show. After she dressed and Jayna left to go take care of the merch table, Kelly pulled Ian aside. She'd been thinking a long time about this and had made a decision.

"It's too close to show time for a quickie," Ian joked.

"That's not what I want," Kelly said. She took a deep breath. "I want to try it."

"Try what?" he asked, then a look of understanding came across his face. "Are you sure?"

"Yes. No. I don't know," she said. "But this anxiety is driving me crazy. I want to feel better. Ritalin just doesn't do it for me anymore."

"I'm not going to talk you out of it," Ian said. "You're a big girl and can decide what you want to do. It could make your anxiety worse, though."

"At this point, I don't care. It's already almost too much to deal with."

"Come with me."

Kelly followed Ian to where the rest of the band sat, getting ready.

"Kelly will be joining us tonight," Ian said.

"Cool," Isaac said. He had already made the lines for all of them. He made one more, a much smaller one for Kelly. Ian showed Kelly what to do. It took her two tries to snort the line. Her nose went numb and she rubbed it.

"This is horrible!" Kelly said. "I don't like this."

"Just—give it a few minutes, it'll be better," Ian said.

Kelly and Ian sat on the couch while the rest of the band moved around, getting a few other things ready. Ian stayed with Kelly until he knew how she reacted to the drug. Kelly got up to get a bottled water, and felt happier than she'd been in a long time.

"Oh my God," she said, bringing the bottled water back to the couch. "This is—weird. I feel great right now."

Ian smiled.

"See? Isn't it fantastic?" he asked.

"I don't know about that." She took a drink of her water. "But I feel like I could sing for hours. I want to go out there right now. I totally get why you guys like this."

"Well, we have to wait," Ian said with a laugh. "We'll be out there soon enough."

"We've made a true rock and roller out of you," Jake said.

Kelly wasn't sure if that was a good thing, but at that moment she did feel very connected to the band and the music. When it was time for the band to go out to the side of the stage to wait, they followed Dean out, laughing and singing as they walked.

"My, aren't we all in a good mood," Dean said.

"Kelly's finally come to the dark side," Isaac said.

Dean turned his head quickly to Kelly. Jake laughed.

"Did you get whiplash there, Dean?" he joked.

"You didn't," Dean said, ignoring Jake.

"I did," Kelly told him.

"Well, no one can say this hasn't been an interesting tour. Are you okay?"

"I'm good!" Kelly said.

"Well, break a leg. Please, not literally, Kelly," Dean added.

"Thanks!" Kelly said.

It was time for them to go out. They went out in their usual order, Kelly coming out last. She went to the mic and took it off the stand and walked to the edge of the stage.

"How's everyone doing tonight?" she asked.

The crowd screamed and cheered.

"We're Fate Struck and we're here to rock and roll!"

With that, they went into their first song.

***

Ian watched Kelly work the stage, interacting with all of them and the fans. She walked across the stage as she sang, and waved at the fans in the first few rows, often bending down to sing directly to them. During Jake's solo, Ian went up to stand by Kelly, and when she started to sing again, she gave him a little playful push away as she ran to the other side of the stage. He laughed and went back to his mic. Kelly looked happier onstage than she had in a long time. She'd been so worried about Greg and his threats that even though she seemed okay onstage, she wasn't her happy self. She now looked as she did when they played those early gigs.

At the midway point of the show, Kelly introduced the band. After she introduced everyone, Ian did the honor of introducing her.

"And this is the 'rock and roll gymnast', Kelly Brennen!"

The cheers for her were as loud as his. Kelly smiled and kissed him on the cheek before the band launched into the next song.

At the end of the show, Kelly took off her shoes, and Ian panicked a little. Would the coke make her try to do something she really shouldn't do onstage? He watched as she got into position and did the aerial and then an Illusion turn, much to Ian's relief. They all waved as Kelly grabbed her shoes and left the stage.

In the dressing room, Ian mentioned his concern.

"I'm glad you didn't do anything else onstage," he said.

"Like what?" Kelly asked.

"Well, I didn't know if you'd try to do a backflip or something in your state of mind," Ian said. "I didn't know if the coke would affect your decision-making."

"Nope, it didn't," Kelly said. "Also, this brace on my wrist is a reminder not to do those for a while."

Back on the bus, the band and Jayna had a couple of drinks before Kelly excused herself to go to bed.

"Crash and burn," Isaac said.

"Yeah, but it's something I'm used to after taking Ritalin," Kelly said.

After Kelly left, Jayna asked about the remark.

"Well," Ian said. "She decided to try cocaine tonight."

"What? And you let her?" Jayna asked.

"We're not her parents or babysitter, Jayna," Isaac said. "She's a big girl and can decide what she wants to do."

"I know, but I didn't realize she was that stressed and that tired."

"She is, thanks to Greg's bullshit," Jake said.

"Which will hopefully end soon," Dean said. "I just got a call from the police, saying they have a lead on Greg."

Chapter Sixteen

Dean gave Kelly the good news the next day when she'd awakened.

"About time," Kelly said. "What did they say?"

"They have the make and model of his car," Dean said. "No license plate, though."

"Damn it," Kelly said. "I guess it narrows it down a bit."

They pulled into the parking lot of the venue the next day at 3 PM. Dean went inside to check in then came back and walked with them to the dressing room, bringing their bags with them.

Since they had a few hours to kill before sound check, the guys went to a local bar while Kelly and Jayna stayed inside the dressing room. Kelly didn't feel adventurous that day and really didn't want to give Greg any chances to do anything to her. Though if he was going to, he'd already had plenty of chances. She just didn't feel like pressing her luck.

At sound check, the guys had a snort of coke before going out. Kelly didn't want any, preferring to wait until show time, when she needed the energy to give a good show. She didn't want to get addicted, and tried to be careful about using it.

A month later, they were on their last shows of the tour, which was another two-day festival, this time in Northern California. They would be playing on the same stage as The Disciples of Man, the headliner on one of the three stages there. All the buses parked behind the stage the band would appear on. Fate Struck's bus was one of the first ones there, so they got a fairly close spot near the stage.

"That'll be nice for leaving the stage," Isaac said.

Band buses constantly pulled into the lot all day, filling it up. The shows were scheduled to go on Saturday and Sunday. Since Fate

Struck arrived early, they had more time to check things out. Dean left for half an hour and when he came back he had a surprise for both Jayna and Kelly.

"Marty!" Jayna shouted when she saw her husband come onto the bus. He was followed by David, Kelly's brother.

"This is a nice surprise," Kelly said as she hugged her brother.

"We thought since you were in California we'd come up and see the shows," Marty said.

"I'm so happy you did," Jayna said. "I've missed you so much."

Jayna and Marty went outside to walk around and visit privately.

"So what's new?" David sat down on the couch.

"I finally took my wrist brace off," Kelly said, holding up her left arm.

"Everything good with it?" he asked.

"It's a little stiff, but I'm working on it," she said, showing him a couple of the exercises she did for it.

"Great!"

That night, Jayna and Marty took the back room to sleep in, and David stayed on the bus in one of the bunks.

"I don't know how you guys sleep in these for months at a time," David said while they ate breakfast. "It feels like a coffin."

"You get used to it," Jake said.

Fate Struck went out to do the line check of their monitors in sunglasses and hats to try to keep cool and shaded from the July sun. David had an All Access pass and took some footage on his phone to post on their social media pages.

Back on the bus, Kelly and the guys got ready for their show. Kelly took a quick shower, then used the back room to get ready while the guys used the hallway between the bunks and front of the bus. Jayna helped Kelly with her hair as usual. Since it was so hot outside,

Kelly wore her hair in two ponytails on top of her head, Jayna using the curling iron to curl Kelly's hair into spirals.

"I doubt they'll stay like that, though," Jayna said.

"It's okay," Kelly said. "I just want it off my neck while we're out there in the sun."

Kelly dressed in her black shorts with red fishnet tights covering her legs, and a loose glittery short-sleeved blouse.

"Don't you look cute," David said when she came out.

"Trying to stay cool yet covered," Kelly told him. She got a bottled water and drank half of it down. "I really don't want a repeat of Arizona."

"Neither do we," Dean said.

She finished the water and then opened a hard lemonade. As it got closer to show time, they had their shot of Fireball, David and Marty joining them. Jayna and Marty went out to the merchandise tent while Kelly stretched her legs and back. Isaac got what they now referred to as the "show time line-up"—cocaine—ready at the dining table. The guys, including David, did their lines, then Kelly went over for hers.

"Okay, that's something I never thought I'd see," David said as Kelly snorted her small line.

"Yep, she's become a true rock star," Isaac said.

"Only before shows," she said as she sat down and laced on her purple Chucks.

Dean showed them the way to the waiting area by the stage. Kelly brought a cold bottled water and her hard lemonade with her.

"Break a leg, little sis," David said before he went to the VIP area to watch the show and take more video of the band's set. Marty would join him just before show time.

The band took the stage right at 7 PM, just as the sun was low in the sky, shining right into their faces. They all wore sunglasses until the sun had dipped below the horizon. Kelly took hers off and, remembering what happened at the Taste of Long Beach when they flew off her head, hung them on her mic stand.

At the end of their set, the band went to the front of the stage for their photos, then Kelly did her aerial and Illusion turn, much to the delight of the fans, and with a wave she ran off the stage.

Back on the bus, Kelly fell onto the couch.

"I really hate performing in the heat," she said. "It zaps my energy."

"You looked pretty energetic to me," Jake said.

"Yeah, I left it all onstage."

"You know the remedy for that," Ian said. He meant coke.

"Naw, I'm good," Kelly said.

They rehydrated themselves and rested for an hour, then went back out to the VIP section to watch The Disciples of Man's set, David included. They got there, right in front on Adam's side, just as the band began their set. Erik found Kelly and locked eyes with her for a moment, then continued to move around the stage.

At the end of The Disciples of Man's set, the band went offstage, with Stevie telling them to come to their bus. Before Kelly could leave, however, several fans behind the VIP section asked Kelly for photos and autographs. She handed her bottle of Mike's to David to hold while she signed photos for the fans.

"Is that your boyfriend?" one young man asked.

"Hardly," Kelly said, laughing. "This is my brother David."

Some of the fans wanted a picture with both Kelly and David so they posed for a few before leaving.

They found The Disciples of Man's bus and knocked on the door. It opened and Stevie stood in the doorway.

"Come on in, guys!" he said, stepping aside to let them in.

The party was in full swing, with several women for all the guys there. Kelly felt a little out of place since she didn't care to hook up with anyone. She finished her hard lemonade and poured a rum and coke for herself.

"Be careful there, Kel," Ian said. "Remember what happened last time?"

"I will," Kelly said.

"What happened?' David asked.

"Just never you mind," Kelly said.

Jayna and Marty came over for one drink before they went back to the bus. Kelly found Paul and sat down next to him.

"Not really your scene, is it?" Kelly asked.

"The partying I can handle," Paul said. "These women can be assertive."

"Yeah, they don't care who they hook up with as long as it's a rock star. They've even tried to hook up with me."

They watched as several women vied for the attention of each guy there, including David, who also wanted to stay faithful to Tessa.

"No judgement from me," Kelly said. "I know you're trying to stay faithful to Alexa. Just remember—we'll be home in two days."

"Yeah, I know," Paul said, and he downed his Jack and coke and went to pour another.

Kelly sipped her rum and coke and surveyed the room. There were literally two girls for every guy there. Isaac had his arm around one woman as they watched a game of beer pong while another had her arm around Isaac's shoulders. Kelly looked around for Ian but couldn't find him, which meant he was already in the back lounge with someone, probably Junie, whom he met the last time the band was up that way. Jake sat on the couch across from Kelly with a dark-haired woman, making out with her. Stevie leaned against the fridge while a woman kneeled down in front of him performing oral sex. Paul came back a moment later.

"At least there's a lot of booze," Paul said, holding up his cup.

"Yes, there is."

Various alcohols and mixers filled the small dining table, and everyone helped themselves. There was also bottled waters, which were hardly touched, and energy drinks.

A little later, Erik got a game of beer pong going. Stevie had zipped up and he and Erik played against a few people.

"Let's go watch beer pong," Kelly said, standing up. "We can do that without having someone with us."

They went over and stood next to Isaac and watched the game, which now had Erik and Stevie playing against two band members from one of the metal bands. So far Erik and Stevie were losing. They only had one cup left, and the other team finally got the ball in the cup, and Erik drank. Kelly and Paul joined in the applause, and Erik and Stevie stood up and took a bow, Erik swaying just a little as he straightened up again. He saw Kelly standing there and smiled.

"Hey, you're still here," he said.

"I am," Kelly said.

"Did you get something to drink?"

Kelly held up her red cup.

"Good! We'll turn you into a proper rock and roller eventually."

Kelly smiled but didn't say anything. She didn't want to encourage him or lead him on. She knew he wanted to have sex with her, but that wasn't going to happen.

Half an hour later, Kelly and Paul went back to their bus. Neither of them were comfortable there with everyone else indulging in one thing or another.

Jayna and Marty were still awake when they got in, but Dean had gone to bed, and the roadies were out somewhere with the other roadies.

"It's pretty crazy over there," Jayna said.

"Yes, it is," Kelly said, sitting on the couch. "Paul and I were out of place there."

"Alexa's a lucky girl to have you," Marty said.

"It was so hard," Paul said, shaking his head. "Kelly reminded me that we'd be home in two days, and I'll see her then. That helped a lot."

"I also won't judge if something does happen," Kelly said. "I know Isaac absolutely adores Hayley, and Jake is completely in love with Missy, but it happens. Not my place to tattle."

"How did we get so lucky to have you as our singer?" Paul asked, kissing her cheek.

"Isaac had the good sense to know a fabulous singer when he heard one. Or two, in our case," looking at Jayna, who smiled shyly.

"I think I'm going to go to bed," Paul decided, standing up. "Gonna call Alexa before I sleep. Good night, all."

"'Night, Paul," Kelly said.

Jayna and Marty followed suit a few minutes later.

"David and I are flying back tomorrow afternoon," Marty said.

"Does he know that?" Kelly asked. "He was having a lot of fun over there."

"I'll smack him around if he's not awake in time," Marty joked.

Jayna and Marty went to the back lounge to sleep.

That left Kelly up by herself. She wasn't going to wait up for anyone, and washed her face, changed into her pajamas and got into her bunk. Just as she pulled the curtain shut, she heard the rest of the band stumble in. They did try to be quiet when they came into the bunk area, but Dean had to tell them to keep it down. They slurred their apologies and soon there was no sound except for the various sounds from the bus.

Fate Struck played the next day in the same spot as the previous day. Kelly left her hair down and by the end of their set her hair clung to her face and neck. The guys had all taken off their shirts and the sweat had made all of their make-up run and smear. After their set, they dried off, changed their clothes, and walked around the festival area before going back to watch The Disciples of Man play, watching from the VIP area in front of the stage again.

After Disciples' set, Fate Struck followed them to their bus for the after party. Disciples would be continuing on to Oregon while Fate Struck headed home the next day.

"Did your brother leave today?" Erik asked.

"Yeah," Kelly said. "He and Marty left late this morning. Davy was hurtin' when he left, though. He called when they landed and said he was taking a nap once he got home."

"He's a pretty cool dude," Stevie said.

"Yeah, I kind of like him," Kelly said.

With it being the end of their tour, Fate Struck partied a little harder than the previous night, even Kelly. She loved being on tour and entertaining the fans, but she'd be glad to get home and have a normal part of life for a little while. Kelly poured herself a rum and coke and watched as Jake and Adam played Quarter Bounce. Adam lost.

They got talking about the feature in *Stripped* the guys did, Erik saying how bold of them to do it.

"It obviously didn't hurt your band at all," Erik said.

"Didn't you do something similar?" Kelly asked.

"I did!" Erik laughed. "I'm surprised you know about it, Miss Goody-Two-Shoes."

"Not as innocent as you think she is," Ian said.

"Are you doing a layout soon?" Stevie asked, grinning broadly.

"Nope. Not gonna happen," Kelly said.

"Hopes around the world are crushed," Erik said.

"They'll live."

Kelly finished her drink and went to pour another, then watched some of the guys play a video game. Ian excused himself to use the bathroom. As she stood there, someone came up behind her and started to play with her hair. Thinking it was Ian, she patted his hand. When she felt a ring, she turned around and saw Erik there.

"I thought you were Ian," she said.

"Nope, just me," Erik said. "Why would Ian be playing with your hair, anyway?"

Oops.

"He's one of my best friends and he'll come up and do that from time to time," she said. It wasn't a lie. He did do that sometimes. In fact, all of the guys had come up to her and played with her hair, or put their arm around her shoulders. They did that with each other, minus the hair-playing.

"Oh. I thought maybe you and he had something going on."

She wasn't about to tell him anything about that. She turned back to the game, and Erik continued to play with her hair, then moved to giving her a neck and shoulder rub. Kelly tipped her head from side to side.

"I guess I'm a bit tight," she said.

"Yes, you are," Erik said.

Kelly finished her drink and poured another, telling herself that's the last one. She'd had very little to eat after the show and the alcohol had gone to her head. The lightheadedness made her slightly unsteady, and Erik caught her as she came back to watch the game.

"Are you okay?" he asked.

"Yeah, I just should've eaten more," she told him.

Erik went and got her a small sandwich from the fridge.

"Here." He handed her the sandwich. "I don't want you to get sick."

"Thanks." She took a bite of the sandwich as they continued to watch the guys play the game.

Kelly finished the sandwich and cheered along with everyone as Ian won the game. Stevie took Will's place and they started again. Erik moved Kelly's hair to the side and kissed her neck. She closed her eyes as tingles went through her body. His kisses were so light, barely there, yet she felt them down to her toes. She took a long drink from her cup then set it on the counter, turning to Erik to return the kisses.

He took Kelly's hand and led her to the back lounge and shut the door. Kelly felt lightheaded, but not just from the alcohol. Erik's kisses were intoxicating. In her current state, she thought of nothing but the moment—his gentle touch, the scent of his skin, the way he said her name.

Erik peeled off his shirt, then pulled off Kelly's blouse. He ran his hands over her skin as he kissed her, then unhooked her bra and took it off. He took her breast in his hand as he kissed his way down, taking the nipple in his mouth. She arched into him. He put his arms around her and pulled her to him, kissing her neck, then lay her back down while he unbuckled his belt and took off his pants. Kelly did the same, kicking her pants to the floor.

Lying there naked, Erik ran his hand down Kelly's body, sending tingles through her again. She wanted him at that moment, even after all the times she'd told him no before. His rock star good-looks—his shaggy light brown hair, hazel eyes, and toned body with several tattoos—were undeniably attractive. She didn't care about anything at that moment. Erik kissed her all over, his hands touching her in places that drove her crazy. He grabbed a condom from the side table, rolled it on, and then entered her. He smiled as they started to move together.

"You've done this before," he whispered.

"Yes, I have," she said.

"That's hot."

This time she smiled and they rolled over until she was on top. He took her breasts in his hands as she moved on him, and she touched herself, making Erik groan. They rolled over again, and he held her as he came, breathlessly saying her name.

When the waves stopped, Erik rolled off her. They spooned together, Erik pressing up against her. He had one hand on her breast, and she covered his hand with hers.

"Oh my God," he said into her hair. "That was better than I'd hoped for."

Kelly chuckled.

"Did you think I was still a virgin?" she asked.

"Kind of," Erik said. "Ian's right—you're not as innocent as I thought."

"No, I'm not."

"Since Greg was your boyfriend, you've obviously been with him, but he didn't teach you all that. I bet it was someone in the band."

"I'm not saying."

"Was it Isaac? Or Ian? I bet it was Ian."

"I'm not saying."

"Whoever it was did a damn good job teaching you."

Kelly smiled, but the smile faded as she realized what they'd done. She had said this wouldn't happen. She didn't want to do that to his wife, but here she was, in bed with a married man. Tears formed and when she sniffled, Erik turned her over to face him.

"What's wrong?" he asked.

"I didn't want to do this to your wife," she said softly.

"You didn't," Erik said. "*I* did. And I told you before, she knows. When I'm on the road, I like the company of gorgeous women. I love my wife very much, and when I'm with her, no one else matters. You don't need to worry."

"But I…"

"This is why everyone likes you. You care about other people. You're hot as fuck. You're a goddess on that stage, but you think you're just a nerd. That's what makes you hot."

Kelly didn't say anything. She was overwhelmed by what she felt and by what Erik said.

He leaned on his elbow and looked Kelly in the eye.

"I know we said we wouldn't do this. This is my fault, but I'm not sorry. Can we still be friends?"

Kelly thought about it. It certainly wasn't just his fault. She let it happen.

"Yes, we can still be friends—if this doesn't happen again. You gotta try harder to not let your hormones run rampant, and I have to not drink so much when I'm around you."

"Okay," he said. "I promise."

They got dressed, and Kelly sat on the edge of the bed, her face in her hands. *God, what did I do?* She had truly become a rock star, sleeping with the lead singer of another rock band.

Erik sat next to her and rubbed her back to comfort her. She raised her head and took several deep breaths to push down her anxiety before she stood up to go back and join the party.

***

Isaac watched as Kelly and Erik came out of the back lounge. Though she tried to hide it behind a smile, the guilt was all over her face. He knew what had just happened in there and he knew she wasn't happy about it.

Kelly said something to Erik, and he kissed her on the cheek. She smiled and then made her way over to Isaac.

"Hey," Kelly said. "Sorry to interrupt. I'm going back to the bus."

"Are you okay?" Isaac asked.

"Yeah, I'm good," she said.

"Okay, I'll see you in the morning," Isaac said.

He watched her leave, then went back to the woman he was with. A few moments later, however, his phone rang. He pulled it out and saw Kelly's picture and number. He answered it.

"What's up?"

Kelly wasn't on the line, though he could hear faint talking, and figured she must have butt-dialed. But as he listened more, it sounded like two people arguing.

"Hey!" Isaac shouted. "Shut up and listen."

Everyone got quiet on the bus and Isaac put it on speaker.

"How did you even get in here?" Kelly was asking.

"It's dark, so it was easy," a male voice said. "Plus, there's a lot going on here, no one paid any attention to me."

"Well, you can just turn your ass around and leave."

"Ooh, someone's learned to swear," the voice said. "Hanging around the guys has really changed you."

"You'd better believe it, Greg."

"We gotta get out there!" Ian said, jumping up.

Everyone ran out and across the parking lot. They could see two people standing in front of a bus. When Greg saw them coming, he ran off. Some of the guys ran after him, and Ian, Isaac, Jake, and Erik ran to Kelly, Ian grabbing her and holding her.

"Oh my God," Kelly said. "I was hoping you got the call, Isaac." She buried her face into Ian's neck.

"You're shaking," Ian said. He hugged her tighter. "You're okay now."

Stevie, Will, and Paul came back, and several people had stepped out of their buses to see what the commotion was all about.

"We lost him," Will panted.

"Goddammit," Isaac said. He embraced Kelly from behind, still in Ian's arms.

"That was pretty smart to call one of us," Erik said.

"I was actually texting Isaac, to get a bump because I felt like crap, and when Greg stepped out in front of me, I just held my phone for a minute, hit Call, and hoped it went through. I was shaking so bad I wasn't even sure I'd hit Call."

"We gotta tell Dean," Ian said.

"I called him as we were walking back," Paul said. "He said he'd call the police."

At that moment, two police officers walked up to the group, and the band members on the other buses quickly went back inside. Erik and his bandmates gave their statements while Kelly and her bandmates went to their bus so Kelly could sit down while she gave her statement. Jayna got Kelly a water.

It took about an hour for everyone to give their statement, and when the police left, it was nearly three in the morning.

"How am I going to sleep tonight?" Kelly asked. "This turned into a fucking nightmare."

"I've got something to help you sleep," Isaac said.

"Of course you do," Dean said. "You're a walking drugstore."

"I'd take anything at the moment," Kelly said.

"Be careful what you wish for," Ian said.

Isaac went to his bag and rummaged around for a moment, then came back with a small bottle.

"Just over-the-counter allergy medicine," he said, responding to Dean's inquiring look. He shook out two tablets into Kelly's hand. She popped them in her mouth and drank them down with water.

"I don't want to sleep alone tonight," she said.

"I'll stay with you," Ian said.

"Walking a fine line there, dude," Isaac said.

"Don't worry about it," Ian snapped. "We'll leave the door open, okay?"

"Look," Kelly said. "I'll sleep in my own bed, and Ian can just sit with me until I go to sleep."

"You're okay with that?" Isaac asked.

"Yes," Kelly said. "I'll probably be asleep pretty soon anyway after taking the meds."

***

Kelly got into her bunk, plugged her phone into the charger, and lay down. She left the curtain open by her head, and Ian sat on the floor and held her hand with his left hand while smoothing her hair with his right. It only took Kelly a few minutes to fall asleep. He carefully extracted his hand from hers and quietly closed the curtain to her bunk.

Ian went to the front lounge where everyone sat. He was steaming.

"What the hell did you mean?" Ian asked Isaac. "'Walking a fine line'?"

"It just seemed to me that you're getting a little too close to Kelly," Isaac said calmly. "I don't want the band to break up because of it."

"There's nothing more to our relationship than what we've said."

"You don't want anything more?"

"No," Ian said. He took a deep breath, realizing that his reaction to what happened that night might have looked like something else. The fact was, he *did* want something more with Kelly, but it was a moot point. He said more calmly, "No. We're just friends. I consider her my best female friend. We talked a lot during rehearsals in high school while the rest of you took your weed break. Our relationship is complicated, but I asked her the other night if she was still okay with our arrangement, and she is. She doesn't want anything else. I care for her like I care for you guys, we just have a little something...extra."

"Okay," Isaac said. "I'm sorry I misread the situation."

"It's all good," Ian said. "I know what it looked like out there, but it's really not anything more than making sure she was okay."

Get it together, Ketchner. She's off limits.

Chapter Seventeen

Kelly looked out the window as Artie pulled the bus up in front of Dean's house and the house never looked so good. While she'd loved entertaining and doing the shows, this tour was more nerve-wracking than the previous one, with all the drama from Greg, and some she'd brought onto herself.

Artie opened the door for them and they all stepped off.

"So glad to be home," Jake said.

Hayley got out of her car and Isaac ran up to her and picked her up, kissing her as he did so.

"God, I missed you!" he said.

Marty had come to pick up Jayna, Missy came for Jake, and Alexa for Paul. They all helped gather up their belongings and divvied out the remaining snacks while Bailey, Scott, and Sam unloaded the gear and took it to the studio before heading home. David had come to pick up Kelly and they dropped Ian off at his home.

"Thanks," Ian said as he got out of the car.

"You're welcome," Kelly said. "See ya in a few days."

Ian waved as David drove away.

Kelly took her belongings to her room, and then flopped down on her bed, happy to be on something that didn't move, and she didn't have to worry about keeping her stuff out of the way. While everyone got along well, it was hard living in such cramped quarters. It was something they got used to, but it was nice to sometimes be in a hotel or get out at a rest stop while Artie took care of the bus.

Once Kelly had most of her things put away, she came out to the living room where David worked on another video.

"So are you recovered from the other night?" Kelly asked.

"Mostly," David said. "I drank way too much that night."

"It's easy to do," Kelly told him. "It's happened to me a few times."

"How was the show last night?"

"It was good! It's what happened later that ruined the night."

"Uh-oh. What happened?"

"Greg showed up."

David paused the video and turned to Kelly. "Are you kidding?"

"Nope. I was walking back to our bus and he just stepped out in front of me."

"Jesus."

"I'd been texting Isaac, but when I saw Greg I hit Call, and he fortunately got the call and he and everyone else came running out. Scared Greg away and they lost him."

"Did you call the police?"

"Yeah, they came and took statements from everyone. I'm sure they and the other bands there were happy to have the cops around."

"I'm glad you're okay. How scary."

"You're telling me! I was scared shitless."

"Hopefully that also scared Greg into staying away from you."

"I hope so, too, but I doubt it. He's really flipped."

Kelly's phone rang. She looked at it and saw her mom's picture. She hit Accept.

"Hi Mom!" Kelly answered.

"Hi, sweetheart," Mom said. "I'm so glad you're home."

"Me, too," Kelly said. "It's like coming home from a long vacation. It's fun while you're gone, but you're glad to be home."

"Can you and David come over for dinner tonight? We want to celebrate your being home."

"I'll ask, hang on." She turned to David. "Mom wants us to come to dinner tonight."

"Sure, I'm free," David said.

"Okay," Kelly said into the phone. "We'll be there."

"Fabulous! See you around five o'clock."

"Okie dokie. Bye, Mom."

Just before it was time to go, Kelly changed out of her sweatpants and t-shirt and into jeans and a short-sleeved purple blouse. She laced on her Chucks and brushed her hair and was ready to leave with David.

They arrived a few minutes later and walked into the house.

"Hey Mom, we're here!" Kelly called out.

"In the kitchen!"

Kelly and David went to the kitchen where their mom was just setting the table.

"Want some help?" Kelly asked.

"Here," Mom said, handing Kelly the silverware.

Kelly placed the silverware at each place setting while David set out the glasses.

"Dad will be home in just a few minutes," Mom said. "He called to say there was an accident on the way home and he's taking a different route."

Just as Mom got the lasagna out of the oven—Kelly's favorite—Dad walked in.

"Hey, pumpkin," Dad said, hugging Kelly. "We're so glad you're home."

"Me, too," Kelly said.

"Hi, David," Dad said, patting him on the back. "You look much better than you did yesterday."

"It's amazing what water and sleep will do for a person," David said.

Kelly had done just that on the trip home. She knew she had drunk too much, but rehydrated and ate so she'd feel better by the time they got back home. What bothered her right now, though, was that their parents didn't get on David for over-indulging like they had with her. A bit of a double standard that she didn't like, but she didn't want to ruin her first night back, and left it for now. But she'd mention it soon.

Dad went to change out of his office clothes and came back and sat down at the table. Mom, David, and Kelly sat in their usual places and Mom started to serve everyone.

"How was the trip back?" Dad asked.

"It was good," Kelly said, pouring dressing on her salad. "No traffic except through L.A. and we made it home before the rush hour traffic."

Kelly told them about all the different places they played and what other bands they saw at the two festivals they played at.

"The Disciples of Man is heading up the coast right now," Kelly finished. "So they won't be back for a few months."

"They're such nice boys," Mom said.

Kelly choked on her salad and David pounded her on the back a couple times.

"I'm good," she managed to say. "Thanks."

They were nice guys, but Mom didn't know the whole story and she wasn't going to explain it to her, either.

"They're great to work with," David said. "Very easy, like your band, Kel."

"Yeah, they're a fun group," she managed to say. She didn't hate Erik, she just wasn't too happy with him or herself at the moment. She'd get over it, though—eventually.

Mom talked about her weekly Canasta game with her friends, and Dad talked about his new photography hobby.

"Yes, he's been going out every weekend to take photos," Mom said. "They're really good."

"Maybe you could be our official photographer," Kelly said, without thinking. *No, that would* not *be a good idea.*

Luckily, Dad thought that, too.

"No, I'm too old for that sort of thing," Dad said. "I'll leave that to David and other professionals."

Kelly breathed easier.

After dinner, Mom brought out lemon cake for dessert.

"We need to get some weight back on you," Mom said. "You look like you lost some."

Kelly hadn't checked the scale, but her clothes did seem a little loose.

"Yeah, I burn a lot onstage," Kelly said, "and the festival this past weekend was so hot, I'm sure I sweated a few pounds."

Mom cut the cake and passed a piece to everyone.

Kelly and David stayed a couple hours, until Kelly wanted to get to bed early.

"It'll be nice to sleep in my own bed tonight," she said.

When Kelly and David got home, David asked Kelly if she wanted to go out with him and Tessa.

"No," Kelly said. "I wasn't kidding about wanting to go to bed. I may not sleep all night, but it will be nice to be in own bed."

"Okay, I'll see you tomorrow," David said.

"Have fun, and tell Tessa I said 'Hi'."

"I will. Goodnight."

Kelly changed into her pajamas, brushed her teeth—in her own bathroom that she didn't have to share with anyone—and got into bed. She turned off the light, opened her e-reader, and started to read. Before long, she kept dropping the e-reader, having fallen asleep. She closed it, put it on the shelf, and closed her eyes.

***

Isaac reached over to Hayley and played with her blonde hair as she drove them home.

"You're gonna make me have an accident," Hayley said, smiling.

"I'm just so glad to be home with you," he said.

He'd been with several women on the road, but none were as beautiful as Hayley, and they were only a poor substitute for her. He suspected she knew what he did on the road, but she never said anything, and he would much rather be with her.

Hayley pulled into the parking lot of their apartment complex and parked in their spot. Isaac got his bags out from the trunk while Hayley gathered up the bags of snacks and they went upstairs to their apartment. Isaac dropped his bags on the floor and immediately grabbed Hayley around the waist and kissed her greedily, then picked her up and carried her to their bedroom.

Afterwards, they lay in bed, cuddling each other. Isaac had missed her so much. He stroked her hair and gently kissed her face all over.

"I cannot believe how lucky I am to come home to you," he whispered.

"It's nice to have you home," Hayley said.

They got up and dressed and Hayley made dinner while Isaac unpacked his bags. He sorted out the dirty laundry, hung up the clean clothes, and put his toiletries back in the bathroom. By the time he finished, Hayley had dinner ready. Isaac and Hayley took their plates to the living room to watch a movie while they ate.

At bedtime, Isaac got into bed and pulled Hayley close.

"It's always nice to be back in my own bed," he said.

***

A few days later, Kelly logged into her bank account and saw that a large amount of money had been deposited into her account from Dean's management company. Earnings from the tour! She hadn't expected that much, but they must have done better on this tour than she thought. Kelly also saw that she'd gotten a royalty payment from Tyrian Records, for record sales and show appearances. She hadn't checked her account for a few months and saw that she'd been getting regular deposits from Tyrian Records. She finally had enough money for the new car she'd been wanting for a couple years, but couldn't afford. Now she could buy it outright.

Kelly went to look at cars, David going with her to help her out with what to look for and what to ask, and after visiting several places and spending three hours looking, she finally settled on a brand new blue Hyundai Accent.

"Congratulations on your new car!" the salesperson said, shaking Kelly's hand.

When they got home, Kelly asked David to take her picture next to her new car, and after editing her license plate out, posted it on her personal social media pages. The guys and Jayna came over to see the car a few days later, with the guys commenting that they were getting new cars soon.

"Just something to show for our efforts," Jake said. "Getting what I want for fun."

She and the guys got together a few times over the next month to rehearse, then at the end of August, they went to their high school reunion barbeque.

There were a lot of cars already parked on the street. Kelly had to park down the street, where she turned off the engine and waited. She didn't really want to walk up by herself, because even though she'd gone to school with everyone, she was afraid a lot of people would come up to her and she didn't do well with a crowd of people on her own.

Just when she had decided to just go for it, Jayna and Marty pulled up. Kelly got out of her car and met them as they walked to the backyard.

"I'm glad you showed up just now," Kelly said. "Hi, Marty."

"Hey, Kelly," Marty said, kissing her on the cheek.

"Didn't want to face a crowd?" Jayna asked, smiling.

"Exactly! I know they're our friends, but it would be like after we did the duet for choir—everyone coming up to us. I was okay with it then, but I'm sure this could be ten times worse."

"We'll stick with you," Jayna said, and they walked up together, entering the backyard through the gate. When they walked in, a lot of their classmates turned to look at them. Kelly pretended not to notice, but it seemed every eye was on her. A few came up to her and Jayna to greet them, even some people who they barely knew back in high school. Kelly and Jayna were polite, but Jayna gave Kelly a skeptical look. Kelly nodded slightly. *They just want to say they knew us.*

Kayla, their senior class president in high school, came over to them as their classmates finished saying hello to them.

"I'm so glad you guys could come," she said warmly. "I was afraid you wouldn't be coming because you're too busy."

"We try to make time for things like this," Kelly said. "But it just happened to be when we had nothing going on."

"We've all warned Jessica not to start trouble with you," Kayla said. "I'll kick her out if she's in bitch mode."

"Thanks, I appreciate it," Kelly said.

"Well, we all know how she is. She's bringing her current boyfriend, but you can't be too careful with her."

Kelly laughed.

"You really can't," she said.

Kayla told them where to find the drinks, and then ran off to talk to the caterers. Marty went and got the drinks, handing Kelly a hard lemonade.

"Thanks," she said.

A few minutes later Isaac and Hayley arrived, followed by Jake and Missy. Lots of heads turned to look when they came in as well.

Marty hung out with Isaac and Jake while Kelly and Jayna went over to talk to their old teammates from gymnastics.

"Emily!" Kelly said as they walked up to the group.

"Oh my gosh!" Emily threw her arms around Kelly. "You guys came!"

"Wouldn't miss it," Kelly said, smiling.

Emily moved to Jayna, hugging her tight.

"I'm so glad you're here! We were just talking about the exhibition we did last year," Emily said. "Your brother did such an amazing job on the video."

"Right? It turned out really well," Kelly said. "He's been doing a lot of videos, both corporate and music."

"I was happy he included everyone in the video," Tinley said. "Some people were afraid it would just be about you."

"And we all know who 'some people' is," Emily said.

"Yeah, I made sure that everyone was included, even *her*," Kelly said.

"Kelly's too nice sometimes," Jayna said, putting her arm around Kelly's shoulders.

"It was only fair," Kelly said. "She *is* a good gymnast."

"Speak of the devil," Emily said, nodding toward the gate.

They all turned and saw that Jessica and her boyfriend had just walked in. Kelly turned back around quickly.

"Great," Kelly said. "I had kind of hoped she wouldn't come, but Kayla said she'd told her to behave."

A few minutes later Jessica came up to the group. Some of the girls greeted her with a hug, but the others just waved or nodded their head to her. Kelly took no notice of her until she spoke directly to her.

"Kelly," Jessica said.

"Jessica," Kelly said, turning to her.

"Fancy meeting you here. Aren't you supposed to be on the road or something?"

"Nope, we're done touring for now," Kelly said. "It worked out really well to be here."

"How was touring?" Tinley asked. "Was it all parties and hot guys?"

Kelly laughed.

"I wish!" she said. "Not a lot of parties except at the festivals, but nothing too outrageous. Hot guys—I met a few from other bands, but that was pretty much the extent of it. Meeting them was cool, but I'm not into one-night stands."

"Oh, don't be modest, Kelly," Jessica said. "Tell us who you've slept with."

Kelly turned to her.

"Jessica, I swear to God if you don't shut it, I'll shut it for you."

A couple of the women in the group snickered, which made Jessica even madder. She turned and left in a huff.

"Damn it, I wanted to see a smack down," Ian said as he walked over to the women.

"Hey," Kelly said. "Kayla said she talked to her, but I don't think it helped."

"I'll go talk to her," Ian said.

"Is that a wise decision?" Kelly asked.

"It'll be fine," Ian said, and he walked over to Jessica and her boyfriend.

"Enough about me! Emily, you've got some big competitions coming up, don't you?"

Kelly had been following some of her former teammates and Emily had gone back to elite gymnastics to try to make the Olympic team. She had to participate in several qualifying competitions around the world before the trials.

"Yes! I'm so nervous," Emily said. "There's a lot of talented girls—younger girls—out there."

"You're just as talented as they are," Jayna said.

"Absolutely! I'll be watching and waiting, but I know you'll make it," Kelly said.

"Thanks for the vote of confidence." Emily smiled shyly.

"Then you can one-up Jess," Jayna said.

"Oh, didn't you hear? She's trying out, too," Tinley said. "She left college and went back to elite last year after the exhibition."

"Well, she's good, too, but my money's on you, Em," Kelly said.

After talking with their friends, Kelly and Jayna went back to Marty and the guys, who had been joined by Paul and Alexa. Several of the guys' friends were talking to them, but when Kelly walked up, they all turned to talk to her, Isaac smirking at their reaction. The same guys who wouldn't give her the time of day back in high school. Now that she was a famous singer, they seemed to want to know her. Kelly had had a crush on a couple of them in high school, and she spoke with them, but wasn't sure if they really wanted to know her better, or just wanted to sleep with her. She did notice that Dillon, who had asked her to the prom and she turned him down, after which he called her some choice names, stayed far away from her.

Kayla got on the microphone to let everyone know that dinner would be ready in a few minutes and they could form a line at the table.

After they got their food, the bandmates sat at a table together. The two guys who had spoken to Kelly earlier sat next to and across from her at the table. Ian sat on the other side of her while they ate.

"So, do you miss gymnastics at all?" the blond guy, Danny, asked.

"Not really," Kelly said. "I've always wanted to sing. Gymnastic was just something I was good at, and is fun. I guess if singing hadn't worked out I'd have gone to college and continued with gymnastics there."

"We're glad it worked out," the dark-haired guy, Mike, said. "I've got both your CDs and listen to them all the time."

"Awesome!"

"And your picture on my wall," Danny said.

"I'm flattered," Kelly said, trying to not make a big deal out of it, but felt her face flush, knowing that people she went to school with now had her photo on their walls.

"What, you don't have my picture on your wall?" Ian asked in mock dejection.

"No offense, Ian, but we really don't want to see you with your clothes off," Danny said, referencing his pictorial in *Stripped.*

"Your loss," Ian said, and he took a bite of his burger.

After dinner, the DJ played some songs and people got up and danced. Ian danced with Kelly a couple times, in between dancing with other women there. An upbeat song came on and Danny asked Kelly to dance.

"Sure," she said. He took her hand and led her out to the dance floor, which was the cement patio. As she danced, she thought about what was happening. Should she give these guys a chance, or pass on them like they passed on her in school? She decided that if either of them asked her out, she'd go out with him and see what happened. They were both cute, and she'd known them both in school, so it wasn't as if they were strangers, they'd just never interacted much in school.

Jessica left Kelly alone for the rest of the evening, although she seemed to be following her with her phone out. *Probably taking photos of me with the guys I'm dancing with*, she thought. *It'll be all over social media tomorrow. I should warn these guys.*

"Just to let you know," Kelly said when they'd finished dancing. "Jessica's got it in for me, and I think she's taking pictures of us. It'll be on our band page tomorrow, I'm sure, with some false caption."

"I think I can handle it," Danny said, glancing over to Jessica, who hurriedly put her phone down.

"As long as you know what you're up against," Kelly said. "I just get that a lot from her."

People started leaving at 11 o'clock, thanking Kayla for hosting the reunion. Danny gave Kelly his phone number, and she gave him hers. Mike gave Kelly his, too, though he admitted he'd conceded to Danny.

"You never know what can happen," Kelly said.

"Very true," Mike said, and with a wave, he left.

"I hope to see you soon," Danny said, kissing her cheek when they got to her car.

"I'll give you a call sometime in the next couple of days," she said.

"I look forward to it," he said, and he opened her car door for her. She got in and he gently closed it, then walked to his car.

Sure enough, the next day when Kelly looked at Instagram, Jessica had posted about Kelly and the guys she was supposedly leading on, even getting a photo of her and Ian sitting next to each other.

"How many guys does Kelly actually have?" read the caption with each photo.

"Ugh!" Kelly said. She read the comments, which were mostly sticking up for Kelly, especially from those who had gone to the reunion.

"Kelly danced with a couple guys," one reply read. *"Is there some law against that?"*

"OMG! Kelly's single! I guess she's not supposed to talk to more than one guy. <sarcasm>," read another.

"Jessica, you need to get over your obsession with Kelly."

"What are we, back in high school?"

"Ian's in the band with her. Is she supposed to ignore him?"

Kelly decided that if Jessica wanted to play the same high school games, she'd just have to learn to ignore her. *At least she can't post on our band's Facebook page anymore,* she thought.

Jayna called a few minutes later.

"Have you seen…" Jayna started.

"Yep," Kelly said. "Jessica's at it again."

"I know Ian talked to her last night, but it looks like it didn't do any good."

"I didn't think it would. I wonder if someone could talk to her boyfriend."

"I did some calling around and the word is that he thinks what she's doing is funny and thinks she'll get bored with it. It's been five years. She's not getting bored with it."

"We need to just ignore her," Kelly said. "Take away the audience and I think she'll stop."

"Worth a try. I'll message people on all the platforms and tell them," Jayna said.

"Good luck! And thanks for watching out for me."

"You're welcome. She's just getting annoying now."

Later that day, when Kelly checked the band's social media again, all the comments to Jessica's posts had stopped. Jessica tried to get things going again by posting more photos, but no one replied to them, except for a few who agreed with her. One of the replies said that it must be true since no one is replying to the contrary. Kelly wanted to reply to that so badly, but it would only fuel Jessica more.

After a couple of days, the comments and posts stopped.

"Finally," Kelly said at the band's rehearsal. "Jessica is getting a little scary."

"Hopefully not replying will make her stop altogether," Jake said.

"Only time will tell," Ian said, as he and Isaac made lines for everyone. "Kelly? You joining?"

Kelly hadn't used cocaine since they were on tour and really hadn't missed it, but she'd also been feeling down the past few days, thanks for Jessica's antics.

"Sure," she said.

After their hit of coke, they got busy practicing for a couple of one-off shows. At the end of practice, Kelly got a text. She pulled out her phone to see who it was from.

"I hope to see you soon," the text from Danny read.

"So, you going out with one of them?" Isaac asked.

"I might," Kelly said. "They didn't even notice me in high school, but now that I'm a well-known singer, they want to know me."

"Yeah, I got that impression, too," Ian said, "from a lot of guys there."

"I might go out with him and see what happens," Kelly said.

Kelly texted back.

"Me, too."

When she got home, she called Danny.

"I really wasn't sure I'd hear from you," Danny said. "I figured I'd text you and see what happened, and you replied back!"

"Sorry I didn't text sooner," Kelly said. "Been dealing with the Jessica situation."

"Oh, yeah, I saw that. What's her deal?"

"When I joined the band back in high school, she thought I was trying to steal Ian from her. I have no interest in him other than as a friend, but even now, Jessica is jealous and won't let it go."

"Sounds like a nightmare," Danny said.

"It can be, but we're learning to deal with her."

"Would you like to go out for dinner tomorrow?" Danny asked.

She knew this would come up, him asking her out, but it still made her just a little nervous. Wouldn't hurt to give it a try, though.

"Sure!"

They made plans for Danny to pick Kelly up at 6 o'clock the next evening.

"I'll see you then," Danny said.

Kelly went to make herself a snack in the kitchen as David came home.

"Hey, Kel," David said. "What's up?"

"Not much, except I'm going on a date tomorrow night."

"Really? With who?"

"Someone from school. We talked at the reunion and he asked me out."

"Fantastic!"

"Well, we'll see how it goes. He never even looked at me in school, so I'm sure this is just because I'm well-known."

"Gotta start somewhere, I guess," David said, grabbing a beer from the fridge.

"Yeah," Kelly said. "It's just dinner, so it should be okay."

Chapter Eighteen

At 5 o'clock the next day, Kelly started to get ready for her date. She showered and while her hair dried she dressed and put on her make-up sparingly, going for the natural look for the night. She pulled on a pair of cotton pants and a lavender blouse, and slipped her feet into her ankle boots. She ran a brush through her hair and was ready fifteen minutes early.

She'd given Danny the directions and the security guard at the gate buzzed them to let them know Danny was there.

"Yes, you can let him in," David said. Danny pulled up a few minutes later and came to the door. Kelly opened the door and asked him in for a minute.

"Davy, this is Danny," Kelly said. "This is my brother, David."

"Nice to meet you," Danny said, shaking David's hand.

"Likewise," David said.

"Well, I'll see you later," Kelly said as she picked up her purse.

"Have a good time," David said.

Danny opened the car door for Kelly and she stepped inside. Danny got in and pulled away from the curb.

"You look very different," Danny said.

"I do?" Kelly asked.

"You don't have your stage make-up on or your flashy clothes."

"Ha, not for a date," Kelly said.

"You look so…normal."

"I am pretty normal," Kelly said. *This isn't going well*, she thought.

"You look great, anyway."

Whew!

Danny got on the freeway.

"I hope you like Stonefire Grill," Danny said.

"I love that place," Kelly said.

"Great! I was afraid it was too ordinary for you."

"I've got simple tastes."

Danny pulled off the freeway and drove to the restaurant and parked. He went around and opened the door for Kelly. She got out and they walked into the restaurant and got in line to place their order.

They found a table to sit at, and so far no one had noticed her, which was why she had downplayed the make-up and clothes. She didn't want to draw attention to her and Danny, wanting to have a quiet dinner with few interruptions.

The server brought their food a few minutes later. Kelly had ordered a Caesar salad with chicken, and Danny had ordered ribs and mashed potatoes.

"Their salad is to die for," Kelly said between bites.

"Their ribs are really good, too," Danny said.

"I've had them, too. They *are* good."

Danny talked a little about himself while they ate, telling Kelly what he did for a living, which was working at a sports magazine.

"That's gotta be fun," Kelly said. "Do you get to go to games or try stuff out?"

"Yes, we get a lot of both of those," Danny said. "I love going to baseball games, so they send me a lot."

"Sounds interesting."

"It is. I get to talk to some of the players, but mostly I just interview one player and do a story on him."

"Awesome!"

After dinner, Danny drove them to a nearby park to walk around the lake. As they circled the lake, a couple of young men of about fifteen years old ran up to them.

"Are you Kelly from Fate Struck?" the taller one asked.

"I am!" Kelly said with a smile.

"See, I told you," he told his friend.

"Can we get a picture with you?" the shorter boy asked.

"Is it okay with you?" Kelly asked Danny.

Danny looked slightly annoyed, but agreed.

The taller boy got out his phone from his pocket and he and his friend stood next to Kelly and he took a selfie.

"My sister will never believe this," he said.

"She will with the photo," Kelly said.

"Thank you for the selfie!" the shorter boy said, and they ran off again.

"Sorry about that," Kelly said. "It happens sometimes."

"You could tell them no," Danny said.

"I could, but we have a good reputation with the fans. We try to be nice to them. It makes life easier if we just give them what they ask for—within reason—and then they move on."

"I guess I'll have to get used to that if I'm going to date you."

They headed back to the car after that. Kelly didn't want any more interruptions since Danny seemed put-out by it. *That's one strike against him,* she thought.

Danny drove her home and walked her up to the door.

"I had a good time tonight," Danny said. "The fans non-withstanding."

"So did I," Kelly said.

"Can I call you?"

"Of course!"

Danny kissed her on the cheek and made sure she got inside before he walked away.

David was in the living room, working on another video.

"How was the date?" he asked.

"It was all right," Kelly said.

"Uh-oh, what happened?"

"Nothing really happened. A couple of fans came up to me while we were walking at the park and he seemed a little annoyed that I didn't tell them to go away. They just wanted a selfie, which I gave them."

"Are you going to see him again?"

"I'll give it another go and see what happens. I'm just really gun-shy after Greg."

"I don't blame you! He's crazy."

Kelly went into the kitchen for a bottled water to take to her room.

"I'm going to bed," she said.

"See you in the morning," David said.

Kelly got a text from Danny the next afternoon, asking her if she'd like to go to a movie the next night.

"Sure! Sounds great!" she replied.

"I'll call you later," he texted back.

Kelly's phone rang after dinner. She saw it was Danny and hit Answer.

"Hey, Danny," she said.

"Hi! Is this a good time?"

"Yeah, I just finished dinner."

"Great! Hey, so there's a new movie out with Harrison Ford and Julia Roberts—I think it's a comedy-adventure movie."

"Sounds good. I love Harrison Ford."

"Awesome! I'll pick you up at five-fifteen tomorrow. The movie starts at five-forty-five."

"I'll be ready," Kelly said.

"Great! See you tomorrow," Danny said.

Kelly was ready for Danny when he came by the next day. She still dressed down for the date, not wanting to draw attention to herself. She had pulled her hair back into a ponytail and wore jeans and a flowery blouse with her purple Chucks.

Danny drove to the mall where the movie was playing at the theater there.

"I used to work here," Kelly said.

"You did?" Danny asked.

"Yeah, when I was in high school, just as I joined the band."

"I guess the band worked out better for you?" he joked.

"Just slightly," Kelly said with a laugh.

They walked up and got their tickets then went inside and saw it wasn't very busy, only two other people in front of them at Concessions. Kelly recognized one of the girls working there and waved to her.

"Oh my God!" the girl, Sarah, said. "Kelly!"

Kelly and Danny walked up to her open register.

"I'm so happy to see you!" Sarah said.

"I'm glad to see you, too."

"What can I get for you two?"

Kelly and Danny told Sarah what they wanted, chatting away while Sarah got the items for them, treating her like a former coworker instead of a celebrity. When they were ready, Danny paid.

"Hey, let me radio Alex," Sarah said.

"Oh my gosh, is he still here?" Kelly asked.

"Yeah, he's an assistant manager now. He'll be happy to see you." Sarah radioed Alex and he came up a few minutes later.

"Wow! This is unexpected," Alex said, hugging Kelly.

"I haven't been to the movies in ages," Kelly said. She introduced Danny to Alex and they shook hands.

"I guess you've been a little busy," Alex said, grinning.

"Yeah, you could say that."

"We miss you here," Alex said.

"You always kept it light," Sarah agreed.

"Aw, I miss you guys, too."

"We better get going if we want to see the movie," Danny said.

"You're right," Kelly said, then she turned to her friends. "It was good to see you two!"

"See ya!" Sarah said.

They got to their theater just as the lights went down. They found their seats and waited for the movie to start.

Two hours later, the movie ended and the house lights came up halfway as the credits rolled. Kelly and Danny gathered up their trash and threw it away on their way out of the auditorium.

"That was a great movie!" Kelly said.

"I thought so, too," Danny said.

"Hey, I need to hit the restroom."

"Me, too. I'll meet you right here after," Danny said.

They went to their respective restrooms. As Kelly washed her hands, someone came out of a stall and did a double take.

"No, you're not," the young woman said.

"I'm not?" Kelly asked with a smile.

"You're not Kelly Brennen," the woman finally said.

"I am, actually," Kelly said. "I used to work at this theater."

"What a weird place to meet a celebrity," the woman said.

"What's your name?"

"Alice."

"Nice to meet you, Alice! What movie did you see?" reverting to usher mode for a moment.

"The new Marvel movie," Alice said.

"Was it any good?"

"It was fantastic!"

Kelly dried off her hands.

"It was nice to meet you," Kelly said, tossing the paper towel into the trash can.

"Nice to meet you, too, Kelly!"

Kelly walked out. Danny waited just across the hall from the women's restroom.

"Ready?" he asked.

"Yep!"

They talked about the movie as Danny drove her home. Kelly invited Danny in for a drink.

"Sure, just one," he said, following her inside.

Kelly got Danny a beer and herself a hard lemonade.

"Whoa, hardcore there," he said, nodding at her drink.

"Yeah, I'm not a big drinker, though it has happened a few times," she said.

When they finished their drinks, Danny said he should go, and Kelly thought he looked disappointed when she didn't ask him to stay.

"Hey, there's a work party on Friday. Would you want to come with me?" he asked.

"That's going semi-public," she said. "We're still figuring things out."

"It's not a big party," he said. "And we'll just say we're school friends—which we are…"

Barely, she thought.

"…and we reconnected at the reunion, but we're not serious yet."

Kelly thought about it for a moment. The way he said it, it sort of sounded okay, even if it only partly true.

"Okay," she finally said. "But we keep it light."

"Of course. I'll text you the time tomorrow."

"Sounds good."

He kissed her on the cheek and left.

Danny texted Kelly the next day with the time of the party and when he'd pick her up. She replied back that she'd be ready for him.

Kelly went over to talk with Jayna later that day, to tell her what's been happening.

"Dipping your toe in the waters," Jayna said.

"I guess I have to sometime," Kelly said. "But it all seems weird. Not the dating part, but his sudden interest in me."

"Maybe he finally saw what he missed in high school," Jayna said.

"I hope that's all it is."

As Kelly sat in her room later, she got a text message. She picked up her phone and her heart sank. *Greg.*

"I see you're trying to replace me," he wrote. *"You'd better watch your back."*

Damn it, he's still watching me. She texted Dean to let him know and forwarded the messages to him. The anxiety rose up inside her again. She looked around her room for the bottle of Ritalin, but couldn't find it. She didn't have any alcohol in her room, either. She went out to the kitchen and poured herself a shot of Fireball, drank it down, and poured another. David followed her in and watched.

"What's wrong?" he asked.

She turned to him.

"Greg texted me just now, pretty much telling me he's still watching me."

"Son of a bitch," he said. "I'm so glad we live in a gated community, otherwise I'd get a guard over here."

"Yeah, I think I'm okay here, but I don't want to be cooped up."

"Just make sure you let Danny know what's going on. Not fair to him that Greg's an asshole."

"I'll let him know, in case he'd rather not take me to his office party."

That Friday, Kelly got ready an hour before Danny would pick her up. She figured since it was a party, she'd have to dress up a bit more. She wasn't going to wear her stage clothes—way too flashy for a work party. She put on her plain black flared pants with a purple flowery blouse, and her ankle boots. She left her hair down, but curled it with her curling iron, and applied her make-up somewhere between normal and stage make-up. She didn't want to draw attention to herself, but she figured she'd be noticed anyway going with Danny.

She was ready by the time Danny came to pick her up. She answered the door and Danny's eyes widened in surprised.

"That's what I'm talkin' about," he said.

"Is it too much?" she asked. "I didn't know what to expect."

"No, you look perfect," he said. She got her purse and followed Danny to his car.

"I have to tell you," Kelly said, "my ex, Greg, sent me another text, saying to watch my back. If you'd rather not take me to the party, I understand."

"He's really been stalking you, hasn't he?"

"Yes, and it gets a little annoying."

Danny pulled away from the curb.

"Where we're going, he can't hurt you, and I'll be on the lookout for him."

Kelly relaxed a bit.

"Thanks."

They arrived at the party, which was at an upscale bar in Orange County. They walked in and the crowd was a little bigger than Kelly had hoped for, but still small—about thirty people. An older gentleman came up to Danny.

"Good to see you, Daniel," the man said.

"Thank you, sir," Danny said. "Mr. Robbins, this is my friend Kelly. Kelly, the owner of the magazine, Ed Robbins."

"Pleasure to meet you, sir," Kelly said, shaking Mr. Robbins' hand.

"Lovely to meet you," Mr. Robbins said. "Glad you could come. Daniel says you're some kind of singer?"

"Yes," Kelly said. "I sing in a band."

"How wonderful," Mr. Robbins said. "I hope you enjoy yourself tonight. We're celebrating one of Danny's articles getting picked up by a news agency to follow up on."

"Oh, how nice!" Kelly said. "Thank you, sir."

Mr. Robbins moved on, and Danny led Kelly to the bar.

"What can I get for you?" the bartender asked.

"I'll have a glass of Moscato, please," Kelly said.

"Gin and juice, please," Danny said.

The bartender got their drinks and Kelly and Danny walked around, Danny introducing Kelly to everyone. A few people didn't know her or the band, but several did, and they gushed over her and told Danny how lucky he was. Kelly tried to downplay the attention, but Danny didn't let her too much, telling his coworkers about her albums and the tour she'd just finished.

They made their way to the food table, which had finger sandwiches, chips and dips, fruits and veggies, and a variety of desserts. They put some food on a plate and then moved around some more, Danny talking to his friends and showing Kelly off.

He wants a trophy girlfriend, she thought. Kelly pulled Danny over to a corner.

"If it's okay with you, would you mind not making a big deal out of my career?" she asked. "I know you want to let everyone know, but I'm really not that famous, and I prefer to stay in the shadows when I'm not onstage."

"Yeah, okay, sure," Danny said. "I just want everyone to get to know you."

"I understand. It just embarrasses me sometimes with all the attention."

"No worries," he said. "I think you've met everyone, anyway."

After that, Kelly enjoyed herself a little more. Some of his friends and coworkers did ask her a little about her career, but they mostly just talked to her like a regular person, asking if she liked sports or read any magazines, preferably theirs.

"I haven't unfortunately," Kelly said. "But I guess I'll have to check it out sometime."

"Kelly was a gymnast in high school," Danny told them.

"Oh, so you know a little about sports," the tall brunette woman said.

"A little," Kelly said, smiling.

A short time after Mr. Robbins presented Danny with a small plaque, Danny asked Kelly if she minded if they left.

"No, not at all," Kelly said. "I'm a bit tired anyway."

They said their goodbyes to everyone, then left.

As they drove, it looked like Danny was headed to the beach. Kelly didn't mind; she actually liked the beach at night, listening to the waves.

Danny pulled into the parking lot and into a spot facing the beach. They could just see the waves breaking on the shore in the moonlight. He rolled down the windows to enjoy the sea breeze.

"The beach is so beautiful at night," Kelly said.

"I love the smell of the salty air," Danny said.

They sat watching the waves for a long time. It relaxed Kelly, something she really hadn't done in a long time and needed after going to the party.

Danny put his arm around Kelly and gently pulled her over next to him on the seat. It had been a long time since a guy had put his arm around her like that. The guys in the band had put their arm around her shoulders, but not in the same gentle way. Theirs was more of a friendly, brotherly way.

After he'd had his arm around her for a few minutes he cupped her chin in his hand and turned her face to him.

"You are so gorgeous," he said.

She smiled shyly, and then he kissed her lips. Her heart raced and her body tingled. His kisses were gentle at first, then more eager. He moved to her neck, her hands in his hair. They kissed for a long time and she was happy doing just that. She wasn't looking for anything else just then after being with Greg and then what had happened on the tour. She wasn't ready for anything else with Danny.

Kelly felt Danny's hand slip under her blouse to her back, to unhook her bra.

"Wait a second," Kelly breathed, pulling away.

"What's wrong?" Danny asked.

"This is only our third date. Aren't we jumping the gun here a bit?"

"You're a rock star," he said. "I thought you'd be used to this."

She moved back from him and looked him in the eye.

"You thought wrong," she said bluntly.

"Come on, babe," Danny pleaded, taking her left hand, trying to pull her back to him. "Isn't this what you expected? You've got a guy in every city, right?"

"No, I don't," as she yanked her hand from his. Her face grew hot, her mouth set in a line and her hands balled up into fists. "I haven't had sex with one fan on the road. Not one! Guys like Ian are a different story. He's got the girl in every port. I'm not like that."

"That's not what Jessica says."

Wrong words, asshole.

"I don't give a fuck what that bitch says!" She pointed her finger in his face. "She's had it in for me since the day I joined the band. She's a petty, insecure little weasel who thinks everyone should be at her beck and call. Goddammit, Danny. That's it."

Kelly threw up her hands, grabbed her purse and got out of the car. Danny followed her. Angry tears blurred her vision, but she didn't care. She'd walk home if she had to.

"Kelly!" he shouted after her. "Come on! It's just one romp in the car."

She whirled around.

"Oh my God! You don't want me, you want a 'rock star', that's why you mentioned my make-up the other day. You didn't give me the time of day in high school, but now I'm well-known, and all of a sudden you want to fuck me? Guess what? I'm still me, the same girl who sang in choir and did gymnastics and read books. Go to hell."

Kelly ran across the street, nearly getting hit by a car whose driver flipped her off. She didn't care. She weaved her way around the people on the sidewalk and ran into one of the restaurants and went into the bar area. She sat down at a table and tried to look inconspicuous. A server came over to her.

"What can I get you?" she asked.

Kelly wiped her eyes.

"Um, a Captain and coke, please," she said, sniffling.

"Are you okay?"

"Bad date," Kelly told her.

The server left, and came back a few minutes later with her drink. Kelly handed her her credit card.

"You want to start a tab?"

"Sure, why the hell not."

Kelly took a long drink, then set the glass down, staring at it. She should've seen this coming. She should have gone with her gut instinct when he asked her out. He didn't notice her in school, why go out with her now? She wiped new tears away. She was desperate and he wanted bragging rights. Asshole.

She finished her drink, and the server brought her another. Halfway through that drink, she realized she needed a ride home. In her current state, she wasn't about to take an Uber, and suddenly remembering Greg, going outside at all made her nervous. She'd have to call her brother to pick her up. She downed her drink and called David.

"Hey, why are you calling me on your date?' David asked.

"Can you come get me?" Kelly said. "I left the date."

"Say no more. Where are you?"

"I'm at the restaurant right across from the Huntington Beach pier. I don't know the name, but it's under the place with all the blue lights on the outside."

"I know the place. I'll be there as soon as I can."

"Thanks, Davy." She hit *End* and put her phone down on the table.

The server came with another drink.

"Thanks," Kelly said. "This'll be it for tonight."

"Okay, I'll run your card," the server said. "Are you sure you're okay?"

"I will be. My brother is coming to get me."

The server came back with Kelly's card and receipt. Kelly signed what she hoped would pass as her signature, then put the card away.

Half an hour later, Kelly saw David come in and look around for her. She raised her hand and David saw her and came over.

"What the hell happened?" he asked.

"I'll tell you tomorrow," Kelly said. "I just want to go home."

Kelly grabbed her purse off the back of her chair. She felt a little unsteady, so David put his arm around her and helped her walk to his car, parked a little ways down the street.

She didn't say anything on the drive home, the anger building inside her. *I should've known. I should've listened to my instincts.*

Once back at home, Kelly sat down on the couch and started talking to David, not wanting to wait until tomorrow.

"I should've known something was up when he asked about my make-up on the first date," she said angrily.

"He did that?" David asked.

"Yeah. He was surprised that I didn't have my stage make-up on for our date."

"Really?" David asked, incredulously.

"Yeah. But you know, I didn't think much of it at the time. I figured it's just what he expected, because people are often surprised that I'm normal, but then he said I looked great, so I let it slide."

"What happened tonight?"

"We went to his work party, then drove to the beach. I thought we'd just talk or at the most make out in the car. Nope, he went for the gusto and I shut him down. He thought because I'm a singer in a well-known band that I slept with every guy I met. Then—*THEN*—he mentioned that Jessica said I did that stuff."

"Oh boy," David said.

"Yeah. I went off on him. I thought that he didn't like Jessica, too, by some of the things he said at the reunion about her, but he was listening to her all along. I jumped out of his car and started to walk away. He got out and said 'It's just a romp in the car,' I told him where to go and took off."

Tears ran down her face as she finished her account of the nights' events. David sat next to her and put his arm around her and let her cry it out.

"If I ever see that bastard he's going to answer to me," David said.

"Don't go looking for him." Kelly sniffled. "He's not worth it."

Fate Struck had a rehearsal the next day. Kelly was still in a foul mood when she arrived. She hardly said anything to the guys, and threw her purse onto the sofa when they went out to the studio.

"What's got your panties in a twist?" Isaac said.

"Danny, that's what," she spat out.

"What happened?" Ian asked.

"Let's just say that my intuition was dead accurate and I should've never gone out with him in the first place. Fucking prick."

"Whoa! What did he do?" Paul asked.

"He wanted to have sex with me *in his car* and I turned him down, and then he says that Jessica said I'd do it."

"I'll smash his fucking face in," Isaac said.

"David wanted to do that same thing. Don't go after him. He's not worth it."

"If I happen to run into him, all bets are off," Jake said.

"I'm just destined to be by myself. I won't know if the guy wants to be with me for me, or because of what I do."

"I'm sure you'll find 'the one' someday," Ian said. He'd been chopping out lines on the table while they talked. "You want some?"

"Hell, yeah, I do," she said. She wanted out of the funk she was in any way she could.

They took their turns at the table, then started their rehearsal. They had one show coming up in a week at The Constellation Room, and then another one a month later at The Anaheim House of Blues.

As the band rehearsed, Kelly felt the weight lifting off her, and she started to have fun again. She was still angry at Danny, but didn't want to punch his lights out anymore. They worked on a new song that Jake had brought in, then ran through their set list.

"I think we're ready," Isaac said.

"Should be another good show," Jake said.

Dean came out to talk to the band.

"We're already getting asked to do the holiday parties for Isaac's and Kelly's father's companies," he told them. "Is it still a yes?"

"For Kelly's dad, absolutely," Isaac said. "Same price as last year. My dad…"

"Don't punish the company for what your dad does, Isaac," Dean said.

"I know," Isaac relented. "It *is* fun to do. Yeah, my dad's company, too."

"Good," Dean said. "Also, Jim wants to send you back to Europe for a more extensive tour there. That would be in two months starting in October, take a break for Christmas, then back over there after New Years."

"Sounds good," Jake said.

"Great! Anything I need to know?" Dean asked.

"There may be more trouble with certain people soon," Kelly said. "Jessica…"

"Is up to her old schemes. I know—there was just a small thing on Facebook about you and Danny. Jayna's taking care of it."

"Bless her," Paul said. "She has to deal with so much shit."

"She's happy to do it, though she wishes she didn't have to. Some people are just immature and can't let things go. I may have to send her an official letter, telling her to stop harassing you or I'll bring her up on charges. The comments she made on Facebook about you and the guys were ridiculous."

"I can't believe she's still allowed to compete in gymnastics, being as snotty as she is," Jake said.

"I really don't want to get her in trouble at school or with the Gymnastics Federation," Kelly said, "but it's getting out of hand with her."

"You're too damn nice," Ian said.

Chapter Nineteen

They played in Europe for two months. While in Germany, Kelly, Jayna, Ian, and Jake made a short side trip to watch Emily and Jessica compete at Stuttgart. They dressed as inconspicuously as possible to blend in with the other spectators, but a few fans noticed them. They quickly posed for photos with them, and shifted the focus back onto the gymnasts as soon as they could. At the end of the days' competition, Emily won a medal for her floor routine, Jessica got a medal for her vault, and the team won a medal. They cheered loudly for Emily, and applauded politely for Jessica, knowing that they could be put on camera and didn't want to be rude, even though Jessica deserved it.

When the band came back to the states for the parties, they only brought their guitars with them. Dean rented drums, amps, and a PA system for the band to do the holiday gigs. It was cheaper to rent than to have their equipment shipped back then shipped again to Europe.

The night before Isaac's father's company party, Dean asked them to meet at his house to go over a few things.

"And, saving the best for last—the band has been nominated for Best New Group and Song of the Year for both the Fan's Choice Awards, and, get ready for this—the Grammy Awards!"

Kelly sat in stunned silence with her mouth hanging open as the rest of the band shouted and stood up and hugged each other. Ian pulled Kelly up and hugged her tight. She finally smiled and came out of her shock and hugged the others. She had never thought they'd be nominated for an award, and to be nominated for a Grammy? She was glad she'd been sitting down because she would have fainted.

"Are you serious?" Isaac asked.

"Yep! I submitted a few things to be considered and you were picked. They want you to perform on the show, also."

Kelly's heart skipped a beat.

"Oh my god," she said, finding her voice.

"That's fantastic!" Jayna said, hugging her friend.

"When is this?" Ian asked.

"Four months from now," Dean said. "Plenty of time to rehearse and prepare."

"What song do they want us to do?" Isaac asked.

"Jealousy Rules," Dean said, "which is nominated for Song of the Year."

"Cool beans. We'll work on that during our next rehearsal," Jake said.

Dean brought out a bottle of champagne and glasses to toast their nominations, even pouring himself one.

"To Fate Struck!" he said, holding up his glass. The band did the same and they drank.

"I have a really good feeling about this," Isaac said.

"It's amazing to even be nominated," Kelly said. "I didn't realize we were on anyone's radar."

"Tyrian Records has been promoting you quite a bit," Dean said, "and you saw how the crowds reacted to you. You're all bigger than you think."

They were riding high as they went to the company party for Isaac's father. Isaac's father didn't introduce that band this time, preferring to stay clear of his son, and Isaac didn't seem too upset by it. Kelly did thank him for hiring them again for the party and he was civil to her, almost nice.

Since they'd be home for all of December, Dean threw a birthday bash for Isaac's and Ian's birthdays that month at his house. Erik from The Disciples of Man and his wife Catalina came, as well as Will and Stevie. Evan and his wife Michelle and Jesse from Chellis came. They invited Maggie but she wasn't able to make it because of her touring schedule. Friends from high school whom they'd kept in touch with also came. Danny was not invited.

The DJ that Dean hired played music for the night, mixing in dance songs with classic rock songs. A few people danced but mostly everyone mingled.

Ian came around and asked Kelly if she wanted to join them for a hit of coke. She normally didn't outside of performing or rehearsal, but wanted it that night. She hated to admit it to herself, but she enjoyed the high. Her problems didn't seem as bad when she was high on cocaine. Isaac had the lines cut out when she and Ian got over to the table. Erik, Stevie, and Jesse were already there. Erik did his line, then noticed Kelly there.

"Kelly?" he said, not believing his eyes.

"She's finally become a proper rock and roll star," Ian said.

"The wonders never cease," Erik said.

Kelly snorted her line.

"It happens," she said, wiping her nose.

Hayley came and sat next to Isaac just after his turn. He put his arm around her and kissed her cheek.

"Hello, my gorgeous wife," he said.

"Hello, my gorgeous husband," she said. "Having fun tonight?"

"Of course," he said. "But looking forward to having more fun with you later."

She leaned over and kissed him.

"Can't wait," she said quietly, but Kelly heard her and smiled. She was glad they were together, and happy that Isaac still went back to her even after being with groupies. She knew he loved Hayley.

Later, Kelly talked with Stevie and saw Erik and Catalina coming over to them.

"Shit," Kelly said softly.

"What?" Stevie asked.

"Maybe trouble," she said.

"Hey, Kelly," Erik said.

"Hi," Kelly said hesitantly.

"I know that Erik fools around when he's on tour," Catalina said, getting right to the point.

Kelly swallowed hard. *This is it, I'm dead.*

"I know he's fooled around with you," Catalina continued.

Kelly's heart dropped.

"I can explain," Kelly said quickly. Catalina held up her hands.

"He comes back to me and treats me like a queen. His flings don't concern me unless he stops coming back to me. I'm not mad. He wanted me to tell you myself, because he told me how upset you were. You are one of a kind, Kelly. Most women don't care who they hurt." With that, Catalina kissed her on both cheeks and walked away. Erik remained, and Kelly let out a long, ragged breath.

"Now do you see?" Erik asked. "It's okay."

"Doesn't make it right, though," Kelly said. "But thank you."

Erik kissed Kelly on the cheek and followed his wife to the drink table.

"Catalina is very easy-going," Stevie said.

"What was that all about?" Isaac asked. Hayley had come with him.

"Catalina was explaining to me that she knows her husband fools around and she's okay with it," Kelly said, glancing at Hayley as she talked.

"I think I'd like to stay blissfully unaware," Hayley said.

Kelly thought Isaac looked slightly relieved by that.

***

Isaac made the rounds to everyone, thanking them for coming to the party. Hayley wanted to leave, and he was anxious to go, too. He wanted to make love to his wife, and he wasn't about to do it there.

Back at home, he had a bump of coke while Hayley changed her clothes. When he climbed into bed with her, she kissed him, but paused for a moment.

"You know I don't mind you having the occasional hit of coke," she said. "Please don't let it get out of hand."

"It won't, baby," he said. "Thank you for caring so much."

"You're my husband and I love you," she said. "I want you around for a long, long time."

"I will be," he said. He kissed her greedily as they made love.

Hayley slept afterwards, but Isaac couldn't sleep just yet. He got up and went to the living room and turned on his computer. Inspiration had hit him and he wanted to get his thoughts down before he forgot them.

Two hours later, he finally felt like he could go to sleep. He saved his work, turned off his computer, and went back to bed. Hayley looked so beautiful sleeping, her hair spread out on the pillow. He took off his sweat pants and got into bed beside her, put his arms around her and finally fell asleep.

Isaac woke up the next morning with a slight headache and a dry mouth. He rolled over, looking for Hayley, but she had already gotten up. He sat on the edge of the bed and pulled on his sweatpants, then got up to use the bathroom. He grabbed a shirt to put on as he walked to the kitchen where Hayley was making breakfast for the two of them. Bacon sizzled in the pan and blueberry pancakes were on the griddle.

"Hey beautiful," Isaac said, wrapping his arms around Hayley's waist.

"Good morning," she said. "Are you ready for breakfast?"

"Absolutely!" he said. "It smells delicious."

She finished with the pancakes, then turned off the stove and took the bacon out of the pan, letting them drain on a paper towel before putting them on plates. Isaac took a couple of pancakes from the pile and he and Hayley sat at the table to eat.

"What's going on today?" Hayley asked.

"I don't think I have any band related stuff today," Isaac said. "So I am all yours for the day."

Hayley smiled.

"Just what I like to hear," she said. "Let's go do something!"

They tossed around some ideas and finally settled on going to Disneyland. Neither of them had been in a couple years and wanted to go see the new attractions.

Isaac and Hayley spent the day going on the rides, enjoying the day, acting like the newlyweds they were still. They held hands as they walked, kissing and hugging as they stood in line for the rides, but not being discourteous to the people around them. Isaac got recognized only a few times and the fans were quick with their interaction, only wanting a selfie with him. Hayley patiently stepped aside during those times.

"I'm sorry," Isaac said after the fourth encounter.

"It's okay," Hayley said. "I'm used to it, and I expect it. I'm glad you're so approachable and kind to your fans."

"Well, they're the ones that made us, so we try to be cool with them."

They left the park as the sun set and stopped at In & Out for dinner on the way home.

"This was a nice day today," Isaac said.

"Yeah, it was," Hayley said. "We need to do more of those when we can."

***

Kelly spent Christmas with her family at her parents' house. David brought Tessa with him to lunch, then they opened gifts. David gave Kelly a framed photo of the band onstage in Europe, taken from the video he did for them.

"This is amazing!" Kelly said. "Thank you!"

"I know you'd never do it for yourself," David said. "But I thought it was a really cool photo."

"It's really great."

"I made one for the guys and Jayna, as well."

"Oh, they'll love it!"

After they had opened all the gifts, Dad put in a DVD of *Love Actually* to watch.

As the movie credits rolled, David and Tessa stood up.

"We've got to get to Tessa's family's get-together," David said.

"Thank you for coming," Mom said, hugging David, then Tessa.

"Our pleasure," David said. He hugged his father, then Kelly. "See ya later, pipsqueak."

"Is that a reference to my height?"

"Wouldn't dream of making fun of a rock star."

"Uh-huh," Kelly said, smiling. She was glad her brother still joked with her. "See ya."

An hour later, Kelly got ready to leave.

"We're doing a gift exchange at Dean's," she said.

"Tell the boys and Jayna 'hello' for us," Mom said.

"I will."

She disappeared into the kitchen for a moment, then came back with a huge tin of homemade cookies.

"Take these to share tonight," Mom said.

"Oh, the guys will love these," Kelly said.

She hugged her parents, then went out and drove to Dean's house.

"Finally!" Jake said when Kelly arrived. "Now can we open presents?"

"You're just like a little kid," Ian said.

"I brought cookies from my mom," Kelly said, setting the box on the coffee table. Jake took the top off and grabbed two cookies.

"Mm," he said, closing his eyes. The rest of the guys and Jayna took a few as they opened gifts.

After the gifts were opened, Dean poured everyone a glass of champagne to make a toast.

"Here's to a great year next year," Dean said. "And a fantastic rest of the European tour."

"Hear, hear!" they all said as they clinked glasses and drank.

Two weeks later they flew back to Europe to finish their tour. They had played extensively in continental Europe before the break; now they headed to the UK and Scandinavia for the next month.

Kelly loved being in England. She felt more at home there than anywhere else, except for California. After they arrived at their hotel in London, Kelly and Jayna went out to explore the city. They found a tea shop where Kelly bought several teas, including her beloved Lady Grey tea, and a tea cup and saucer set.

"We might be out on the road," Kelly said, "but I want to have some luxuries."

They did a lot of walking and a lot of shopping while they were out. By the time they got back to the hotel, Kelly had bought quite a few more things. Jayna kept her spending to half as much.

"Just remember you gotta find a place for all that when we fly back," Isaac said.

"Yeah, I know," Kelly said. "Maybe I'll ship it instead."

"Probably cheaper than paying for the extra luggage weight."

It was nearly time for sound check, so they got everything together to take with them. They would come back to the hotel after the show, then the bus would arrive the next day to drive them for the rest of the time in the UK.

After sound check, Kelly took a shower at the venue. She didn't realize how tired she was from walking until she finished. She got dressed and rested for a bit, then put on her make-up and once her hair was dry, styled it with Jayna's help.

The opening band finished their set and while Bailey and Scott made the change-over, the guys and Kelly had their hit of coke before they went out to wait on the side of the stage, Kelly grabbing a bottled water and a bottle of hard seltzer. When it was time, they went out in their usual order, with Kelly coming out just in time to ask the audience, "How are you doing tonight?" before starting the song. The fans shouted their enthusiasm for them as the band played.

At the end of the set, the band came to the front for their bow and photo, then Kelly did her aerial and illusion turn. The fans cheered and Kelly waved as she ran off the stage.

Backstage, Kelly and the guys rested while they rehydrated with water. One photographer, Max Bryant, had been given permission to come in before everyone else. He was a famous band photographer and had taken some shots of them onstage, and now went around the room and took photos of the band. The band was getting noticed and Max wanted to be one of the first to document them as they became more famous.

After half an hour, Dean let in the backstage pass holders, mostly press, but some fans had passes as well. The press talked to the band, asking questions about their next album and the remainder of their tour.

The party continued at the hotel in Dean's room later that night and into the morning. Out of the prying eyes of the press, Isaac kissed a woman he'd brought with him to the hotel, then disappeared with her for almost an hour. Ian and Jake did the same, but Paul and Kelly didn't have anyone with them and they were quite happy with that. In fact, Kelly excused herself and went to her room, where Jayna was already preparing for bed.

"Not into the party scene tonight?" Jayna asked when Kelly came in.

"No, not tonight," Kelly said. "I'm just really tired from the show and from walking around today. But it was a fun day!"

"Yeah, we haven't done that in a long time."

"It was nice to have some girl time."

Kelly took off her make-up, washed her face, and put on her pajamas. She sat cross-legged on her bed and scrolled through some of the photos from that nights' show on social media.

"There's a lot of good photos here," Kelly said. "I think I'm finally comfortable seeing photos of me onstage."

"Not so geeky-looking?" Jayna asked.

"No, I still look like a dork, but these photos manage to make me look decent."

Kelly scrolled a little longer, then put her phone on the charger and got under the covers. Before she turned off her light, she got a text.

"Who could that be from?" Kelly asked. She opened the text and saw it was from Dean. "Oh my God!"

"What?" Jayna asked.

"This is the best fucking news ever!" Kelly exclaimed. "Greg's been caught!"

Chapter Twenty

Kelly looked at her phone the next morning and saw she had over a hundred texts and calls from everyone, congratulating her on the good news. Even better than that, she'd had the best night's sleep in a long time.

"This is fantastic!" Kelly said.

"I can't even imagine how you must feel," Jayna said. "I'm so happy for you!"

"Thank you! I need to talk to Dean and get all the details."

Kelly texted Dean to see if he was awake.

"I am," he replied.

"I'm coming over in a minute," Kelly texted.

She and Jayna got dressed quickly and then went over to his room. Ian and Paul were there as well. Ian got up and embraced her, then dipped her and kissed her. Once Ian let go of her, Paul kissed her cheek.

"So what happened?" Kelly asked, sitting on the couch. "How'd he get caught?"

"He got caught at the airport," Dean said. "He tried to board a plane on a fake passport."

"What an idiot," Paul said.

"He tried to run but airport security caught up to him. He's in jail as we speak."

Kelly laughed out loud. A huge weight had been lifted off of her and she could finally stop being afraid to look into the audience from the stage.

"What a moron," Kelly said.

Dean's phone dinged, indicating a text. He looked at his phone.

"Jake and Isaac are coming over," Dean said.

Seconds later came a knock on the door and Dean let them in.

"Have you heard?" Isaac said.

"Yes! Isn't it amazing?" Kelly said.

Isaac hugged her tight.

"You gotta be feeling pretty great right now," he said.

Jake kissed her cheek.

"So happy for you!" he said.

"This is, like, the best day ever!" Kelly said.

After disparaging Greg for a few minutes, Dean suggested they go downstairs for breakfast. Everyone agreed and they all went to the elevator.

They were seated right away, and they talked more about Greg's capture.

"Hey," Kelly said. "Can we add in Pink's song 'So What?' to the set list just for tonight?"

"I think we can figure out how to play it in that time," Isaac said.

"Sure, no problem," Jake said.

"I mean, it doesn't have to be perfect, just enough to get the point across."

"You betcha!" Ian said.

They finished their breakfast and went upstairs to pack. The bus would be there to pick them up in an hour to take them to their next venue, about a two-hour drive up the coast.

On the drive, the guys got their acoustic guitars out and Isaac drummed on the table as they worked out the song to do that night and by the time they pulled into the parking lot of the venue, they had a pretty good knowledge of it, which they would work out more at sound check.

With a few hours to kill, the band went off to explore the city. Kelly felt so much better and more relaxed as she, Jayna, and Ian walked around Birmingham.

Back at the venue later, Fate Struck went out to do their sound check. After making sure everything worked, they ran through the Pink song. Kelly had the lyrics up on her phone, though she changed just a couple of words to "ex-boyfriend" and "bail" and after a couple of run-throughs, they deemed it good enough for the show.

As it got closer to show time, the band snorted their half-gram each of coke, except for Kelly, who had less. They went onstage and started their set.

Halfway through, Kelly told the fans what had happened that day.

"Today I got some great news," Kelly began. "My ex-boyfriend, who has been harassing me and stalking me for the past year, was finally caught!"

The audience cheered, and Kelly had to wait for them to quiet down somewhat to continue.

"So, in honor of that, I wanted to sing this song and dedicate it to him. It's not our usual genre, but I thought it fit the situation a bit. Sing along if you know it."

Jake played the intro and the crowd cheered louder than before. Kelly took the mic off the stand and moved around the stage as she sang. When she got to the chorus, she stood at the front of the stage, legs slightly apart, and one hand held up in the air as she sang about being a rock star. At that moment, she totally owned that stage. She ran back and stood on the drum riser next to Isaac when she sang about being next to the drummer in the song, and Isaac hit the drums extra hard, making Kelly smile. The guys got into the song as well, singing along with the na na na's of the chorus, and coming to the front of the stage with Kelly at the end of the song.

The cheers were deafening for the band and the song, and Kelly smiled broadly. She turned and high-fived Ian, Jake, and Paul as they went back to their positions, then ran over to high-five Isaac.

"That went over really well!" Isaac shouted over the cheers.

"It really did," Kelly said. She took a sip from her water bottle, and Isaac started the next song.

After the show, the press wanted to talk to Kelly about Greg's capture. Dean granted access to them for half an hour.

"You must be relieved that Greg's been caught," one reporter asked.

"It's a tremendous relief," Kelly said. "I've hated having the feeling that he was going to turn up somewhere. I've seen him a few times in the audience in the States, but he'd always avoid being caught."

"He also sent you threatening texts message, too," another reporter said.

"Yes, he has. I've blocked his number several times but he'd just get a new phone. We've turned everything over to the police. That, and with the incident in Jakarta, should put him away for a while."

The reporters asked a few more questions, then Dean kicked them out and let in the pass holders.

They all celebrated that night by having a few drinks with the fans, toasting the airport security for catching him. Kelly desperately wanted Ian that night. She texted him, asking if he wanted to go to the bus.

"*Sounds like a great idea*," he texted back.

Kelly staggered out to the bus, followed by Ian a few minutes later. She hadn't gotten to the back lounge before Ian came up behind her, turned her around, and kissed her greedily. They walked into the room and Ian kicked the door shut with his foot then locked the door.

"Do you want a bump?" Ian asked, pulling out his little bag of coke.

Kelly hesitated only for a moment.

"Sure," she said.

After their hit of coke, Kelly sat on the bed and scooted back, Ian crawling on top of her, kissing her face and neck. Every sense seemed to be heightened. Ian's touch was soft yet sent tingles through her, and his kisses were just the opposite—hard, eager kisses, his tongue tangling with hers. They took off each other's clothes and got under the blankets.

Afterwards, they got dressed and went back inside before Dean texted them. The party was still going on backstage, however. They walked in together and got strange looks from some of the people there. Jayna came up to her.

"Everything okay?" she asked.

"Yeah," Kelly said. "Why?"

"You just seem a little out of it."

"I drank too much earlier, but I was celebrating!"

"And then some," Jayna said.

"Yeah, well, I'm happy that Greg is finally getting what he deserves and I don't have to be afraid I might see him anymore."

"That is a good thing," Jayna said, smiling.

Finally, Dean started his rounds, thanking people for coming to the show, and the guys and Jayna and Kelly got their belongings together to go back on the bus for the drive north to Scotland.

Kelly got up the next day when it was nearly noon. She and the others hadn't gotten to sleep until 3AM after the excitement of Greg being caught and the subsequent celebrating. She grabbed her phone off the charger and then got out of her bunk and shuffled to the bathroom, then to the dining area to make a cup of Lady Grey tea and some toast. Jayna was awake already, along with Dean.

"Good, you're up," Dean said.

"Why?" Kelly asked hesitantly.

He held up his phone to show Kelly the photo on *The Gossip Spot* website of her and Ian coming into the dressing room together.

"So? Doesn't mean anything," Kelly said, but inwardly her heart dropped.

"I can spin this away, but you two have got to be careful if you don't want people talking," Dean said. "Don't make my job harder than it already is."

"You're right," Kelly said, stirring sugar into her tea. "I'm sorry. Not something I want to be hit with first thing in the morning."

"Not my favorite thing, either. Jayna's already taking care of all the social outlets."

Jayna looked up and nodded.

"You-know-who is really running with this," Jayna said.

"Of course she is."

"But I've calmed everyone down by posting you had gone someplace quiet within the venue and Ian had gone to the bus. It was just coincidence that you two came in together."

"Jayna, I don't know what I'd do without you," Kelly said, kissing Jayna's cheek. "And Dean—thank you. I appreciate everything you do for us."

"I know you do," Dean said. "Just be careful."

When Ian and the rest of the guys got up, Dean told them what happened.

"But it's taken care of?" Isaac asked.

"Yes," Dean said. "But like I told Kelly, we all need to be careful."

"It's fucked up that bandmates can't even walk into a room together without people making comments about it," Ian said.

"I hate that you have to lie for us." Kelly looked at Jayna.

"I'm just stretching the truth," Jayna said. "Not an outright lie, really."

"The same goes for all of you," Dean said to all of them, but looked at Isaac and Jake. "Things will get out eventually if you're not careful."

"We'll be careful," Isaac said.

"I'm actually surprised that no one has posted a picture of you two making out with the ladies after the shows," Jayna said.

“Yeah,” Isaac said somberly.

“Okay, so that fire has been put out. Greg is being arraigned today,” Dean told them. “I’ll keep you posted on what happens.”

“Thank you,” Kelly said. “I hope no one posts bail for him.”

“I think you have a lot of fans hoping for the same thing,” Dean said.

While they’d been talking Ian had chopped out lines for everyone.

“Kelly?” he asked.

She held up her tea cup.

“No, I’m good with my tea.”

“Jayna? Dean?”

“No thanks,” Jayna said. She hadn’t started and wasn’t about to.

“Pass,” Dean said.

The rest of the guys snorted their coke, then got breakfast for themselves from the cupboard.

They arrived at the venue in Edinburgh early that afternoon. They got out of the bus and went inside. While Dean took care of business, the band and Jayna were directed to the dressing room. The band took their bags in and got things set up, then Dean gave them the go-ahead to go explore the area.

Kelly loved the rich history of the city, and she and Jayna walked the Royal Mile and did some shopping before taking a tour of the Edinburgh Castle at the end of the street.

By the time the tour finished, it was nearly time for sound check. Kelly and Jayna quickly walked back to the venue, arriving only a few minutes late. The guys were already onstage. Dean had Kelly’s in-ear monitors, and she grabbed them from him and ran out to the stage.

“I’m so sorry!” she said as she put in the monitors and clipped the battery pack to her pants.

“We just barely started,” Jake said.

"Well, I should have paid better attention to the time," Kelly said. "But the tour of the Castle was fantastic."

During the show, Kelly radiated confidence onstage like the previous show. A weight had been taken off her with the news of Greg's arrest. Being onstage was fun again instead of a point of stress for her. They did the Pink song once again during their set and the fans loved it and sang along.

On their way to their next city, Dean let Kelly know about Greg's arraignment.

"He was denied bail since he's a flight risk," Dean said.

"Fantastic!" Kelly said.

"They're going to call you as a witness, obviously. The trial is set to start the week after we get home."

"That'll be a fun 'welcome home' party," Isaac said.

"I'll be happy to help put him in jail," Kelly said.

"He may not get much jail time, but it'll be something," Dean said.

The band headed home three weeks later. The tour had been fairly successful, though only two sold-out shows, but a lot of fans had shown up to the shows. During those three weeks, performing had become fun again for Kelly. She didn't have to worry about Greg showing up, and it showed in her performances. She had a little more energy when she did her skills at the end of the shows.

Kelly always felt kind of down after coming home from touring. It was always a let-down from the high they all experienced while playing music almost every night. She was happy to be home, however, to be able to sleep in her own bed.

It took Kelly a few days to get back into the routine of being back home—going to bed before midnight, getting up before noon, and eating real food and not fast food. She went shopping to buy herself some fruits and vegetables to snack on, as well as other things to make dinner a few times that week for herself and David.

"I'm going to get spoiled with you making me dinner," David said as they finished their meal.

"It's not much," Kelly said. "Since I really can't cook, but it was fairly easy to make."

One thing Kelly had to prepare for was testifying at Greg's trial the following week. While she knew what she needed to say, she was nervous about seeing him again, even though she knew he could no longer hurt her. She'd have to relive her apprehension of going onstage, and she didn't relish that thought.

The band met at Dean's house later that week to go over a few business things.

"You've got another gold single," Dean said. "This time in England."

"Awesome!" Isaac said.

"They'll ship it here, because I told them we weren't going to fly over there again when we were just there."

"Great, because I really didn't want to stay in another hotel for a while," Ian said.

"And Kelly wouldn't be able to go because she's got to testify at the trial," Dean reminded them.

"Are you nervous?" Jake asked.

"A little," Kelly said.

"We'll come for moral support," Isaac said.

"That'd be fantastic," Kelly said.

The next day Kelly went to her parents' house for a Welcome Home dinner along with David.

"What's next for the band now?" Mom asked.

"I think we get a break for a few months, except for appearing at the award shows, then we'll probably start writing for the next album," Kelly said. "Then it starts all over again. We're gaining some momentum here in the US, so we'll be headlining all the shows we do from here on out."

"And then another tour?" Dad asked.

"Probably," Kelly said, "but that's a ways off. And I'm hoping we don't do it in the winter. It gets really cold sometimes on the bus, even with the heat on."

"And at least one source of rumors has been dealt with," David said.

"Thank God," Kelly said. "Now if we could just deal with that bitch Jessica…" She paused, then said, "Sorry. She just gets on my nerves so much she brings out the worst out in me."

"I know, honey," Mom said. "I also have to realize it's the element you're in, and can't blame the boys on that."

"Well, I know you don't like it, so I'll try to be better."

On the eve of the court date, Kelly showered then got into bed, but had a hard time falling asleep. She ate a couple of gummy edibles to help her sleep, then set her alarm for 6 AM, to be at the courthouse by 8 AM.

That morning she got up and ate breakfast, then got ready to go to court. Dean thought it would be best to have someone drive her there, since this was a high profile trial, with her being the victim, and hired a driver and bodyguard to take her, the guys and Dean to the courthouse.

The driver pulled up in front of the courthouse and he and the bodyguard stepped out first, then opened the door for Kelly and the rest of them, then Dean and the bodyguard walked them all up to the entrance. Kelly was nervous and this was one of the rare times she didn't smile as the cameras went off around her, and she didn't make any comments to the reporters there.

Once inside, they were led to the courtroom where they sat and waited for Greg to be brought in and then the judge entered. Kelly thought the orange jumpsuit suited Greg well. The judge read the charges aloud to the courtroom.

"How does the defendant plead?" the judge asked.

"Not guilty," Greg's attorney said.

The guys gasped and shouted out comments as the judge banged his gavel on his desk.

"I'll have order in this courtroom!" he said.

What the fuck? Kelly thought.

Rock and roll.

Song Lyrics for Fate Struck's Second Album

It's All On You

(Kelly Brennen, Ian Ketchner, Isaac Landry)

1st Verse:
Your obsession with me
Drives me insane
But I'm not afraid
And I won't be claimed
You want me for yourself
But you're gonna get burned

Chorus:
It's all on you
The jealousy you keep
I won't be caged
I'm breaking free from the chains

2nd Verse:
You watch like a predator
Ready to strike
You've distorted our love
Made it perverse
Threatening harm
You're making things worse

Chorus:
It's all on you
The jealousy you keep
I won't be caged
I'm breaking free from the chains

The Hunted

(Jake DeHerrera, Isaac Landry, Paul Slaney, Ian Ketchner, and Kelly Brennen)

1st verse:
Stepped off the plane in Jakarta
Looking forward to the show
Instead we got detained
By the cops looking for blow

Chorus:
You wanted your revenge
For being done wrong
You think we're the hunted?
We'll fucking hunt you down

2nd verse:
Spent several hours waiting
Shit turned upside down
Where you thought was something
Nothing could be found

Chorus

3rd verse:
Now you'll always be looking,
Looking behind your back
I hope to God they find you
In prison you'll never lack

Chorus and Fade

The Cheerleader

(Kelly Brennen and Jake DeHerrera)

1st verse:
Gotta lift you up
Pat you on the back
Atta boy, atta girl
Yeah, I'll tell the world

Chorus:
Gotta give, give, give
Until I give it all
When do I get mine?

2nd verse:
I cheer you on
Scream it far and wide
What have I achieved?
Does anyone know?

Chorus:
Gotta give, give, give
Until I give it all
When do I get mine?

Meet Me in Room 315
(Ian Ketchner)

1st verse:
I'm stalking the night
Looking for you
I crave you despite
The danger pursued

Chorus:
Meet me in room 315
We'll give in to our lust
Will our desire demean
What we feel is just?

2nd verse:
I want to feel you
Taste your desire
Let the ecstasy ensue
Our bodies on fire

Chorus

Bridge:
I want you, even if it's wrong,
I need your body, to taste you, to feel you,
I want it all tonight.

Chorus and Fade

Thank you so much for reading *Flipped,* Book Three in the Rock and Roll Gymnast Series. If you enjoyed it, please consider leaving a review on Amazon or Goodreads and tell your friends! If you found any typos, etc, please email me at jedi_anegram@hotmail.com.

I started this story, intending it to be just one book, but Kelly's story wasn't finished with one book. I wrote every day for a year to see if I could (developing that habit) and I wrote this book, the third in the series, in about three months. I wrote four books in this series in that year, and I'm still going! Book Five is nearly finished and I have ideas for Book Six, which should be the final book in the series.

I'd like to thank the writing communities I'm a part of, both online and here in Colorado. Christine Whitmarsh and Ink Authors, Sparkly Badgers of Facebook, Bryan Cohen, 500 Words a Day, 20 Books to 50K, and Pikes Peak Writers have all been a great help to me whenever I need it. You rock!

Thanks to…

Ian Bristow for creating another beautiful cover.

Rebecca Camarena for editing.

All the bands I have watched and loved over the years that continue to inspire me.

Special thanks to my family—Reid, Vincent, Carter, and Aerin, Tony, Wolfe, and Mya for their love and support, as always.

Dedicated to all who aspire to be something. Follow your dreams!

Other books by Margena Adams Holmes

The Rock and Roll Gymnast Series

Fate Struck (Book One)
Routine (Book Two)

The Elixir Series

The Elixir War
The Elixir Deception
Evalycer's War
Coming Soon! The Elixir Vengeance

Dear Moviegoer Series

Dear Moviegoer: Tales From Behind The Velvet Curtain
Dear Moviegoer 2: Unmasked Mayhem

On The Line

Dark Harmony

Moments From A Lifetime:
A Collection of Poems and Short Stories

www.ingramcontent.com/pod-product-compliance
Lightning Source LLC
LaVergne TN
LVHW091033080826
845145LV00002B/482

* 9 7 8 0 9 9 8 7 9 6 1 7 8 *